"WOULD YOU HAVE ME TELL YOUR FUTURE?"

Taziar started at the sorcerer's question, trying to look nonchalant yet feeling as if he'd already been caught stealing from the man.

"If you'd like," he answered, while, beneath the table, his fingers crept toward the sorcerer.

Mordath's face locked in an expresionless pall. He made an arching gesture with his arm.

Taziar's hand skittered from the fur-lined trim of Mordath's robe to the corner of a pocket. He edged his fingers inside and came upon a smoothed, rectangular gemstone.

A sibilant quality entered Mordath's voice, "I see a sudden, violent death at the whim of an irate Dragonrank sorcerer!" His fist crashed against the tabletop, and Taziar recoiled, using the movement to flick the stone into his palm.

"Witless servant! Leave before I set you and this broken-down box of timber to flame. . . ."

MICKEY ZUCKER REICHERT
has also written:

GODSLAYER

SHADOW CLIMBER

MICKEY ZUCKER REICHERT

DAW BOOKS, INC.

DONALD A. WOLLHEIM, PUBLISHER

1633 Broadway, New York, NY 10019

First Printing, July 1988

1 2 3 4 5 6 7 8 9

PRINTED IN THE U.S.A.

For Gullinfaxi, in memorium
and for
My grandparents, Carl & Dora Halpern
May they live forever.

Acknowledgments

I would like to thank Dave Hartlage for brutal critiques; Joel Rosenberg, Ray Feist and Janny Wurts for believing in "pay forwards"; Dwight V. Swain (whom I've never met); Sheila Gilbert for being the world's best editor; Don and Elsie Wollheim for treating me like family; Arthur and Sandra Zucker who actually are family; but mostly for Gary who has to put up with me until death do us part.

CONTENTS

Prologue 13

CHAPTER 1:
The Shadow Climber 35

CHAPTER 2:
Betrayed 53

CHAPTER 3:
Buchorin's Mercy 66

CHAPTER 4:
Shylar's Haven 80

CHAPTER 5:
The Comforts of Wyneth 96

CHAPTER 6:
The Kielwald 125

CHAPTER 7:
The Bounty Hunter 140

CHAPTER 8:
The Hunted 164

CHAPTER 9:
The Days of Glory 188

CHAPTER 10:
Another Betrayal 208

CHAPTER 11:
Dragonrank Magic 230

CHAPTER 12:
The Dragon's Wrath 254

CHAPTER 13:
The Price of War 271

Epilogue 296

Note to the Reader

The astute reader will realize that the world of the *Shadow Climber* corresponds to an area of Ancient Germany across the sea from the Old Scandinavia where *Godslayer* was set. The historical and geographical inaccuracies are purely intentional. They will be explained painlessly in subsequent volumes. The forthcoming sequel, *Dragonrank Master* will continue the adventures of Al Larson as well as those of some of the people from this novel.

PROLOGUE

Sunlight slanted through the forest of oak and hickory, sheening from the smoothed hide tents of Cullinsberg's army. Perched on a rotting stump in the Danwald Wilderness, Ilyrian chewed the end of his stylus, watching the soldiers settle in for the evening. To his right, five guardsmen butchered a red deer for the evening meal. Ahead, a row of tents obscured Ilyrian's view. Through the spaces between, he watched a cavalryman brushing the flank of one of the striped horses which had become the baron's trademark.

Ilyrian set his stylus to the paper, bored with chronicling the guardsmen's routine. But, as Army Information Liaison, his job was to report even the most mundane affairs of the soldiers to Baron Dietrich and to review their performances to the last critical detail. He scribbled, "Approaching sundown: Bannruod, Ehren, Thuodobald, Berg, Waldifrid prepare meal."

A branch snapped. Ilyrian glanced up at a solidly-built soldier who addressed him briskly. "Captain Taziar wants you in his tent, sir." Without further clarification, he turned and marched away.

Ilyrian clapped his ledger closed. Discomforted by the summons, he fidgeted. *Why would the high commander wish to meet with a political officer now?* He clambered to his feet and wound through the maze of tents. *We've already discussed our next offensive. In the ten years of war against Danwald's barbarians, he's never deigned to discuss details with me, nor to simply chat.* Ilyrian scowled, aware of information about himself he would rather Captain Taziar Medakan did not know.

Ilyrian threaded between the last sequence of camps and stopped before the commander's tent. He took a deep breath and loosed it slowly, not wishing to look suspiciously distressed by the captain's calling. Still tense despite the maneuver, he raised the flap and stepped within.

An oil lamp bathed the interior of Captain Taziar Medakan's tent; its flame swayed in the breeze of Ilyrian's movement. Light flickered over the simple, wooden furnishings. The captain occupied a chair before a cluttered desk. His tanned muscles bunched beneath the thin linen of his uniform. The well-kept brass of his buckles glittered. Black hair shadowed eyes gray and hard as stone. "Don't bother to sit, Ilyrian." Taziar's voice was a graveled bass. "This won't take long."

Ilyrian swallowed. Despite a decade in the baron's service, he still felt unsettled by the captain's icy glare. "I—I don't understand."

The captain's eyes narrowed. He clamped a hand over the disarray before him, and a stylus disappeared beneath his massive fist. "I have evidence you've been dealing black market drugs to my men."

Though true, the accusation jarred Ilyrian. As

the youngest son of a nobleman, he had received
only a piddling inheritance at his father's death.
Unwilling to toil like a commoner and embittered
by the station fate accorded him, he had considered murdering his elder brothers. But aside from
its illegality, the latter course posed practical difficulties. Two of his brothers were warriors, and the
last had been apprenticed to a blacksmith, swinging the hammer until his muscles bulged. Without
recourse, Ilyrian had used cunning and his father's status to attain his political position. Careful
dealings with the baron of Cullinsberg and the
money from his black market sales had already
drawn him nearer to promotion. Now, Captain
Taziar Medakan threatened to destroy ten years
of manipulation with a single accusation. Ilyrian
gathered breath for denial.

But the captain waved a hand in scornful dismissal. "Save your words, Ilyrian. I'd sooner trust
a street beggar."

Ilyrian scowled, infuriated by the insult.

Captain Taziar rose, his demeanor threatening
yet composed. "I'm telling you now to give you an
opportunity to stop without bringing you up on
charges. What my men do in their free time is
their own business. But I won't tolerate anyone
undermining their abilities as warriors or endan-
gering their own and their companions' lives."
Taziar retook his seat, his expression bleakly for-
bidding. His voice went soft. "Dismissed, Ilyrian."

Ilyrian drew a ragged breath. Without the in-
come from his drug sales to the soldiers, he knew
he could never buy his promotion. His tone went
shrill with feigned offense. "I'm innocent! I . . ."

The captain's fist slammed to the tabletop, scattering papers like fluttering ghosts in the lamp-light. "Dismissed, Ilyrian! Get out of my tent before I change my mind and try you today."

Anger spun ideas through Ilyrian's mind. He whirled and stormed through the tent flap. Immediately outside, he collided with a soldier. With a muttered curse, he pushed past. The warrior shoved Ilyrian back with an open violence. The nobleman staggered. He snapped his head about to confront the other man. It was Aird Moor, one of the baron's fiercest bowmen and his most successful scout.

Aird Moor grinned. "Sorry, Ilyrian," he said with mocking insincerity. Without awaiting a reply, he entered the captain's tent.

Rage burst like flame across Ilyrian's mind. Hatred flared against the indiscretions of a peasant soldier and the captain who could destroy his reputation with a single report. *He'll ruin me.* The nobleman no longer harbored any doubts. *Captain Taziar Medakan must die.*

Ilyrian tromped to the edge of the camp and sat, cross-legged, on a bed of pine needles. For a silent hour, he stared at the captain's tent, alternately cursing Taziar and vowing bitter vengeance. At sunset, he watched Aird Moor and Taziar leave for dinner. Ilyrian remained, his appetite lost, his fury dulled to cold calculation. His vigil continued as the captain returned to his tent alone and later, wandered into the forest to relieve himself. Then, Ilyrian's lips framed a smile, and cruel excitement suffused him. He flicked open his ledger and wrote. "Well after nightfall: Captain Taziar disappeared into the woods for an indeterminate period of time."

*   *   *

Nearly two hundred of Cullinsberg's citizens gathered before the platform at the city gates, drawn there by the towering threat of the gallows. Despite the huddled, sweating mass of people, a shiver traversed young Taziar Medakan. He backstepped, glad for the reassuring warmth of his mother against him. She clapped a palm to his shoulder in reassurance, but her hand trembled and her fingers gouged his flesh.

Though twelve years old, Taziar stood only as high as his mother's breasts. He knew he would never attain the resplendent proportions of the father after whom he was named, nor even those of a normal man. Craning his neck, he surveyed the crowd. Most wore the homespun shirts and britches of Cullinsberg's peasantry, but the number of nobles seemed disproportionately high. Guards and soldiers, in uniforms of red and black, stood in tense clusters among the citizenry. Taziar recalled the many times these same people had watched in awe as the baron bestowed honors and medals of heroism upon Captain Taziar Medakan, young Taziar's father. But this time, Taziar knew they had come to see his father die.

Helpless tears welled in Taziar's eyes. *This can only be a nightmare.* He imagined himself in bed, attempting to find a different reality to disperse the cold terror of what he hoped was only a dream. But the crowd remained vividly clear. Their whispered conversations left him no choice but to believe. He rubbed tears away with hands toughened from tree climbing. Suddenly, he wished the calluses which scratched his eyelids had been won from practicing the sword maneuvers his father had taught him rather than from boyish antics.

A stately-looking man dressed in finely-woven linen trimmed with red silk stepped to the platform. The crowd fell silent. Again, tears blurred Taziar's vision, and his father's last words to his son rose in accusation: "A warrior dies twice, once for himself, and once for his loved ones. You must remember. I have already died. Someday, I will not return from a battle. Your mother will cry, but you must remain dry-eyed. You are my son, and you must understand. My soul is long gone. My body will have only left to join it and leave me at peace." Taziar's hopelessness fled before a rush of righteous anger.

The man on the platform raised his arm. He addressed the crowd, his voice a dramatic baritone. "Listen all. Listen well. We have gathered in the sight of sacred Aga'arin to witness the execution of Taziar Medakan, supreme commander of Cullinsberg's marshaled armies, found guilty of high treason against our most holy baron, Lord Dietrich."

Nervous whispers ran through the massed group. Taziar's small hands balled into fists. Behind him, his mother shivered, her breaths emerging in short sobs. Neighbors' hissed inuendoes during the course of the trial had wounded her deeply, and she had wasted to a frail skeleton. Taziar winced and clung to her, numbly aware he might lose both parents in one day.

The nobleman continued. "Lest anyone doubt this most harsh application of punishment, it must be remembered that Captain Taziar Medakan has committed the most heinous of crimes and the one act unforgivable to soldiers: the sin of cowardice."

Taziar shook his head, certain of his father's innocence, yet helpless to intervene. He watched in pained silence as the speaker produced a bound ledger.

"According to the notes of our Army Information Liaison, Captain Taziar Medakan's actions have seemed suspicious for some time. We find multiple entries documenting his late-night disappearances." He flipped through the pages. "On the sixteenth day of the month of high suns, barbarian gold was discovered in the captain's tent, an odd finding for one violently opposed to attacking villages or plundering, even to add to the baron's treasury. Captain Taziar Medakan denied knowledge of the incident."

The speaker turned more leaves. "On the twenty-first day of that month, Captain Taziar Medakan hid his men at a woodland camp rather than participate in a flanking maneuver he had arranged. As a result, the frontal troop was decimated. The captain claimed a messenger informed him the frontal forces had been delayed. Citizens, the messenger denies leaving the frontal troop, and two of our brave soldiers and our liaison swear he was at the front at the time the so-called message was delivered. Taziar Medakan's apparent concern for his own welfare cost the lives of over a hundred of his loyal men. Their only crime was to follow orders he, himself, chose not to obey. His treason caused the deaths of your husbands, fathers, and sons. If anything, this punishment is too lenient. Full retribution must be gleaned from Aga'arin's hand in the afterlife, beyond the boundaries of our world."

Shouts of indecipherable condemnation rose from the crowd.

The speaker cleared his throat, then finished in an overrehearsed monotone. "As a duly appointed priest and executioner for the city-state of Cullinsberg, I sentence Captain Taziar Medakan to death by hanging on this fifth day of the harvest month in the seventeenth year of his high lord's reign. Hangman, proceed."

Taziar's mother moaned. Her fragile frame went rigid. Tears drenched Taziar's collar. Stung by his mother's grief, he huddled closer, silently beseeching the expectant figures of Cullinsberg's citizenry. He located six guards clustered behind his mother: Pluchar, a younger warrior who had often shared drinks with Taziar's father; Salik, the man who'd commanded the troop decimated by Captain Taziar's presumed treason and, as the second in command, the one most likely to benefit from the captain's death. Young Taziar did not recognize the other men. *Damn you! You know he's innocent.* He imagined the soldiers drawing swords and rushing the platform in defense of their commander. But the men remained silent and attentive, guiltily avoiding Taziar's gaze.

Taziar's father mounted the platform, led and flanked by spearmen. The captain wore a simple cloth tunic and breeks, stripped of the proud blacks and reds of his uniform and his badge of rank. His hands were bound behind him, yet otherwise he looked no different than when he'd left home for the last of his many battles against Danwald barbarians. His black hair lay neatly combed. He carried his immense, swarthy form with a quiet dignity. His head remained high, and his eyes swept the crowd with friendly interest.

Though not unexpected, Captain Taziar's courage unsettled his son. Hangman and executioner adjusted the ropes and pulleys, but Taziar could not tear his gaze from his father. Casually, the captain's gray eyes scanned the crowd, singling out and focusing upon each soldier in turn. Taziar noticed that not one of the men dared to meet his father's pointed stare. Then the captain looked directly at his only child.

Taziar caught at his mother's skirt. Though distant, his father's eyes seemed clear, gray and soft as clouds. Yet urgency lurked in their depths, a driving force which goaded Taziar to action. His gut drew into a tight knot. His eyes locked on his father's, attempting to read the older man's last request, yet still too young to understand the demand for vengeance.

Captain Taziar Medakan spoke, his voice devoid of bitterness. "Taziar." The crowd went silent, surprised the accused would waste his last breath by speaking his own name. "My son," the captain finished softly. "I *was* betrayed."

Taziar turned his gaze toward Salik, but the new, young captain stood with his head bowed. The tears on the soldier's cheeks looked unmistakably sincere.

The hangman flicked a loop of rope over the head of the former supreme commander of Cullinsberg's army. The elder Medakan remained still, accepting. He neither flinched nor shied, even as the hangman drew the slip knot tight to the base of his neck and signaled the pulleyman below.

Shock numbed Taziar's mind. No longer able to believe in dreams, he surrendered to a fear which crushed his chest until he felt unable to breathe.

The pulleyman yanked the rope, hand over hand. The sisal went taut. The force lifted Captain Taziar Medakan from the ground. His wife's pained scream was lost beneath the cries of the crowd. She went suddenly limp and dropped to the ground.

"Momma!" Taziar whirled to comfort her. Tears burned his eyes like poison. But immediately, his father's plea returned: *Your mother will cry, but you must remain dry-eyed.* Ruthlessly, Taziar crushed his urge to weep. He glanced toward his father. The captain's skin had gone deathly pale; his gray eyes bulged. Then, the man who had so many times anticipated death in combat and had faced his execution fearlessly, bucked and jerked reflexively to retain his last moments of life.

Sorrow slapped Taziar with the force of a sea gale. His vision washed to a painful white. He wanted to run until the world collapsed about him, climb to the new star which, by Mardain's religion, would hold his father's soul. And he needed to be alone.

The crowd shifted to aid Taziar's mother, many the same people whose whispered slurs had so weakened her. A hand clapped Taziar's shoulder, and a gruff male voice sounded in his ear. "Taz?"

With an oath befitting a mercenary, Taziar broke free and ran. He crashed into a peasant. Impact sprawled him in the dust. Pain shot through his nose, but it seemed inconsequential compared with the emotional agony of watching his father die. Again he pushed into the masses, flailing his arms.

Gradually, a path cleared before him. A reedy voice cursed him, and others echoed blasphemies as he thrashed blindly through the crowd. Once free, he darted into the city streets.

Taziar ran without direction. Though slight, he was strong and lithe. The sun had disappeared beneath the horizon before he paused to catch his breath, deep in an unfamiliar sector of the city. Leaning against the mud-chinked logs of a dwelling, he heard voices and footsteps in the roadway, but discomfort and disinterest rendered their words unintelligible. Soon, the speakers rounded the corner of the building, dressed in the uniforms of Cullinsberg's guardsmen.

A lump formed in Taziar's throat. He felt the warm sting of beginning tears and bit his cheeks to keep from crying. Unable to control his grief and fearing to violate his last vow to his father, Taziar again raced into the street. He dodged through the roadways, their darkness broken only by the faint shimmer of moonlight.

Taziar's headlong flight brought him through a narrow alley. He charged between the buildings' hulking shadows, blind to the rusted cooking pot and the ten figures lounging around it. Suddenly, spent coals crunched beneath Taziar's sandals. His shin cracked painfully against iron. The pot rolled, splashing hot soup across his thighs. Impact bounced him to the ground. He rolled from instinct, abruptly aware of angry shouts around him.

Taziar struggled to his feet. Before him stood nearly a dozen people, their hair long and frazzled, their expressions hostile. "Clumsy bastard!" one screamed. "Get him!"

Taziar spun and raced down the alleyway. His

legs ached from his already overlong run and his collision with the cooking pot. Fear and exertion soaked him with sweat. The pursuing footfalls closed rapidly. Though running for his life, Taziar gained a strange pleasure from the rush of excitement his terror inspired. For the first time, he could momentarily forget his father's death.

Suddenly, a storefront loomed before Taziar, its wooden awning protecting a porch load of firewood. Cornered, Taziar whirled. His pursuers fanned into a half circle before him. Panting, Taziar studied them in the moonlight. Closer, he recognized them as youngsters, some no older than himself. At least one was female. All of them wore tattered clothing, much of it far too large.

The oldest and tallest of the street rogues sneered. "We've got him now."

Another's voice grated with threat. "Let's kill him."

The girl tossed her blonde tangle of hair. "He ruined our dinner."

"Whacha mean?" A muscled teenager with a scarred face glowered at Taziar. " 'e is dinner. I'll skin 'im."

Taziar bit his lip, heart pounding. He backstepped into the shadow of the awning.

A child who appeared no older than seven piped up breathlessly from the back. "You gonna kill 'im first, Blade? Or just skin 'im?"

Frantically, Taziar cast about him. His gaze missed nothing: the ten rogues who baited him, blocking escape through the alleyway; the painted brown door of the store, its padlock clearly evident; the awning which towered two arm's lengths over his head. Fear heightened his senses. His mind channeled solely on the menace before him, allowing him to forget the trial which had occupied his thoughts and nightmares for weeks and the mother he had left lying in a crowd of Cullinsberg's citizens.

Blade crouched. "I think I'll just skin 'im." A knife appeared in his fist. Moonlight glittered off the blade, carving its edge into sharp focus. He closed on Taziar, his steps graceful and precise as a cat. The others followed, brandishing sticks, expectant and ready.

Taziar glanced from Blade to the awning to the approaching gang. Breath rattled in his chest. His fists tensed and loosened. With a howl of purpose, he leaped. His fingertips hooked the edge of the awning. He hung there for a moment, anticipating the cold sting of the knife. Leaf mold slicked his hands, and his grip faltered. He hissed in frustration.

Taziar shivered, remembering the gnarled oak at the city limits. Elbows bent, he swung his body up and over the awning. More accustomed to branches, he misjudged the force of the maneuver and crashed to the top of the awning. Wood slivered through his britches and into his knees. Shouts rose from the crowd below him.

Taziar darted across the awning, his footfalls thundering on the thin layer of pine. He came to the far end and stopped abruptly. He whirled. A sandy-haired teen was hoisting his wiry body to the awning with a boost from his friends. Taziar looked down. A jump would land him back in the alley, surrounded by street toughs. Cursing, he glanced upward.

Stars littered the sky. The moonlight revealed

each mud- and sod-chinked log which supported the store. At the corner, the edges of wood overlapped, forming hand and toe holds Taziar could have climbed even when he was six. Without hesitation, he scrambled to the roof.

Taziar spun, seeking an escape from street rogues hungry enough to follow him to a rooftop and eat him. The stores on either side of the alley stood taller than the one he had climbed. The rift between the buildings gaped, wide enough so Taziar dared not trust himself to jump without plummeting to his death. His palms went slick with sweat. Fear blurred the neighboring buildings to gray shapes. He inched forward and peered over the side. Two of the ragged youths had gained the awning. The sandy-haired climber was nowhere he could see, until a grubby fist appeared over the rooftop.

Taziar leaped forward and stomped on the groping fingers. Their owner yelped and withdrew his hand with a string of ripe oaths. "Spread out! Up the other corners."

The street youths scattered. Taziar crouched, uncertain. Soon, he heard the scrape of climbers from other parts of the building. He scuttled to an edge as the climbers' heads appeared over every side. They clambered to the rooftop and closed in on him: four boys and one girl. None appeared friendly. The sandy-haired youth nursed his hand, glaring.

Taziar shivered closer to the edge. "Come any closer and I swear I'll jump. I'd rather splash my blood all over the street than be eaten." With effort, he feigned a grimace of cold purpose.

The eldest, who seemed to be the leader, stopped,

staring with unconcealed incredulity. "Are you stupid or crazy?"

The street toughs went still.

The leader continued. "Hey, be calm. We's only teasing. You ruined our dinner. We thought you owed us some fun. We're not gonna eat you." His four followers broke into uproarious laughter.

Taziar hesitated. He studied the faces before him. The leader towered over him, the size of a grown man. A few years older than Taziar, the sandy-haired youth was long and lanky, built for running and climbing. Beside him, a youngster with mahogany-colored hair and eyes shifted from foot to foot. Though close to Taziar's age, he stood far taller and nearly double Taziar's weight. The girl watched intently, but said nothing. The last of the group was the child who had goaded Blade.

Now more embarrassed than frightened, Taziar tried to regain his lost dignity. "Yeah, well. I wasn't afraid."

The street rogues chuckled. The girl's blue eyes sparkled. "Then why'd ya run?"

Taziar defended his honor, naturally adopting the poor grammatical speech of his pursuers. "There was ten of ya." He screwed his face into a mass of wrinkles, hoping he looked tough. "Now that you're only five, I'll take all of ya."

Again, the gang howled with laughter. Taziar felt relieved that Blade was still on the ground. The children on the roof seemed like petty thieves, but he harbored no doubt the knife-wielding ruffian would have killed him.

The reddish haired boy gestured at Taziar. "Easy on 'im, now. 'e's just a child. 'e ain't no bigger'n

Mouse." He gestured at the seven year old who matched Taziar perfectly for height and breadth.

Humiliation exploded to anger. Suddenly goaded beyond thought of consequence, Taziar screamed. "I'm not a child. I'm almost thirteen."

Blade's voice wafted clearly from the ground. "Quit playin' and take 'is money. 'e's gotta pay for what 'e spilled."

The leader looked questioningly at Taziar who shook his head. The older boy hollered over the edge. "He ain't got no money, Blade."

"Then kill 'im and come down."

The girl winced in sympathy. The leader rolled his eyes. "Easy, Blade. What's got your fire burnin'?" He addressed Taziar. "He don' mean nothing."

Anger tinged Blade's answer. "Why ya takin' the baby's side, Waren. He ain't one of us."

Taziar bit his lip, fighting the urge to counter Blade's insult.

Waren shouted. "Well, maybe he should be one of us. He climbs better'n Rabbit. And he's small. He'd fit 'bout anywhere."

Taziar said nothing, not at all sure he wanted to become a street rogue, but quite certain he wanted to prove himself as hardened as the youths who confronted him.

"We already got Mouse," Blade argued.

"Mouse ain't gonna stay small much longer. This boy says he's thirteen."

Blade snorted. "And ya believes 'im?"

Waren shrugged. "Why not?"

Rabbit leaned over the edge, his tone gruff with the impatient rudeness only a brother could voice with impunity. "Listen, maggothead. You're so damned worried about your dinner. You know the baker leaves his third-story window open. I know I can't climb up to his shop."

For some time, no reply followed. An unfamiliar voice floated to the rooftop. "He does owe us dinner . . ."

Waren nudged Taziar. "So, how 'bout it? Can ya climb to the third floor of a bakery?"

Taziar smiled, glad of the distraction. "No problem," he lied.

Taziar's walk home along the cobbled stone roadways reawakened the mental anguish the excitement of stealing rolls had displaced. Concern for his mother quickened his pace, but it was nearly midnight before he reached the aging, sod-roofed structure of moss-chinked oak which served as his family's cottage. He paused only long enough to realize the door had been left unlatched, then entered and pulled the panel shut behind him.

The reek of alcohol pinched Taziar's nostrils. Discomfort gnawed at his chest. He had never seen his mother drink, and his father had confined his occasional consumption to the local tavern. But his mother lay on her raised straw pallet. She had drawn the handmade table to her bedside, and it held a ceramic jug, a small vial, and a knife. The candles in the wall sconce sputtered in the breeze from the closing door. Purple wine stained the blankets pulled up across her chest.

Taziar cried out in terror. "Momma!" He ran to her side. "What's the matter?" Self-loathing filled him. *May the gods forgive me. How could I leave her alone when I knew she would never survive without Father?*

His mother spoke, her voice weak but soothing. "Nothing's wrong, Taz. It's all right."

Taziar caught his mother's arm, his every breath painful. "What do you mean it's all right?" The strong-willed woman who had inspired Captain Taziar Medakan's heroics had withered, body and soul, to a form unrecognizable to her own son.

"I want you to do something for me." Wine slurred her words, but her voice held an urgency Taziar dared not ignore. "Then you'll go live with your uncle on his farm near Vesberg."

"No!" Taziar crouched before his mother, dizzy with fatigue and the acrid fumes of the wine. "I want to stay with you. Father told me to take care of you." Grief choked off his words. "I know I'm just ... I'm just ... small." Resentment twinged through him. "But I'll find a way to protect both of us, even if I never get big enough to use a sword."

Taziar's mother stroked his knee. She stared at the ceiling. "You don't need to take care of me, Taz. I'm going to be with your father." She smiled strangely.

Blankly, Taziar watched her. Her expression frightened him. "But Father's dead."

Taziar's mother continued as if he had not interrupted. "Your father told you to be brave. There's one last thing you must perform for me, something I'm too weak to do myself. Your father would call me a coward. That's all right. But he wouldn't want his son to be a coward, too." She paused, as if struggling with a decision, then continued with more resolve. "Promise me, Taz. Promise you'll do what I ask."

Taziar gripped his mother's arm with both hands.

The burden of his last vow to his father, not to cry, still ached within him. "Anything, Momma," he said hoarsely.

She turned tear-glazed eyes to him, dark and soulless as the dead. Aga'arin's priest had slain not only her husband's person, but his character as well. Taziar could not know the torment in his mother's heart nor the depth of her concern for her only child. But she knew that as long as he remained with her in Cullinsberg, he would be only the traitor's son. On his uncle's farm, he would become just another pair of hands. He could learn to take care of himself, a lesson she could never hope to teach him.

Taziar's mother reached a hand to his head and tousled his black hair fondly. She turned her other arm, palm upward, to reveal a string of dark salve which ran from the inner point of her elbow to her wrist. She seized the knife on the bedside table and held it as she spoke. "I'm going to lie here. I want you to cut along this line as deeply as you can." She indicated her arm. Turning the knife, she offered its hilt to Taziar.

Taziar cringed to the stone floor. Its cold dampness seemed to fold around him. "I can't do that." Fear ground through him. "Momma, I could never hurt you." He recalled the many times his mother had comforted him when he felt frightened, nursed him when he was ill, and encouraged him against all doubts.

Her demeanor went hard, her eyes unforgiving. She prodded the hilt against his hand, still warm from her grip. "You must."

He shied away.

"You already promised, Taziar Medakan. Would

you have your father look down from Mardain's star and see his son a coward and a liar?"

Taziar closed his hand about the haft, seeking a means to free himself from a vow he dared not fulfill. "Father said to protect you," he whispered. "Don't make me do this."

She turned her gaze back to the ceiling. "Get out," she hissed.

Her rejection stung Taziar. "I—I don't want to leave you."

Taziar's mother's chin jutted beneath a nest of tangled hair. "The whole world has turned against me. Neighbors talk behind my back, and everyone calls your father a coward and a traitor. The only way you can protect me now is to do as I ask." Her mouth pursed with displeasure. "If you're willing to break a promise to your mother, I don't want you here."

Tears welled in Taziar's blue eyes, and this time no vow in the world could stop them. His hand on the knife went slick with sweat. Gently, he laid his mother's pallid arm on the pallet for support. The blade fumbled from his grasp and dropped to the floor with a clink of metal.

Glad for the delay, Taziar retrieved the knife and raised it. He felt hollow and empty.

"You promised, Taz," his mother said.

Taziar gritted his teeth until his jaw throbbed. Tears transformed his mother's arm to a blur. He imagined her flesh as a white plank, the dark line of salve a crack in the floorboards. The self-deception allowed him to plunge the blade through the crook of his mother's arm. The whetted steel bit easily through muscle and sinew then jolted against bone. Taziar's stomach lurched. A sudden rush of grief forced him to avert his gaze. He ripped the knife downward, driven to finish the gruesome task as quickly as possible. His mother screamed and jerked away. Warm blood splashed Taziar's hand, and the movement wrenched the dagger from his grip.

Taziar watched in horror as his mother struggled to rise, fighting the death she had previously welcomed. But she gathered only enough strength to roll from her pallet to the floor, blood splattering the stone like spilled wine.

"Momma!" Taziar's pulse pounded in his ears. Fingers spread, he stared at the mother's blood which stained his hand like a living presence of evil. He dropped to his knees. A strangled sob emerged from his throat, and he vomited until his gut ached.

CHAPTER 1

The Shadow Climber

"The day is for honest men, the night for thieves."
—*Euripides,*
Iphigenia in Tauris

Taziar Medakan crouched beside the madam, Shylar, on the second-story floor of Cullinsberg's whorehouse, studying Ilyrian through a hole in the floorboards. The nobleman's craggy face and tiny, close-set eyes inspired an initial aversion. Ilyrian paced, knotting his fingers. His gaze swept the room in a predatory manner.

Taziar flicked unruly black hair from his eye. "Who is he?"

Though average height for a woman, Shylar stood half a head taller than Taziar. Cross-legged on the bare wood, she met his blue eyes levelly. "His name's Ilyrian. He's the baron's personal adviser and one of the men up for the prime minister's position."

Taziar watched Ilyrian pry at a knothole in the wall, apparently oblivious to his audience. "Did he tell you that, or did you find out from other sources?"

Shylar shook her graying curls and regarded Taziar from a creased face which had once been beautiful. "Both. He's worked with the underground before, mostly semilegal things to aid his rather rapid rise to power."

Taziar nodded, glad to have Shylar and her informers to do his background work. In his younger days, he preferred to leave court intrigue to his gang fellows. He could never bring himself to understand the mentality which allowed the baron and his administration to turn against his father after more than a decade of meritorious service.

Shylar continued. "Ilyrian's taken a few bribes. Used to deal black market when he first came to Cullinsberg from Vesberg. He's a noble's child, a younger son. He served as our Army Liaison five . . . ten years ago."

Taziar repeated, considering. "Army Liaison?" Suddenly, Shylar's description seemed to fall together. "It was eight years, about the time my father . . ." Grief rushed down upon Taziar, suffocating him. A lump formed in his throat, making him unable to finish. His mind conjured images of his father, proud with his badges as captain of the baron's army, then swinging, lifeless, from the gallows. With effort, Taziar forced aside the memories. Dismayed that his father's execution still affected him so deeply, he finished quickly and euphemistically. ". . . passed away. My father spoke of Ilyrian once. Thought he might be supplying mind-hazing drugs to his warriors. His sales destroyed the soldiers' judgment and caused a number of good men's deaths. Ilyrian is a lizard."

Shylar shrugged. "The lizard has money. You don't have to like him to steal for him."

Taziar sighed, aware he could never escape the intense morality instilled by his father. Despite a thousand of Waren's lectures and Blade's growled threats, Taziar had limited his thefts to those who could afford them and shared his spoils with beggars and drunkards.

Shylar leaned closer to the floor, following Ilyrian's movements. "Since the baron rules by divine right of Aga'arin, his sect has a strong say in the appointment of our prime minister. But the high priest doesn't like Ilyrian." Again, Shylar met Taziar's gaze. "So, our client needs a blackmail tool, an object he could threaten to destroy if the clergy didn't sanction him. He wants you to steal an artifact from the temple."

"Aga'arin's chalice." Taziar dropped to his haunches, considering. The golden goblet could make any thief rich, even if its intricate designs were lost to recasting. His fee would have to include the item's value as well as reflect the difficulty of its theft. Taziar stared at Ilyrian. The nobleman ceased pacing, sat on the room's only chair, and picked idly at his crotch. Taziar leapt to his feet. "Forget it, Shylar. You know I don't handle politics. Why didn't you call Badanor or Faldrenk?"

Shylar rose. Irritation tinged her voice. "Because Ilyrian requested you."

Taziar paused. "Me?"

"He asked for the Shadow Climber."

Taziar scratched the back of his head, surprised the notoriety of his secret persona had spread so far. Secure in the knowledge only Shylar knew his true identity as Taziar Medakan, the junk merchant, he shrugged. "I'll have to disappoint him. I don't deal in politics." He headed for the doorway.

Apparently thinking Taziar was beyond range of her voice, Shylar mumbled. "Just as well. I'd hate to see you mauled by lions."

Shylar's challenge intrigued Taziar. Not for the first time, his love for action and the intimation he might fail became his weakness. Hand on the doorknob, he turned. "Lions?"

For an instant, the corners of Shylar's mouth twitched upward with realization. She bit her cheeks. "Guard lions patrol Aga'arin's courtyard." Her face twisted in a grimace of regret. "Don't take this job."

Taziar shook his head. He pictured the chiseled stone walls of the temple and considered its overtended gardens. Aga'arin's priests had wrung a wealth of gold from Cullinsberg's peasantry for its upkeep. *Perhaps some good might come of robbing pompous clergymen who are bigger thieves than me and my fellows.* "I'll do it."

Shylar seemed about to speak, but she held her tongue. She pulled a leather pouch from the pocket of her shift and tossed it to Taziar. "Then I guess this is yours. He promised twice the amount when you complete the job."

Catching the sack, Taziar peered inside at a fortune in gems. Without bothering to count them, he tossed it back to Shylar. "Keep this as your share."

Shylar kneaded the gems through the leather. Her dark eyes widened. Apparently dumbfounded, she stammered. "J-just ten percent, you generous idiot! I can't take this."

Taziar smiled. "A fraction of that could buy my

ale for years. You have connections. Put the money to good use. Use it to restore the underground's hideaways. Buy a guard or two." He waved. "Give the girls a few nights on the town." He caught the doorknob.

Again, Shylar spoke softly. "Shadow?"

Taziar faced her.

Shylar hesitated, as if unsure. Then, boldly, she continued. "You're too damned moral for this kind of work. If you just want the thrill, why don't you go legal and become a guard like your father?"

Shylar's question awakened a storm of emotion within Taziar. He recalled the respect the other guards accorded his father as captain, and how quickly it had turned to scorn after his father's death. Some of the war atrocities his father had described and the treatment of prisoners in Cullinsberg's dungeon sickened Taziar. The thought of taking another life sent a shiver of dread through him. He stared at his tiny hands, deeply scarred with calluses from climbing and recalled that his father stood half again as tall as himself and nearly twice his current weight. Unable to share his inner thoughts even with Shylar, Taziar parroted a remark Rabbit had once made in jest. "The baron needs soldiers who can see over the heads of their striped steeds."

Without awaiting a reply, Taziar exited Shylar's room.

Six nights after Taziar Medakan's conversation with Shylar, a crescent moon grazed the shadows of Cullinsberg's evening. The "thieves' moon" he called it, and it was no coincidence he chose to prowl on this particular night. The moon's reflected light traced the outline of the temple to Aga'arin, but it was not bright enough to reveal faces with any clarity. Dressed in black linen from his hood to the soft socks which covered his feet, Taziar knew his form blurred to invisibility in the night's dank haze.

At the base of the wall which surrounded the temple, Taziar removed a soft pouch from the tie about his neck and rummaged through its contents. It held a roll of twine, a second sack, and three quarters' weight of chopped pork laced with sleeping drug, a deterrent for the lions which prowled the temple courtyard.

The wall around Aga'arin's temple stood as tall as two men, a wide, white blur in the darkness. Taziar replaced his pack on its neck strap. He paused, listening. By habit, his senses sifted the normal sounds of night: the insects' chirrups, the gentle whoo of an owl, the exchanged howls of distant wolves. Beneath the familiar music of the night, Taziar heard the rustle of weeds under large paws in the temple courtyard.

Delicate and practiced as a cat, Taziar caught handholds in the irregular stonework of the wall and scrambled to its top. When he ran with the gang of rogues, his companions bragged he could climb a straight pane of glass. While their claim was exaggerated, Taziar knew he could find irregularities where other men could scarcely imagine them.

Crouched on the wall top, Taziar Medakan studied the courtyard which spread beneath him like a map. Stone walkways bordered well-tended gardens with benches for outdoor prayer sessions. Summer flowers of saffron and blue waved in the breeze, too fat to close completely to buds for the night. Taziar flattened against the stone. Short as a woman and less than a hundred weight, he found hiding easier than most men. This fact, and his habit of wearing black for night jobs, had concealed his identity as the notorious Shadow Climber for more than five years.

Seeing no movement in the courtyard of Aga'arin, Taziar snaked a hand into his pouch, retrieved a fistful of meat, and dropped it to the walk. The pork impacted stone with a barely audible plop. From beyond one of the flower gardens, a tawny shape leaped toward him with a menacing growl. Taziar recoiled, despite the safety of his position on the wall.

Twice the size of a large dog, the guard lion moved with the grace and speed of a house cat. Taziar balled another piece of meat and tossed it toward the beast. The lion retreated to a crouch. It sniffed the air like a dog, circled the meat twice, and pounced on the offering. From the far side of the temple yard two more guard lions appeared as the first finished the pork in a single bite.

Taziar wadded meat in his fist and wrinkled his nose at its slightly spoiled odor and the grease which slicked his palm. He tossed the meat toward the lions. It bounced from one beast's nose, and the first snatched it with a warning growl at its companions. Taziar swore softly. One lion aware in the compound could foil his plan, and he was running low on pork. While the first lion chewed, Taziar tossed the remainder of his drug-laced meat. The two latecomers to the feast devoured their portions, and Taziar smiled in relief.

Waiting for the drug to take effect, Taziar pondered the events which had brought him to the baron's temple. He thought little of Ilyrian and his designs against the temple, but he cared even less for Aga'arin's preachings. *A god of precious metals.* Taziar pursed his lips and stuffed a sliding comma of hair back beneath his hood. *An excuse for manicured gardens, pretty women, and ungodly wealth for that fat priest, Buchorin. And, with the foolishness of the obsessed religious fanatic, the baron sanctions Aga'arin's temple.*

The first of the lions staggered. White foam bubbled from its muzzle. Taziar winced and looked away. Larger amounts of the sleeping drug could kill, and caution had forced him to err toward overdosing. Slowly, he glanced back into the temple grounds. One lion fell. Another wandered in chaotic circles. The third sat, whimpering. Still, Taziar waited. The drug would make its victims unpredictable before it took effect completely.

Taziar redirected his thoughts to the evening in the whorehouse when Shylar questioned his profession. She had always treated him like a son, perhaps because of his youth and size or because he had become an orphan before his thirteenth birthday. But his obsession with action was the product of a restlessness he could never satisfactorily explain to her, or even to himself. When he had looked upon his father's writhing body eight years ago, the world seemed to explode around him. Bound by his promise not to cry, he tried to drive sorrow aside in other ways, performing feats which he now realized should have killed him. But with each success came a natural elation. Soon, he found himself seeking a means to reactivate the euphoria which allowed him to forget, as addicted to his own excitement as other men were to the drugseller's herbs. His love for the impossible remained. Unfortunately, so did his grief.

The lions sprawled, motionless, on the stone path. With a sigh of regretful relief, Taziar lowered himself to the courtyard. He moved through the gardens with practiced agility and speed. His blue eyes, narrowed and darting, sought movement among and beyond the buds. The heavy, sweet odor of flowers filled the court. At the base of the cut stone temple, Taziar paused to readjust his hood. Behind him, stems rattled. Taziar jerked his head toward the sound. A tawny shadow sprang at him.

With a smothered gasp of horror, Taziar leaped for the wall. Claws raked his calf as his hands caught irregularities in the stone. Fast as a squirrel, he pulled himself to safety. *Idiot!* Taziar berated himself. He watched the fourth of the lions pace hungrily beneath him. His options shrank. With a lion still loose in the compound, if the situation in the temple grew uncomfortable he could not retreat in haste without becoming the beast's repast. He doubted the throwing spike in his belt could do much more than anger it. With no other choice, Taziar continued up the wall stones, knowing the dilemma would still confront him when the time came to make his escape.

Balconies jutted from the temple walls. Four towers rose from the rooftop, a single, narrow chimney between them. Taziar clung beside the closest balcony and listened. Delicate, patterned curtains swung through the opened doorway, fluttering in the summer breeze. Their swish masked any other sounds from the room beyond. Noiseless as a shadow, Taziar slipped to the balcony between rungs of a silver railing which would have made a greedier thief quiver with the injustice of leaving such wealth behind. But Taziar enjoyed the challenges of his trade more thoroughly than its rewards.

Once beyond the swirling curtains, Taziar saw a nightstand, a wardrobe, and a bed. A woman huddled beneath a thin sheet which clung to her nearly perfect form. Brown hair spread across an embroidered pillow, highlighting her full, pink face. Taziar studied her long-lashed lids and her breasts which rose and fell in the pattern of sleep. Watching to make certain his movements did not awaken the woman, Taziar crossed the room to a teakwood door on the far side.

The handle turned without a sound. For the first time, Taziar appreciated the wealth which kept the temple of Aga'arin under constant, careful maintenance. He opened the door a crack and felt a breeze from the open balcony. The curtains snapped in the draft. Taziar bit his lip and glanced at the woman, but she did not stir.

The hallway beyond was empty. Taziar stepped through and pulled the door shut behind him. To his left, the corridor continued as far as he could see. Doors of iron-bound oak and teak broke the walls without pattern. To his right, the hallway ended in another balcony. Someone had propped one of its shutters open for the night. Taziar mentally calculated the time it would take him to cross the passage to the balcony and affix himself to its outer wall. Then, he turned back to the woman's room.

Taziar's forelock of hair had slipped back into

his eyes. He tucked it neatly beneath his hood. His plan required that nothing be visible which could link the Shadow Climber with Taziar, the merchant. He flexed his hands, pleased with a strength far out of proportion to his size from years of supporting his body weight on his fingertips. He relied on fear and notoriety to make him look larger to those few he confronted in his present persona.

Again, Taziar opened the door, stirring air from the balcony. This time, the woman moved. Quick as a heartbeat, Taziar closed the panel and latched it against the breeze. He crossed the room in a bound, pressed his left hand across the woman's mouth, and clamped his right to her neck. "Don't scream." He tightened his grip on her throat.

The woman's eyes shot open, green and wild with fear. Her hands went instinctively to his wrists.

Taziar kept his body beyond range of her feet. "Who guards the chalice?"

She shook her head slightly beneath his fingers.

Taziar lifted the hand on her mouth. His right hand tensed. "Who guards the chalice? How many men?"

Her cheeks went white. "J-just the snake," she stammered.

"By Aga'arin, woman, the truth or I'll throttle you dead." Taziar spoke from his chest and held his face in shadow. "A snake would go dormant in winter." Unconsciously, his fingers worked deeper into her neck.

The woman whimpered. "Please. I swear by my lord. It is a cobra. In winter Buchorin lights a fire in the hearth which warms the room. P-please don't kill me."

The chimney! Taziar eased his hold on the woman, hoping he had not frightened her too severely. Though her revelation gave the information he needed, he continued questioning to mislead her. "Which room?"

The woman's voice squeaked. "Two doors down the left passage on the right."

"Swear it."

The woman trembled. "I swear by Aga'arin."

Taziar released the woman; she rubbed gratefully at her neck. He caught her by the wrist. A sudden jerk dropped her, facedown, to the floor. Breath rushed from her in a gasp.

"Don't look up," Taziar warned. Guilt tightened his chest as he watched the woman quiver like an insect on the floor. "I'm standing behind you. If you move or make a sound, I'll kill you."

Taziar crossed the room with practiced stealth, confident the woman could not know he would never harm her or anyone else. The memory of his mother's slaying still lay like lead within him. In his three years with the street gang and his five with the underground, he had learned to judge people and avoid those with whom confrontation would result in violence.

The linen on Taziar's feet made no sound on the wooden floor. Silently, he opened the door to the empty hall and judged the distance to the balcony. He sprinted through the right passage, leaving the door to catch the cross draft. . . . *two, three, four, five* . . . The door banged shut as he reached the balcony. As Taziar caught his fingers in wall chinks above its shutters, the woman's anticipated scream reverberated through the hallway.

Taziar Medakan pulled his body to the rooftop,

counting softly. Shylar had told him the chalice room contained no windows. Soon, the woman's shouts would mobilize the guards to the chalice room door. But Taziar's talk with Buchorin's concubine had gained the final piece of information which might make his plan successful.

Taziar scuttled across the roof tiles. Shortly, he came upon the chimney between the towers. As he stared into its depths, his hopes fell. Little wider than a pipe, the chimney seemed too small even for Taziar's tiny frame. If so, instead of leading the guards astray, his last maneuver had served only to sabotage any chance of stealing the golden chalice of Aga'arin.

Had he subscribed to a religion, the Shadow Climber might have prayed. But, to Taziar, the sects of Cullinsberg existed only to dupe their worshipers, to squeeze coppers from peasants and gold from the foolish rich. Many of his gang fellows had attended the temple of Karana, mistress of lies and ruler of the hellish afterlife for those who practiced sin; but Taziar saw no point in announcing his dishonorable profession. For this reason, when the baron's guards assailed Karana's church only he escaped execution.

Taziar heard the sounds of the temple coming to life beneath him. He studied the opening again. Climbing to the edge, he shrugged his left shoulder from its socket with surprisingly little pain. After several deep breaths, he tucked the sack into his shirt and wriggled inside the chimney, comforted to think that the guards would never check for a man in the opening, and at the same time dismayed to realize no one would ever free him if he stuck.

The stone walls scraped Taziar's sides through the thick linen of his costume. Ash dislodged from the sides, pattering to the hearth. Though soft, the sound made Taziar cringe as he gradually worked his way to the chalice room. He landed, feet flat, in the soot-speckled hearth.

A table busy with intricate designs held the chalice between two candles nearly melted to their golden holders. Shadows swam in their guttering light. Nearer, a cobra's hooded head reared to strike.

Breath broke from Taziar. Back pressed to the hearth, he seized the spike in his belt. The snake's head jerked toward him. He hurled the spike. It embedded in a glaring yellow eye. The snake's lunge fell short, and it writhed and knotted like a dying worm.

For a time, Taziar remained, watching the snake for any sign of purposeful movement. Human voices beyond the door mobilized him. Avoiding the cobra's death throes, he pulled the pouch from his shirt and lengthened it with twine until it hung past the floor. Without stopping to admire the golden masterpiece of the chalice, he stuffed it into the bag. Within seconds, he started up the chimney as the verbal exchanges below him turned to shouts.

Taziar quelled rising fear and thrilled to the sense of urgency which kept him in this deadly business. Gradually, he squeezed into the shaft. Ash coated his mouth. Even through his clothes, stone scraped skin from his limbs as he pulled himself to the rooftop. The thieves' moon never seemed so welcome. Taziar forced his shoulder back into place. He would pay for the maneuver with pain for the next few days, but it had helped him through an unusually tight space. He hoisted the chalice through the shaft, looped its cord several times around his neck, and started across the tiles.

Feet crashed on the roof behind him. *Damn!* Taziar quickened his pace. He caught a ledge and lowered his feet over the side. He turned his head to judge his distance to the ground. Directly beneath him, the lion watched with obvious interest. *Aga'arin's ass, what else can go wrong?* Taziar scrabbled for a better hold. He heard voices on the rooftop, much closer now, and he froze in position.

Taziar felt the tiles shake beneath the guards' weight. Slowly, he clamped the fingers of his right hand tighter to the ledge and let his left swing free. *That much less for the guards to discover.* The lion crouched beneath him.

A man spoke, far to Taziar's left. "What are you doing?"

Another replied from so close Taziar winced. "Watching that lion. He's staring at me. Wants to make a meal of me." He added in a disgusted whisper, "I hate those damn things."

Taziar's fingers cramped. He tried to rest his free hand against the wall, but he could not reach it from the ledge. *Death from angered priests or lions. I don't know which would be worse.* Sweat and grease slicked his fingers, and his grip slid along the ledge.

The guard's footfalls rang closer. Taziar gritted his teeth, channeling full concentration into his failing grasp. He glanced up. Suddenly, a pale, bearded face blocked his view of the stars. The guard's mouth splayed open. "What's this?" He lunged for Taziar.

Taziar shrank from the guard's groping hands. His fingers ached.

Swearing, the guard reached out awkwardly. "Lytren, here!" Eagerness caused him to misjudge balance. He tumbled, shrieking, from the rooftop.

The lion sprang. Its claws shredded leather like paper. The guard screamed. Taziar's grip gave. He hit the ground, rolled, and froze. Occupied with the writhing guard, the lion paid the thief no heed. Still, Taziar crept toward the outer wall, aware that sudden movement could incite the beast to murder.

Suddenly, light flooded the compound. Women screamed; men shouted. Rocks sailed toward the lion. Taziar broke to a run, clambered over the wall, and hit the ground at a sprint. Not daring to glance backward, he sped through the streets, past his own deserted stand, tarp-covered for the night. He careened through the market, around two rows of cottages, and nearly collided with a scantily-clad streetwalker.

"Sorry," Taziar muttered. He doubled back and dove into an alley. He found niches in a stone and mud wall and worked his way upward. On the rooftop, Taziar rolled to his back. His lungs ached. His heart hammered in his chest. Fighting for breath, he watched the thieves' moon as it slipped lower in the sky.

Nothing remains but the delivery. Taziar folded his hands beneath his head as his breathing became less labored. *What am I going to do with fifteen hundred weight in gold?* Briefly, Taziar considered the advantages of wealth, but the thought seemed too foreign. Once dedicated to achieving the impossible, money became too easily attained and ceased to have value. *Though small, my cottage suits me. I prefer beer to fine wines, and I enjoy my work too much to grow soft and fat in idleness.* Taziar swept to a sitting position and caressed the chalice through the bag around his neck. It seemed to him the money should be returned to the hungry families whose toil paid for its crafting. *Shylar will know the best way to distribute it.*

Taziar rose, relishing the last of his dispersing excitement. He measured the distance to a neighboring building, leaped to its roof, then shinnied down its wall back into the street. Ilyrian had promised to hide his fee in a rain barrel in Ottamant's alley between two stocked warehouses near the river. Taziar would exchange sapphires for the chalice which, thankfully, would conclude his dealings with the baron's temple and Ilyrian.

Taziar traversed a circuitous route through town to Import Street which paralleled Ottamant's alley. Discovering the far side of one of the chosen warehouses, he climbed to its roof and flattened against the tiles. For nearly a quarter of an hour he lay and watched for movement in the alley beneath him. The rain barrel sat to his left, near the warehouse door. The wind tossed a discarded strip of parchment, and it scraped the alley stones. Gently, Taziar unwound the chalice bag from his neck and lowered himself to the ground.

The sky faded to twilight gray. Taziar caught the barrel lid and lifted it from its base. His movement disturbed the surface of the water; moonlight shivered from the waves. Otherwise, the barrel was empty. Taziar shook his head, perplexed. His heart quickened.

A voice from behind startled him. "Be still, Shadow . . ."

Taziar leaped for the wall. His hands settled into irregularities in the mud-chinked stone. Behind him, bowstrings sang. Pain seared through Taziar's shoulder. A cry broke from him. He tried to climb, but the arrow pinned him to the wall.

Taziar's voice became an anguished croak. "No!" As he worked his shoulder free, agony dulled his senses. A final tear freed him, though blood coursed down his side in a warm stream. He turned. A sword point pressed against his throat. Taziar's gaze followed the blade to its wielder, and he recognized the huge, sallow features of Salik Kanathul, the baron's captain. He froze.

"Be still, Shadow Climber," repeated Salik, though this time his words were unnecessary. Arrowheads peeked from the warehouse windows. Seven guards stepped from the doorway and paused at their commander's side. One reached for Taziar. The thief shrank from the hand, but it tore the hood from his head. Taziar's small features, his unruly black hair and moist, blue eyes lay as fully revealed in the twilight as the spreading scarlet stain at his shoulder.

A murmur ran through the guards. Salik held his blade tight to Taziar's neck, and the sharp sting of its touch made the thief recoil. The captain spoke scarcely above a whisper. "Taziar Medakan, son of the same, you are now in the baron's custody."

Blood loss drained Taziar's remaining consciousness before he could reply.

CHAPTER 2

Betrayed

"And oftentimes to win us to our harm
The instruments of darkness tell us truths,
Win us with honest trifles, to betray's
In deepest consequence."

—*William Shakespeare,*
Macbeth

Taziar awoke to the dull ache of his injured shoulder. He rolled to his back. Sudden, sharp pain roused him to full awareness. As he lay still, waiting for the pain to subside, memory returned in a wild rush. With his left arm held immobile against his naked chest, Taziar leaped to his feet and brained himself on the low ceiling.

Head ringing, Taziar dropped to a crouch and explored the tattered muscles of his left shoulder with his fingers. Dried blood flaked onto his palm. Testing the connection between bone and sinew, he wriggled the fingers of his left hand and shook his wrist. Then he flexed his elbow; the motion jogged his shoulder. He winced in pain. Tender-

53

ness and swelling limited movement of his shoulder nearly to nothing.

The only clothing the baron's guards had left Taziar were the thick linen britches of the Shadow Climber. The little thief seized the fabric and tried to tear a bandage from the bottom of one pant leg. But even his strong fingers could not spoil his own handiwork, crafted to withstand the rigors of night work.

Taziar favored his left arm, and the pain dulled to a throb. He turned his attention to his surroundings. He occupied a steel-barred cell scarcely large enough for a dog, its low ceiling designed to prevent him from standing. A dirty, wooden bowl near the door held water. He wet his hand, splashed blood from his aching shoulder, and examined the world outside his prison through the narrow spaces between the bars.

Taziar huddled in one of six cages at the center of the baron's dungeon. Larger cells lined the granite walls, their pattern broken only by a space of wall with dangling shackles directly across from Taziar and a barred metal door down the row through which he could see guards pacing their watches. But, while the central pens were designed like kennels, a solid strip of steel rose from the floor of each outer cell to the height of Taziar's waist. Their bars continued to the ceiling, allowing prisoners to stand.

Taziar's brief examination revealed he was not alone in the baron's disfavor. A man crouched in one of the outer cages near the door, gnawing at a chicken leg. Blond hair hung to his shoulders in limp, damp strings. If not for the movement of his jaws, he might have seemed a statue; every muscle bulged, defined as chiseled marble. Taziar guessed the steel cell lining might reach the man's lower thigh, and he measured easily two and a half times Taziar's meager weight.

Barbarian, Taziar surmised from his father's descriptions. *But the barbarian wars ended years ago. Why have they kept him alive?* He continued to stare. Slowly, the barbarian graced the thief with an answering look. Distance blurred his eyes to pale gray, but they held a wild freedom, unbroken by the cages and cruelty of the baron's guards.

The baron's only other prisoner had not fared as well. The cage to Taziar's right held a scrawny woman dressed in rags. A breast hung free from her tattered clothing, but she made no attempt to cover it. She lay on her back, head cradled in a mass of mouse brown hair. Flesh sagged from her frame. Taziar doubted the barbarian spoke the language of the barony, so he chose to confront his neighbor instead. "Lady?"

The woman gave no sign she heard him. "Excuse me, lady?" Taziar said, louder. He raised his torso until his head touched the roof of his cell. From his position, he could see that her dark eyes were open, though flat and emotionless as the dead.

Concerned, Taziar moved closer. "Lady?" He snaked his right hand between the bars and touched her arm gently.

The woman's eyes sparked to life. Scream after scream ripped from her throat.

Taziar flinched away, torn by guilt, though her actions were irrational and unexpected. He watched with widened eyes as her cries broke to sobs, then stilled to silence.

He whispered tentatively. "Lady? I won't hurt you."

She trembled slightly but gave no reply.

From the steel-barred outer doorway, a voice broke the ensuing quiet of the baron's prison. "She won't answer. After I finish with you, Taziar Medakan, neither will you."

Taziar whirled toward the speaker. The door opened, and two men dressed in the lacquered leather armor of the baron's guard entered the cell block. Taziar recognized one as Pluchar, the warrior who had, on occasion, shared a drink with Taziar's father. The other stood no taller than Pluchar, though he weighed twice as much. He reached for a ring of keys at his belt which was nearly lost beneath moist rolls of fat. Taziar unconsciously crept toward the back of his cell while the obese guard latched and locked the outer door.

Neither of the guards carried a sword, but Pluchar clutched a thick wooden staff. His gaze flicked over Taziar, then dropped to the floor. The fat man turned. He stared at Taziar with the same loathsome interest as a buyer examining a curvaceous, female slave. The corners of his mouth twitched to a cruel smile. Taziar tried to read the guard for some flaw or weakness which might allow him to escape. But he found only the deep-seated viciousness his father had despised.

Pluchar shifted uncomfortably. He spoke softly to his companion. "Go easy. He's Taz's son."

Amusement filled the guard's dark eyes. "If he cooperates, I won't hurt him at all." He walked around the caged barbarian toward the front of Taziar's prison.

Pluchar paced a parallel passage to the back of

Taziar's cell line. The thief tried to watch both men. His back touched the bars which separated him from his neighbor. He pressed his injured arm tight to his chest, unable to banish the memory of Berin, once the street gang's strongest member. Taziar recalled Berin's lifeless body in a sewage trough, days before the raid on Karana's temple which resulted in the execution of Waren's rogues. Berin's skull had been staved in, his skin crisscrossed with bruises, his wrists rubbed raw from shackles. There could be no mistaking the guards' method of interrogation. Now, the threat of punishment raised sweat on Taziar's temples. He fought memory, aware he would need his composure and his wits intact.

As the guards approached from opposite ends, Taziar fixed his attention on Pluchar. The guard avoided his questioning stare. Behind, Taziar heard the muffled clack of keys and the squeal of rusted hinges as his door swung open. Forced to a crouch by the abnormally low ceiling, he spun toward the fat guard.

"Out!" The guard indicated the cell door. Flesh jounced about his elbow.

Taziar recalled his father's stories of dungeon brutality. He froze.

The guard's double chin raised slightly. "Pluchar?"

The staff slid through the bars and jabbed Taziar's side. Off balance, the thief fell. Wincing with pain, he caught at his injured shoulder and scrambled forward to avoid another poke. A fleshy hand caught his upper arm and dragged him from the cage. Even as Taziar tried to gain his feet, a massive fist crashed against his ear, smashing his face to the floor.

Taziar's consciousness swam. All his years of planning and prowling had not prepared him for physical combat. The guard moved surprisingly quickly, with none of a fat man's laziness. The huge hands hefted him like a doll and jammed his chest against the wall. Dazed, Taziar swung blind. The guard caught his arm, ripped it over his head. Cold steel framed Taziar's wrist, and the shackle clicked closed with a finality which jolted him to awareness.

The guard caught Taziar's left wrist. The slight thief screamed. Sweat doused his body. The guard yanked him around with a force which sent tortured waves through his shoulder. He went limp as the shackle pinched closed about his other wrist.

Designed for larger men, the shackles held Taziar so high his feet scarcely met the floor. His breathing quickened to a pant as he realized he stood helpless and exposed before a power-mad guard who could easily slay him. Through painfully dry eyes, he watched the wide blur of his tormentor as the guard took the staff from Pluchar's hand.

"You can go now," the fat man told his companion icily.

Pluchar hesitated long enough to show Taziar an expression of sympathy. He turned and trotted from the fat man's presence.

A laugh of elation rumbled in the guard's meaty throat. He spun the staff from hand to hand with the speed and confidence of a professional. "Who hired you, thief?" He spat the last word as if it was an oath.

Taziar flinched, though the shackles left no room for movement. Irregularities in the wall bit into his back, but the pain seemed minor compared with the threat of torture at the guard's hand. Recalling his oaths of secrecy to the underworld, Taziar said nothing.

The guard's tone rattled with impatient anger. "Speak vermin. Who hired you?" The staff in his fists jabbed toward Taziar's face.

Taziar jerked his head to the right, and wood impacted stone with enough force to dislodge rust from the shackles. Again the staff shot toward him, and Taziar twisted his head to the left. Wood scraped his cheek and smote the wall.

Taziar's heart quickened. Fear huddled like a beast in his gut. He struggled against it, showing the guard only a defiant sneer. *Why should I protect the man who apparently deceived me?* Taziar moved his head to avoid a third strike and answered his own query. *Because the moment you talk, the baron no longer has a reason to keep you alive.*

The staff hovered in its wielder's hand. "Who hired you?"

Taziar replied with the strength of his decision. "You know I can't tell you."

The staff crashed into Taziar's stomach, driving breath from him in a whistling rush. He doubled over. The shackles resisted his movement, jolting his arm right to its injured shoulder.

Leaning smugly against his staff, the guard waited until Taziar regained his breath. Every heartbeat emphasized the nagging pain in his shoulder. The guard and his weapon blurred to a fleshy shadow. "Who hired you?" the guard repeated, soft as a kitten's purr.

Taziar spoke between gasps. "The same . . . one . . . who always hires . . . me." He stalled for time.

The staff weaved before Taziar's eyes. "His name," demanded the guard.

"I . . . don't know," lied the Shadow Climber.

The staff shot forward. Its tip met Taziar's chin and ground the base of his skull against the wall. Taziar's head felt as if it might explode, but he dared not move for fear the pole might slip to his throat. "All right," he whispered.

The staff retreated slightly. Taziar's thoughts stumbled through pain for memory of an underworlder he could name without consequence. "It was . . ." The guard withdrew his staff, and Taziar raised his head. ". . . Nelabarsh."

The staff crashed against Taziar's upper left ribs, shooting agony through his body. "Nelabarsh is dead!" the guard shouted. The staff slapped Taziar's side repeatedly. "Dead men don't pay!"

Taziar's scream echoed through the prison. He fought the bonds which held him. The guard's last words lodged in his thoughts. *Dead men don't pay.* Suddenly, he envied Nelabarsh.

The staff changed direction, came down heavily on his wounded shoulder. Every muscle tightened into a tiny ball. His eyes closed against pain, and his lips writhed open to emit tortured howls.

As suddenly as it started, the beating stopped. Taziar opened his eyes to slits. The staff lunged toward him like a snake. Its tip stabbed into the freshly reopened hole in his shoulder. Pain seared through him like fire. Blood colored the sweat which ran along his arm, directly contrasting with the stark white of his features. Consciousness staggered through red mist. His lips twitched, but he'd lost the urge to force words between them.

The guard pulled his staff, but the pain lin-

gered. Taziar managed to speak in a dull croak.
"Anything. I swear, I'll tell you any name you
want."

The guard relaxed, one hand at the top of the
staff, the other braced at its center. His eyes glittered like black diamonds. His mouth set, the corners bent slightly downward in expectation. "The
real one," he said. "The man who hired you."

"Ilyrian." Taziar's head buzzed, cursing his weakness. He awaited death or release.

The base of the staff flicked upward, slammed
into Taziar's groin. The thief's face contracted in
a soundless scream. His body went limp. Weakness shielded him from the graceless maneuvers
of the guard who unshackled him, tossed his sagging body back in his cell, and slammed the door
on his moans.

"Diseased and dying rat, I'll get the truth from
you." With this final threat, the guard left Taziar
to his anguish.

For some time, Taziar lay on the floor of his
cage until sleep blissfully exchanged torment for
oblivion.

Taziar awoke, curled like a fetus on the floor of
his cell. The jolt to consciousness tightened his
sinews, and pain ground and hammered his body
while memory of his torturer reeled through his
mind. *Karana's hell.* His stomach lurched violently.
He fought the quivering muscles of his gut and
rolled to his hands and knees. Dizziness smothered him in a curtain of black and red.

Taziar waited patiently while discomfort dissi-
pated, and the room returned to clarity. To his
right, the female prisoner lay on her chest, her

eyes vacantly forward. Her tongue flicked through her water dish like a cat's. Taziar turned away while resolve crushed the torment of his badly bruised ribs. *I won't become like her.* He could tell by the lack of scars on her skinny body, her trials had been far different from his own. *I must remain strong.*

Taziar mentally explored his aching body. Nothing seemed broken, and he realized his left side had sustained all the damage. He reached for his own bowl of water. Catching it in his right hand, he poured the warm liquid between his jaws. Most of it sloshed down his chest, and what entered his mouth tasted muddy, but it soothed his dry and swollen tongue. He dropped the empty bowl near a metal dish which held a cold lump of porridge. Yet despite his unappealing fare, the odor of meat rose above the stench of illness and despair.

Taziar shifted his attention ahead and to the left where the barbarian paced with the slow, powerful tread of a caged guard lion. Sinews stretched taut and sprang to position as he moved, more like a beast than a man. The barbarian paused at the door to his cell. Several moments passed before Taziar realized the huge man had met his gaze. The thief reddened, embarrassed at being caught staring at the other man. His eyes dropped to the stripped beef rib bones jutting from the barbarian's dish.

Rage tore through Taziar. A deceitful politician and an overindulgent guard had stripped him of all self-dignity and left him to die in anguish for the price of a trinket. Yet they fed and cared for this barbarian, who had surely murdered several of Cullinsberg's citizens without remorse. Taziar's fist crashed against the bars of his cell with enough force to send waves of agony across his body.

The outer door swung open. Taziar turned. Another man stood at the entry to the cell block with Pluchar and his fat companion. The sight of the man who'd splintered his pride with intolerable tortures washed Taziar's skin in sweat. The battering seemed only moments ago, though bruises and hunger revealed much more time had passed.

The third man tipped his head toward Taziar, and the thief recognized him in the dim light from the corridor. *Ilyrian!* Taziar crouched, jarred by a mixture of hatred and hope. He waited.

"Thank you. I'd speak with him alone." Ilyrian addressed the guards.

The fat man's reply sent Taziar into angry spasms. "He's small, but even desperate mice grow dangerous. Be careful."

"I won't go near him," Ilyrian promised. He started along the path between the cells as the door clanged shut behind him.

Taziar lowered himself to the floor and pressed his back to a corner of the bars. Ilyrian circled the far corner of the central cells and hesitated before the barbarian's cage. The nobleman's back snapped taut and his face screwed to a glare of disdain. Taziar closed his eyes while Ilyrian covered the remaining distance to his cell.

Taziar opened his eyes and fixed a bleary, pain-glazed glare to Ilyrian, who leaned against the wall chewing at his fingernail. Taziar's voice emerged as an unfamiliar whisper. "I hope you've come to release me."

Ilyrian met Taziar's gaze. "Release you?" His laughter thundered through the prison and faded to ugly silence. "After I worked so hard to gather the information to catch you? Such a foolish child."

"So, I was betrayed." Flecks of dried blood on the wall behind Ilyrian brought sour memories of Taziar's torture. *Small wonder the guard thought I lied when I named Ilyrian.*

Ilyrian's features twisted to a chilling frown. "Is lying to a thief betrayal? No matter. To me you served as a pawn to gain the favor of the baron and his priests . . ."

Taziar spit. "Karana damn you, liar."

Ilyrian continued as if Taziar had never interrupted. ". . . The baron wanted a thief with the appellation of Shadow Climber. I happened to gather some information. What a lucky coincidence my timely warning rescued the greatest artifact of the very temple which would confirm me as prime minister." Ilyrian's eyes narrowed.

For the first time, Taziar realized how much the nobleman's sharp features reminded him of a rat. The last stubborn remnants of pride held him silent.

Ilyrian sidestepped. Taziar sensed some inappropriate rage funneled against him. "When I set you up for arrest, I didn't know you were Taz Medakan's son. Years ago, your father menaced my rise to power." He turned on Taziar a sneer of wry amusement. "You can see which of us was destroyed by it."

Outrage filled Taziar, but he controlled the urge to question Ilyrian further. For now, he needed the nobleman's good will. "I've served your purposes, and I'm no threat to your cause. Let me free."

Ilyrian shook sand-colored curls from his cheeks.

"And risk the baron's disfavor? You'll have to give me a better reason than that."

Taziar tried another tactic. "I can get you anything you want."

"As could any of a dozen other thieves." Ilyrian yawned. "I already have what I want. I am the prime minister."

Taziar leaped foward and caught the bars of his cell door. "Anything," he repeated. "Even something you've deemed impossible. I am the Shadow Climber."

"As could any of a dozen other thieves with pseudonyms," Ilyrian amended. "Happy captivity." He waved a hand with bored nonchalance and swaggered from the cell block.

CHAPTER 3

Buchorin's Mercy

"We hand folks over to God's mercy, and show none ourselves."

—George Eliot,
Adam Bede

Voices floated to Taziar from the outer doorway, generously interspersed with laughter. Too distant to discern words, he turned his attention to the bars. Though pitted, the iron remained firm, the spaces between too slight to allow Taziar to squeeze through them. *Trapped. No way out.* Yet Taziar's nature would not permit despair. *Limits are men's delusions, a means to justify failure. If no one has ever escaped the baron's dungeon, I will simply be the first, just as no thief stole Aga'arin's chalice before me.* His own bold thoughts comforted him. From experience, he knew an opportunity for escape would arise in time. He only hoped it would come before the guards killed him.

Across the way and to the left, the barbarian sat in his cell, his back pressed to the wall, arms folded to his chest. Taziar might have believed he slept if not for the unblinking, pale eyes trained on the trio in the doorway.

Ilyrian's baritone rose in farewell. "I care not. Leave his fate to the baron and Aga'arin's priest."

The comma of black hair spilled into Taziar's eye. He ignored it and focused his full awareness on the pair of guards who approached his cell from opposite sides. Ignoring Pluchar, he watched the fat man wrestle his own bulk for the key ring at his belt. Taziar tried to lock his face in an expressionless pall, but discomfort flickered through the china blue of his eyes, and his cheeks twitched involuntarily.

Pluchar rattled his staff against the bars and spoke gently. "We're taking you to Buchorin. I won't hurt you if you don't fight."

Your actions don't concern me. Taziar's eyes trained on Pluchar's fat companion with fanatical interest. He resisted an urge to scuttle to the back of his cage. This, he knew, would only gain him Pluchar's staff in his ribs.

The cell door swung open with a shrill complaint. "Out!"

Struggling with his natural repugnance, Taziar clamped his injured arm to his chest, turned his right side toward the guard, and moved slowly to the door.

Despite his bulk, the guard moved as quickly as a ferret. His moist, pink hand closed about Taziar's wrist, and he tore the thief from his cell.

Stone scraped Taziar's chest. He went limp and passively allowed the guard to subdue him, hoping to avoid the pain resistance might inspire. The guard held him to the floor with a heel in the crook of his back and yanked Taziar's right arm behind him. Concerned for his injured shoulder, Taziar gave his left hand freely. Cold steel closed about his wrists. The fat man fastened another set of fetters to his ankles.

The guard caught Taziar's manacles by the short chain between them and hefted the thief as easily as a cornered kitten. The expression on the guard's jowly face was one of disappointment. *He wanted me to fight*, Taziar realized. The guard took the staff from Pluchar and prodded the thief toward the outer door. *My compliance cheated him out of a chance to batter me.* As Taziar walked with the short, careful tread the shackles allowed, memories of his father's advice resurfaced. "Arrests, patrols, and murder," the older man used to stay. "Never trust a guard who loves his work." It seemed to Taziar the fat man not only embodied this expression; he took a malicious pleasure in executing his tortures.

Slightly exaggerating his condition, Taziar stumbled through the outer doorway nearly into the arms of the three armed guards placed as sentries. One caught him by the shoulder and faced him straighter in the corridor ahead. The maneuver gave Taziar a chance to study the layout of the baron's keep. Ahead, the hallway stretched, without branches, to a sharp left turn. The right-hand wall ended in a long, stone-framed window.

Taziar continued on, reluctant to face the accusations of Aga'arin's priest. The staff jabbed his back, urging him forward. Taziar complied. At the bend in the corridor, he intentionally staggered against the window. The sun hovered over Cullinsberg which lay seven stories beneath him. Light glimmered like gilt from the baron's moat,

seeming unbearably far down. Pluchar caught
Taziar's left arm, and the thief shivered back against
pain. Under ordinary circumstances, he could scale
the wall without difficulty. Injured and shackled,
he would fall to his death.

Unceremoniously, the larger guard spun Taziar
around the bend in the hall and pulled him to a
halt before a door. Farther along the passage,
guards gathered; most watched Taziar expectantly.
Pluchar rapped on the chamber door.

A dark-haired man in the silver-trimmed, gold
robes of Aga'arin's acolytes pulled open the panel
and greeted the guards with a stiffly formal bow.
He stepped aside as the two guards entered with
their prisoner between them. Buchorin perched
on an overstuffed chair, watching the scene with
an aloof scorn. To Taziar, he looked like a spoiled
child grown tired of his toys.

"Kneel," the fat guard commanded. Before
Taziar could comply, the staff slapped the backs
of his knees. His legs buckled beneath the blow,
and he dropped to the floor. While the guards
took positions at either side, Taziar lowered his
buttocks to his heels and avoided the priest's penetrating gaze.

With a pompous flourish of his hand, Buchorin
rose from his seat and stood before Taziar. The
thief stared at the priest's shoes, crafted of white
bear hide brought from the north at no small cost.
Ermine trimmed his robes. "So this is the thief
who tried to despoil Aga'arin's temple." Buchorin's
voice emerged annoyingly nasal and nearly as high-
pitched as a woman's.

Buchorin moved with none of a fighting man's
speed. He caught a handful of Taziar's hair and

jerked his face upward with an angry pull. Forced to meet the muddy, yellow eyes of his accuser, Taziar glared with violent anger.

"Tiny thing, isn't he?" the priest continued. "Surprising he could carry the chalice from its home."

Taziar bit his lip and made no reply.

Buchorin's grip went lax. Burdened with the weight of hatred and humiliation, Taziar let his chin drift to his chest. The priest's fist closed suddenly. He jerked upward. Pain flared along Taziar's scalp, sharp contrast to the chorus of dull aches which served as constant reminder of the guard's torture.

Taziar pursed his lips against the angry tide of thought he dared not verbalize. *Demoralized by a priest who preaches mercy. But what more should I expect from an overstuffed dog who wallows in the riches he convinces his congregation to defer for the afterlife? What singular lack of humanity would allow a holy man who sanctions punishment and reward after death to abuse a helpless man?*

Buchorin's free hand tensed. Taziar flinched. His back hit the guard's plump legs as the priest's palm darted forward. The slap reverberated through the small room. Taziar's cheeks flushed scarlet, more from rising fury than the force of the blow. Stung beyond thought of consequence, Taziar spit in Buchorin's face.

Buchorin recoiled with a yelp of surprised outrage. Taziar's face pinched into a tense mask. The guard's staff crashed across his back. Unable to break the fall with his arms manacled behind his back, Taziar collapsed to the floor. He lay still, hoping the guard might think him unconscious and forego the effort of a second blow. But the fat man caught the chain between Taziar's wrists and hoisted the hapless thief to his feet.

Again Buchorin confronted Taziar. The priest's face had turned dark as spilled blood. He spoke in a sibilant voice, and saliva sprayed from his lips with each forceful word. "I had thought to spare you for Aga'arin's justice in the afterlife. But now . . ." His eyelids twitched as he sought words as reprehensible as his thoughts. ". . . vermin, the guards can have you!"

Taziar went rigid. He fought to maintain the quiet control he had known through all his thefts. But he'd never before heard his death pronounced with certainty. The fat guard jabbed him toward the door, and he staggered, caught in a wave of emotional intensity. His eyes measured acolytes and guards, seeking sympathy in a roomful of enemies, hoping to find one caring man who might later aid his cause. He focused on the fat guard's face. The cruel, dark eyes gleamed with wicked anticipation, and Taziar felt composure slip like sweat from his taut limbs. The door clicked open before him, loud as thunder in the room's warped silence. Together, Pluchar and his companion pushed Taziar through, and the door closed with the same heightened amplitude of sound.

The hall sentries merged toward the guards and their prisoner. Their questions seemed to blend into the numbing rumble of sea in an empty whelk shell. Taziar heard his sentence of execution repeated until the words failed to have meaning. He stumbled through the long hallway between Pluchar and his obese companion. If he received blows or trips or jibes, Taziar noticed none of them. His rational mind raced, lost behind the all-encompassing need to escape before his imminent torture and death.

A jab from the fat guard's staff propelled Taziar forward. The window ledge drove breath from him and returned awareness in a sudden rush. The baron's moat shimmered in the grayness of Cullinsberg's evening. Taziar imagined his body plummeting through the moist air. Somehow, the vision comforted. He had always expected death to come to him in this fashion, a fall from a wall or ledge, the rush of air like the strongest winter wind, the short burst of complete agony followed by the nothingness of the final void. But the fat guard spun Taziar through the corridor. Without a word, he pushed past his companions before the prison's door, unlocked it, and half-dragged, half-carried the thief to his cell.

The cool, stone floor of his cage soothed Taziar's throbbing shoulder. The door shut with a slam of finality, and the guard growled a menacing promise. "Lick your wounds, thief, while you still have a tongue to do it with." As he crossed the row of cells, his receding bootfalls echoed like laughter.

Taziar did not bother to reply. He lay motionless, mentally reviewing the fat guard's techniques of forcing him from the cage. He sagged to the floor, body aching. Dully, he stared into the adjoining cell where the ragged girl sprawled like a broken doll. *They can kill me, but they can't break me. I won't ever become like her!* Vitality surged through Taziar. Memories rushed down upon him. He saw his father, resplendent in the regalia of war. But the older Medakan's face was grave as he stared at the tiny, wiry figure of his son. "Men fight for many causes," said the father, his voice an unsettling monotone. "Religion, faith, the honor of country and ruler, insecurity, and worst of all, joy of slaughter. But, son, let no man convince you he fights for life. Those who love life become farmers and craftsmen and merchants. To become a warrior, a man must kill himself inside. Once he has reached this realization, he fears nothing. No one can do him harm."

Now, pinned beneath the fat guard's threat, Taziar called upon the courage his father inspired. He stared at the barbarian across the walk who watched him with curious sympathy. A slight smile shivered across the wild man's lips, and he seemed about to speak. Instead, he turned away. Taziar's mental strength blossomed to the renewed fury of injustice. *Ignore my plight, uncivilized one. Long after you remain, exchanging glares with that whale of guard, I'll be running through Cullinsberg's streets, climbing to greater heights, inspired by the blood heat of action.*

Taziar lowered himself to his knees. The unspoken tirade dispersed anger, but left him oddly embarrassed and unsettled. For the twentieth time, he checked the bars of his cell for flaws, though he knew he would find nothing major enough to aid his escape. As he tested the door lock again, the outer, barred door to the prison creaked like the planks of a casket as the last nail is hammered in place.

Taziar flinched flat to the farthest corner of his cage. The fat guard rolled like a shadow along the walkway between the cells, passed the barbarian without a glance, and stopped directly at the entrance to Taziar's cell. The keys in his hand rattled like the warning of a striking snake. "Out, vermin!"

Taziar crouched.

The guard's eyes lost their twinkle of pleasure and went hard and dark as death. "If you make me come in after you, I swear this will be as slow and painful as possible."

Taziar crowded so tightly to the cage back, the bars pressed long, red prints against his side. He screened the long-buried memories of his father's words for some description of the dungeons which might furnish an idea for a breakout. *Taz, the worst task of all is prison duty. Like whipped dogs in cages shaped like kennels, men huddle despite your best reassurances. And why should they believe you? Some of the guards handle prisoners unnecessarily roughly. Some of the women have been raped a hundred times . . .*

The cell door swung open. "A slow death then." The guard's voice rasped. His bulk shivered lower. The expression on his face mingled annoyance and anticipation. "The harder you make this, the worse it becomes for you." With a fighting man's caution, he entered the cage.

Taziar's sinews tightened to wire. The images from the past seemed more real than the fat guard's threats. *The only means to pull them from the sacred back corner of the cell and still keep control was to catch a wrist and a handful of hair . . .*

The guard inched forward. He shifted his weight to his legs, and his center of gravity rolled backward. His hands darted toward Taziar.

Taziar dove between the guard's arms. His palms struck the meaty face. The combined force of every sinew of his body drove the guard off balance. The guard's head impacted the cage roof with a ring of metal. Taziar regathered his strength and leaped at the fat man. His head hit the guard's massive stomach, and pain lanced along his neck. But the force of the strike knocked the guard to this buttocks. Taziar scrambled for freedom.

A curse broke from the guard's wide lips. He scuttled out of the cage and caught Taziar's calf. The thief sprawled to the ground. He struggled to regain his feet. The guard's fingers latched onto his throat and wrist and whisked him flat to the walkway. The huge hand shifted from neck to hair, and he hoisted Taziar painfully to shaky legs. Taziar threw a protective arm before his face. The guard readjusted his weight. He loosed Taziar's wrist, and crashed a fist into the thief's gut.

Air whistled through Taziar's teeth, and pain banished all hope of escape. He sagged, fighting to regain his breath. Anguish stabbed along his diaphragm. Taziar was certain he would never breathe again. Even as he gasped with effort, blows rained upon his body until he no longer felt their sting.

Air came slowly to Taziar's starved lungs and rasped painfully in his throat. He raised his arms in a gesture of surrender. But the guard caught his forearms, twisted for momentum, and flung his tiny body sideways. Taziar struck the bars of his cell with a force which drove him nearly to unconsciousness. He lay spread-eagled, awaiting the final blow.

"Stupid, miserable rat." The guard snarled. His breath smelled putrid. Sweat leached through his armor, staining the leather black. Muscled limbs advanced toward Taziar. The little thief gathered strength to dodge, too late. Fat fingers bruised his arms, whisked him about, and pounded his back against the wall where he had been tortured. The world swam. The usually comforting wash of adrenalin had grown stale, replaced by more foreign body chemicals which would dampen both pain and reason. The guard's fist cracked against his jaw. Taziar smiled stupidly despite the blood which colored his teeth. He dropped, curled against the base of the wall.

Again, the guard hefted Taziar. Dizzied beyond comprehension, the thief staggered toward the guard. Instinctively, the fat man recoiled. With a grunt of annoyance, he shifted position, caught the limp thief, and jammed him against the barbarian's cell. Bars pressed into Taziar's back, revivingly cold through rising sweat. The guard's crushing grip on his neck was the only force which held him upright.

Suddenly, from behind Taziar, the barbarian's fist snaked between the bars and wound in the guard's hair. The guard's sneer melted to a grimace. Fear filled his eyes. His fingers went slack, and Taziar slid to the floor. The fat man's voice wafted to him as if from a great distance, grating with threat. "You think we treat you bad now? If you hurt me, hell will seem welcome!"

A deep rumble rose from behind the bars like the purr of a giant kitten. Through the unshakable haze between reality and dream, Taziar recognized the sound as the barbarian's laughter. He struggled to one knee as the barbarian tensed. The guard's head struck the bars with an impact which jarred Taziar to the ground. A single scream rent the tomblike sanctity of the baron's prison. Repeatedly, the guard's head thunked against the cell wall. Flailing limbs buffeted Taziar as the guard bucked in the throes of death. Then, suddenly, the expanse of body flopped to the floor beside him.

Taziar's thoughts narrowed to one idea. *Weapon! I need a weapon.* He rolled toward the guard, turning his eyes from the bloody mass which had served as the guard's head. A delicate search revealed no weapons. No sword hung at the dead man's side. No knives graced ankle, hip, or pocket. The wide belt around the fat man's waist supported only the prison keys. The twigs of metal slid through Taziar's hand and rattled hollowly. The barbarian voiced an unrecognizable expletive. A huge hand, dripping guard's blood, clawed for Taziar.

Dulled by pain, Taziar did not move. The barbarian's reach fell short, and the thief watched in fascination. His eyes rolled to the wild man's face and met a demanding expression and eyes as hard and unquestioning as nature. It took Taziar's mind an unreasonably long time to recognize the obvious. *He wants the keys. And he saved my life.*

Taziar caught the keys and struggled to his feet. He waited for dizziness to pass in a wash of blackness marred by white spots. The barbarian watched expectantly. Taziar's shaking hand jerked toward the barbarian. He flung the key ring at the massive figure beyond the bars and ran.

Again, Taziar's thoughts channeled on a single track. *Escape is only through the dungeon door.* Metal clanked behind him as he half-ran, half-staggered through the cell block. Even as he approached the barred outer door, sense seeped slowly back to his numbed brain. One of the three sentries at the door leaped and spun. "Taziar's loose!" A sword sprang to his hand, reflecting candlelight like stars.

Taziar cursed the fog of pain which dulled his normally quick wit. He wheeled and raced back into the depths of the prison. A voice rose above the hammer of his heartbeat. "I'll get him. He's hurt pretty badly." The door creaked open and crashed shut. Pursuing booted footfalls haunted Taziar through the corridor. The guard was running.

Taziar ran as fast as his failing strength allowed, around the curve in the prison path and past his own cell. Abruptly, the echo of footsteps died, replaced by blaring silence. Taziar whirled. Up the corridor, the barbarian draped the sentry across one shoulder. The guard's neck lay at an awkward angle, and his sword glittered in the barbarian's hand. The barbarian crept soundlessly toward the outer door. Panting and sick with the taste of blood, Taziar followed.

The barbarian pressed near the wall, at a bend in the cell path where the outer sentries could not see him. He readjusted his grip on the dead guard, then effortlessly tossed the body to the floor before the door.

"That's Dolme!" The sentries went cautious. The door lock clicked, and the barbarian crouched. Sword at the ready, one guard entered the cell block. Even as the other made to lock the gate behind him, the barbarian sprang. His blade slid across the guard's throat as he passed. His shoulder hit the barred door. The sentry's strength was no match for the barbarian's moving bulk. The gate flew open and smashed the sentry against the wall stones.

The barbarian never slowed. He charged up the long hallway, Taziar close behind. The layout was exactly as the little thief remembered from his audience with Buchorin. The corridor made a sharp bend to the left. Ahead, the window beckoned, dark as a well mouth. Its silken curtains flapped in the night breeze. At the turn, the barbarian stopped with a grunt of frustration. Taziar pulled up beside him and stared down the corridor.

A multitude of guards lined the hall, all in metal-studded armor and most armed with broadswords. But the barbarian gazed beyond the immediate threat to a growing row of crossbows at the back. Taziar swore. He caught at the window ledge, fighting the mental mist which threatened to consume him. Dangerously far below them, the baron's moat reflected the light of distant stars in a marbled pattern of black and gold.

CHAPTER 4

Shylar's Haven

"Let no one pay me honor with tears, nor celebrate my funeral rites with weeping."
— *Quintus Ennius,*
From CICERO, De Senectute

Taziar Medakan and the barbarian crouched, pinned against the window by guardsmen in the baron's hall. The gray tracing of the outer wall plunged seven stories only to disappear at the waterline. Moonlight winked from the surface of the moat. Groggy from blood loss and beatings, Taziar scrambled awkwardly to the sill. An arrow bounced from its ledge. The sentries blurred to an advancing mass of swords and bows, and Taziar's shadow-clotted senses forced realization upon him. *I'm too weak to climb quickly. They'll shoot me before I reach the ground.* Still unwilling to surrender, he eased his toes into cracks in the wall stones. The barbarian dove through the window. A broad sweep of the huge man's arm slammed into Taziar, toppling him, and an arrow pierced the air where the thief had been.

Taziar plummeted. Wind howled in his ears. He flailed for a handhold, but his fingers sliced only air. He curled to a ball and crashed into the moat. Impact dazed him, jarred agony through his aching limbs. Its shimmering murk swallowed him. Foam spewed, red-stained from the reopened wound in his shoulder. His own weight dragged him deeper. He clawed blindly, trying to swim, but pain and exhaustion robbed him of strength and the dark, greedy water stole all sense of direction. Dizzied and air-starved, he fought for consciousness. His limbs felt lead-weighted. Pain seared his throat, forcing him to breathe, and water funneled into his mouth.

Suddenly, the barbarian's thick fingers closed on Taziar's wrist. A steady pull drew Taziar to the surface. Air rushed into his raw throat, choking him. He felt the barbarian's grip shift to his hair and chin and, with strong swimming strokes, drag him landward. Taziar lay still, feeling water sluice around him until the barbarian released him, limp and sputtering, on the grass-cushioned bank.

Above Taziar, the moon and stars appeared like rents in night's fabric. Then the barbarian's craggy face blocked his view of the sky. He met soft, lead colored eyes which seemed oddly caring. *My father's eyes were gray.* Though irrelevant, the thought clung to Taziar's clouded mind. Memories of his father's words spun through his mind like a song he could not suppress. *A man becomes a hero when he continues fighting though he no longer cares if he dies.* The thought raised a faint flicker of determination. And with the reemergence of will came urgency. He staggered to his feet, and a fit of coughing doubled him over. "Come on!"

His voice sounded hoarse as a whisper. Catching the barbarian's arm, he sprinted across cleared ground into the town proper. The other man followed.

Taziar traversed Cullinsberg's roads from habit. The streets appeared to have grown to endless, bleak tunnels, empty save for his own footfalls and the barbarian's warm breath on his scalp. Every step jarred pain through him. Each tortured breath burned from the grime and water in his lungs. Wind whipped through the alleyways, cutting beneath the dripping tatters of his clothes. His pace had dropped to a painful jog when he rounded the corner of Panogya Street and stopped at the black door of Shylar's whorehouse. He pounded with both fists.

Seconds dragged into eons. A tentative answering tap sounded from the opposite side of the door. Taziar's vision hazed to a gray plain. He forced all his concentration into raising a trembling hand. His head buzzed, masking sound so he could not discern his own sequence of knocks: two . . . pause . . . two . . . pause . . . three. The scrape of the opening bolt seemed distant. The door swung inward, and Shylar studied Taziar and his companion in the moon's wavering light. "Shadow?"

Taziar fixed his jaw to speak. Vertigo buffeted him to oblivion, and he collapsed in Shylar's arms.

For seven days, Taziar lay senseless on a cot in Shylar's whorehouse. Young, beautiful women tended his wounds and, in his brief moments of lucidity, fed him. But to Taziar, the recurring dream memory forced upon him seemed far more real. Caught within his own recollection, he knew

himself as a child on the day of his father's execution. He recalled the older man's eyes and their
gray gleam of urgency which goaded Taziar to
action. He reexperienced the father-driven frenzy
which had sent him racing through Cullinsberg's
streets. Locked in his dream, Taziar relived a pause
to catch his breath and heard the soft verbal exchange of passing guardsmen. At the time, sorrow
and outrage had drained their words of meaning.
Now, comatose in Shylar's whorehouse, Taziar's
mind forced details upon him which he had long
suppressed from memory.

This time, the guardsmen's conversation came
to Taziar clearly. One, pinched-faced and drawn,
spoke in a voice colored with surprise. ". . . Didn't
you know? They locked him in the dungeon. He
battered Ilyrian. Grabbed him by the throat and
made him admit he falsified reports. Even got
him to say he set up the whole thing with the
messenger."

The other guard shook his head. "Ilyrian said
that?"

The first man spat. "Sure. He probably would
have taken full responsibility for poverty, crime
and the war with the bastard's fingers locked on
his neck . . ."

Taziar's thoughts focused. Gradually, the image
faded. He pictured Ilyrian's dark, curled hair and
rodentlike features and recalled the words the
nobleman had spoken in the baron's dungeon:
*Years ago, your father menaced my rise to power. You
can see which of us was destroyed by it.* No doubt, the
charges against Taziar's father had been contrived
by Ilyrian.

Taziar's callused fingers twisted the bedsheets.

Grief dissolved before black rage. "Karana damn you, viper!" His screamed curse echoed through Shylar's hall. *The next blood spilt, Ilyrian, will be yours.* Through a haze of delirium, Taziar dove upon the Ilyrian-figure in his dream.

Wildly, Taziar flailed. One punch met flesh, then a second. Words buzzed into his ear, unintelligible in the blur between nightmare, memory, and reality. Fingers encircled his wrists. He fought blindly. The grip on his skin tightened, pinning him to the bed. Taziar howled, twisting and kicking beneath the coverlet. He opened his eyes; darkness shattered to sudden clarity. The barbarian hovered over him, gaze soft with almost motherly concern. Blood trickled from the corner of his mouth where one of Taziar's frantic blows had landed.

Karana's endless hell, what have I done? Taziar shook his head to disperse the last remnants of dizziness. "I'm all right now." He studied the walls, recognizing the warped, gray paint of one of Shylar's second-floor workrooms. Aside from his cot and the barbarian, the room stood empty.

The barbarian's grip relaxed. He sat, cross-legged, on the floor before Taziar. His voice emerged in a deep singsong. "Feel better?"

Shocked by the barbarian's use of the barony's language, Taziar grimaced. "Yes. Sorry I hit you. I must have been dreaming."

The barbarian tilted his blond head soberly but said nothing.

Taziar made a sweeping gesture. "You speak our language."

The barbarian made no reply. Apparently, he saw no need to address Taziar's self-evident statement.

Taziar pressed further. "How? And why didn't you speak with me in the dungeon?"

"I learned your tongue from a man who wintered with my people." The barbarian answered Taziar's questions in turn. "And talking with you would have been unwise. The guards spoke freely in my presence because they assumed I could not understand their language. I dared not take a chance they might hear us."

Taziar nodded. The barbarian's explanation seemed plausible. "My name's Taziar Medakan."

The corners of the barbarian's mouth twitched upward. He started to speak. "Tazi . . ." His lips split wide and he laughed with enough force to steal his breath.

With effort, Taziar shifted position to support his weight on an elbow. "Why are you laughing?"

Convulsed with mirth, the barbarian gave no answer.

The barbarian's antics turned Taziar defensive. His tone went crisp with annoyance. "Taziar is a fine name. It was my father's name. And his father's name . . ."

The barbarian caught his breath. He forced words around snickers. "What . . . does it mean?"

"Mean?" Taziar raked his hand through his tangled, black hair. "It doesn't mean anything."

The barbarian collapsed in another paroxysm of laughter. "How can a name mean nothing? And why do the women call you Shadow?"

Taziar bit his lip, attributing the barbarian's reaction to cultural differences and a dull mentality. "Because . . ." He paused, then chose his simplest option. "Because that's what Taziar means. It means shadow." He considered, realizing his cover no longer mattered. "And Medakan means climber."

Regaining his composure, the barbarian settled back into his position by Taziar's cot. "I am Moonbear."

The irony was not lost on Taziar. He slapped his palms over his face. *I just defended my name to a barbarian called "Moonbear."* He lowered his hands to his sides, glad to change the subject. "Thanks for saving my life in the baron's moat. I owe you."

Moonbear's face creased with puzzlement. "You were drowning."

Taziar flushed. "I know. You rescued me. Thank you."

Moonbear stared. "You were drowning. You would have died. You owe me nothing."

Taziar knotted his small hands, slightly offended. "Are you suggesting my life is worthless?"

Moonbear seemed taken aback. He stammered, "I . . . I . . . would never think to put gold value on a person's life. You were drowning. I could save you. If I did not, it would be as if I murdered you."

Moonbear's reasoning made little sense to Taziar. "Luckily for me, you didn't seem to mind murdering the prison guard."

Moonbear rocked in place. He spoke slowly. "I do not murder enemies. I kill them. He was an enemy. You are a friend."

Taziar considered. *Moonbear's definition of "friend" seems rather loose.* Not wishing to appear ungrateful, he kept the thought to himself and abandoned the point. "Fine, *friend*. How long have we been here?"

"Seven days."

"S-seven days!" Taziar jabbed his hands beneath the coverlet, feeling the healing scars and scabs from his torture in the baron's dungeon beneath the coarse fabric of an unfamiliar tunic. His shoulder no longer ached.

Shylar's voice echoed Moonbear's answer. "Seven days." She slipped into the room, her plaid frock weaving about her hips. "Too long." Her voice held an unaccustomed harshness. "Tonight, you both must go."

Taziar tensed to speak, but Moonbear's voice cut above his like a whipcrack. "No! Shadow's too sick. He's not ready to travel."

Shylar hissed. "Tonight, you overgrown rag doll. I can't risk any more. Not even for . . ." She met Taziar's confused stare, and tension seemed to dissolve from her. ". . . you, Shadow."

Taziar worked to a sitting position. "Quiet, both of you! I awaken after seven days, and all you two can do is ridicule me and yell at each other. Shylar?"

Gaze fixed on her shoes, Shylar mumbled. "Good to have you back, Shadow." She clasped his hand, squeezing affectionately. "Forgive me. The last few days have been difficult."

Wondering what antics of Moonbear's might have angered Shylar, Taziar rolled his eyes toward the barbarian.

Apparently guessing Taziar's concern, Shylar shook her head. "No. Moonbear's a pleasant enough guest. But I don't think he understands the gravity of this situation." With a crooked wink at Taziar, she tapped her head to indicate some concern about Moonbear's intelligence. "Neither, I fear, do you."

Nausea passed through Taziar. He leaned forward. "They got Aga'arin's chalice back, and they punished me thoroughly." He shrugged. "Soon enough, the town will forget. Of course, I'll need another alias." He laughed alone.

Shylar caught both of Taziar's forearms. Her dark eyes fixed on his face. "Sentries comb the borders of Cullinsberg, letting no one in or out. Patrols in town have trebled. Yesterday, the baron started searching homes for the two of you. Shadow, he's put five thousand weight in gold on your heads! I didn't know the baron had that much money."

Taziar's eyes widened in disbelief. *Three times the value of the chalice for a thief and a barbarian. It makes no sense.* "Why?"

With a heavy sigh, Shylar released Taziar. "No one seems to know. Not even the guards. Whatever the reason, I can't risk having you here any longer. Numerous people pass through every day. For five thousand weight in gold, even one of my girls might talk. Too many lives and jobs depend on this house. A raid here would destroy the underground. And my life . . ."

Taziar flinched. "Say no more. I understand. We'll leave tonight."

Moonbear snarled. "No!" The sudden expletive startled Taziar. "He's too sick to travel."

Taziar swung his legs over the side of the cot. "I'm fine." To demonstrate, he stood. His vision blurred and spun. Weak as twigs, his legs collapsed beneath him. He crashed to the floor.

Shylar and Moonbear glared at one another. Each caught one of Taziar's arms and hoisted him to the bed. Shylar's wrinkled countenance softened. "You have two more days." Striding toward the door, she added, "And may Mardain protect us all." She left the room. The door slammed closed behind her.

Taziar spent a restless night on his cot in Shylar's whorehouse, plagued by the thought of a bounty of such nonsensical proportion. *None of my thefts warrant such effort. As for Moonbear, the barbarian wars ended five years ago. I know of no major hostility since that time.* Taziar rolled to his side. But sleep remained elusive. An image of Ilyrian's face formed in his mind, and his skin washed cold with sweat. The memory of his dream returned. Taziar fought down hatred. *I can't condemn a man on a suspicion.*

Taziar flipped to his other side, noticing, for the first time, Moonbear lying on a pallet beside him. Limp strands of hair had fallen over the barbarian's face, and Taziar watched them dance with each of Moonbear's breaths. Carefully, Taziar lowered his feet to the floor. Dizziness crushed in on him, but this time he managed to remain standing. With the broad-based, deliberate tread of a toddler, he paced. *I will confront Ilyrian and assure myself of his guilt. Then, I must avenge my father's death.*

Strengthened by his decision, Taziar returned to his bed. But, almost immediately, doubts gnawed at his mind. The brave, new oath he had sworn ached in him like a burden. Pledging violence, even against his father's murderer, seemed to undermine the morals he'd embraced since childhood. The idea of killing repulsed him. But his vow of vengeance would not be banished. *Even if I perform no act against the traitor, I need to prove his guilt. I owe it to my father's memory. I owe it to my mother. And I owe it to myself.*

The muscles of Taziar's jaw clamped tight. He forced them to relax, feeling his limbs uncoil simultaneously. Though still burdened by his decision, sleep finally came to him.

A weak beam of sunlight streamed through the open crack of the doorway, awakening Taziar. He sat up. Beside him, Moonbar sprawled in a chair, binding a turkey feather fletching to a smoothed and sharpened shaft. A table before him held half a dozen similar arrows and a ceramic bowl with steam rising. A grain and honey smell twined through the room.

Moonbear smiled. "Good morning. Porridge?" He gestured toward the dish.

Taziar yawned and stretched. He scratched his side, feeling each rib. "Good morning, Moonbear." Rising, he crossed the room, took the bowl, and returned to his pallet. The ceramic felt warm in his hands. Inside, the creamy white cereal striped with raw, brown honey looked inviting. A wooden spoon jutted from the mixture. Grasping it, Taziar stirred.

Silently, Moonbear continued his craft.

Taziar scooped a spoonful of porridge into his mouth, and its warmth suffused him. "So, where you from?"

Moonbear never looked up. "North."

Taziar scraped with his spoon. "North, huh?" He smiled. "Danwald Wilderness?"

Moonbear shook his head. "We call it Danemark. And no. I am from farther north across the sea in a kingdom known as Sweden."

Taziar put his breakfast aside, surprised by

Moonbear's revelation. Stories abounded about the magical lands across the Kattegat, tales of sorcerers, dragons, and golden-haired pirates. "I know of no hostilities between Cullinsberg and the lands across the sea."

Moonbear snorted. "Only because the baron has no ships. We came to visit our cousins in Danemark. But Cullinsberg's guards murdered my friends and locked me in the baron's castle. When I killed a soldier trying to get free, they threw me in their dungeon." He waved a hand in disgust, redirecting the conversation. "Shy Lark gave me something you may need." He reached into a fold of his cloak, withdrew a dagger, and gently tossed it onto Taziar's cot.

Amused by Moonbear's bastardization of Shylar's name, Taziar examined the slim, tapered blade. A bright strip of steel traced the edges, indicating recent sharpening. Its tooled leather grip felt worn and comfortable in his fist. He tucked it into his belt.

Moonbear watched with apparent interest. "You're not a warrior, are you, Shadow?"

Taziar picked up his bowl of porridge, finding the question gross understatement. "No. I'm a merchant." Taking a spoonful of the cooling mixture, he chewed thoughtfully. *The barbarian has twice saved my life. I owe him the truth at least.* "Actually, I'm a thief. The rest of the barony knows it now, so why shouldn't you?"

"A thief?" Moonbear set aside his finished arrow, looking genuinely puzzled. "What is a thief?"

Taziar stared, incredulous. Innocence as simple and complete as Moonbear's seemed inconceivable, but the sincerity of the barbarian's question could not be denied. It unsettled Taziar, inspiring a shame he had not felt since his early days among the street gang. While he considered his answer, his mind wandered to a memory from six years ago. He sat with Rabbit on a warehouse roof, watching the closing-time bustle of Cullinsberg's market. They played a familiar game in which they guessed the contents of each passerby's pockets. Taziar swung his legs, feeling pensive. "So, Rabbit," he asked cautiously. "Does stealin' things ever make you feel bad?"

Rabbit did not hesitate. "No. Do I wanna know why ya're askin'?"

Young Taziar replied, knowing from past experience he could speak openly with Rabbit. "Sometimes I don't like it. I think maybe *I'm* eatin' tonight 'cause I made *someone else* go hungry." He paused thoughtfully. "Ever wish you had an honest occupation?"

"Ya mean would I like ta be the baron's son, live in a castle, have my meals served by gorgeous women, and wallow in riches?" Rabbit's tone went blatantly sarcastic. "No, Taz. I prefer ta live in a alley, feast on rats, and bathe in sewage troughs."

Taziar grumbled, feeling betrayed by the one person with whom he felt comfortable enough to reveal his private thoughts. "Sorry I asked."

Rabbit sighed. "All right, yes. Don't say nothin' to Blade, but sometimes it bothers me, too." His forehead creased with thought. "Then I remember Berin and some of the others who's been caught by guards. If they can kill without carin', I can steal. The baron's soldiers slaughter barbarians every day. Ya think it bothers them?"

Taziar recalled his father's sobering descriptions of war. "It bothered my father."

"Really?" Rabbit seemed unconvinced. "Well, maybe he was as crazy as his son."

"What is a thief?" Moonbear repeated, jarring Taziar from his reverie.

Taziar swallowed. "I . . . take things from other people."

Moonbear shrugged. "Good. If you need things more, they should give them to you. You should not have to take anything."

Moonbear's words confused Taziar. Uncertain how to address such a statement, he pondered a reply.

Abruptly, a high-pitched scream shrilled through the whorehouse hallway, followed by a second. Dropping his handiwork, Moonbear sprinted for the door. Feathers spiraled from his lap, floating to the floor in a wash of gray-barred brown.

Taziar hollered. "Wait! You can't. . . !"

But Moonbear wrenched open the door and galloped into the hall as another shriek rent the air.

Muttering blasphemies, Taziar followed unsteadily. The room emptied into a hallway. At the farther end stood three iron-bossed doors, one slightly ajar. From the room beyond came a pained whine and then a woman's voice, pleading.

Like an enraged beast, Moonbear charged through the portal. The door slammed against the wall. Still some distance behind, Taziar glanced through the entryway. A thick-muscled man, partially dressed in the red and black breeks of the baron's guards, shook a naked woman. Her head bobbed. She screamed again. Early bruises colored her torso.

"Moonbear, wait!" Taziar's hand slid to the dagger in his belt.

Moonbear leaped. He seized the guard's shoulders, spinning the man like a toy. The guardsman's back struck the wall. Surprise crossed his features. His right hand raked toward his sword. Moonbear punched. His fist crashed into the guard's gut. Breath rushed from the guardsman. His face went blank as a mask, and he dropped to the floor. Moonbear turned to the woman.

She clung to Moonbear, sobbing against his chest. He smoothed her hair, whispering words Taziar could not hear from the doorway. The guard's eyes flickered open. Silently, he crouched. Taziar heard the rasp of a drawn sword. Steel flashed as the guardsman regained his feet and rushed toward Moonbear's unshielded back.

A cry of warning caught in Taziar's throat. He forced the word between his lips. "No!" The guard twisted toward him. Taziar sprang. The knife slid in his sweaty grip. Realizing his peril, the guard redirected his strike. Taziar raised his arm to drive his dagger through the guard's defense. Suddenly, his mind colored the blade scarlet with his mother's blood. Panic pulled his strike short. He dodged aside, and the guard's sword whistled by his head.

Moonbear whirled. His punch hurled the guard against the wall. Bones snapped. The guard's dark eyes glazed, and he sank, lifeless, to the floor.

Taziar staggered, smothered by vivid visions of his mother's slaying. Horror wrenched the dagger from his grip. His pulse pounded in his head. Red haze pressed his vision. Sound tumbled against his ears, blending into a meaningless cacophony. Shylar's reedy voice was the only thing which threaded through his consciousness. "Out! Out now! Karana's darkest hell, you've ruined us all."

Taziar clung desperately to his failing sanity. His voice emerged beaten and flat. "We're gone," he said.

CHAPTER 5

The Comforts of Wyneth

"The robbed that smiles steals something from the thief."

—William Shakespeare,
Othello

Rain poured from the morning sky and pattered on the porch steps of Cullinsberg's alehouse, soaking Taziar and Moonbear who huddled underneath the porch. Taziar pulled his borrowed cloak higher over his head, attentive to the roadway to his right and its parallel alley to his left. His gaze followed a beggar woman in a shaggy, weather-stained frock. Water plastered thinning, white hair to her face. Seemingly oblivious, she meandered through the alleyway, stooping occasionally to stir a finger through the sewage trough set between the road stones.

Taziar crouched, peeking around the chipped paint of the stairs to the turbulent sky. Clouds formed a gray net across the horizon, bleak as his thoughts. *The guard would have slain Moonbear.* Taziar's throat tightened. *I owe Moonbear my life,*

but I couldn't kill to save his. Nausea slithered through
Taziar's gut. He buried his face in his palms, trying
to banish the memory of his mother's blood, purple red and smelling of death. The smooth glide
of his dagger through flesh still seemed vividly
real. *I've lied, conned, and stolen. I can move without a
sound through spaces scarcely large enough for a cat,
and I can climb almost anything. I've taught myself to
dodge confrontations and violence.* His hand dropped
to the hilt of the knife tucked in the sash beneath
his cloak. *But I'm a fugitive now. I need to learn to
kill.* The realization sent a shiver of dread through
him.

Apparently sensing Taziar's distress, Moonbear
squeezed his companion's thin wrist. "Are you well?"

Taziar gritted his teeth, resisting the urge to
share his remorse. *It would be like expecting sympathy
for hunting deer from a guard lion.* Avoiding Moonbear's
gaze, he watched the beggar woman track a piece
of human excrement with the interest of a child
with a toy boat in the river. *My father was the most
moral man I know, yet even he could kill.* Taziar lowered his head.

Moonbear's grip tightened. He whispered. "Listen."

Taziar jerked his head up, stiffening. Above the
ceaseless cadence of the rain, he heard the slap of
footsteps in the alleyway. Glad for the distraction,
Taziar motioned at Moonbear to flatten himself
against the wall, shifted to one knee, and craned
around the alehouse steps until he could spy on
the entire length of the alley. Three of Cullinsberg's
guardsmen entered the far end of the alley, dressed
in the coarse, black shirts and breeks which indicated they were on duty. Wind flicked open their
red cuffs. Water slicked the leather hilts and sheaths

of the swords that jutted from their waistbands.

Taziar retreated behind the stairs. "This way." He caught Moonbear's sleeve, drawing the barbarian around the alehouse to the parallel roadway, grateful for the rain which kept the streets barren despite the hour. A five thousand weight gold bounty would translate a glimpse from any citizen of Cullinsberg into instant capture. "Stay here." Taziar's tone left no room for argument. He scrambled up the alehouse wall, flattened to its sod roof, and watched the guardsmen beneath him.

As the soldiers approached the beggar woman, she rose from her sport. One of the men pointed. "Hey, Hildhard! I didn't know your mother was out here."

Another guard snickered. He spoke in a high-pitched jeer. "Ah, Adlar, that's not his mother." Seizing the woman by an arm, he jerked her toward the man who had not yet spoken. "It's his wife."

Angered by the guardsmen's play, Taziar curled his hands into fists. Wet grasses drenched the front of his cloak, penetrating all the way to his tunic. Recalling Moonbear's defense of the prostitute in Shylar's whorehouse, Taziar was glad the barbarian could not witness the guardsmen's antics.

Growling his contempt, Hildhard grabbed a handful of the beggar's hair. "She's your sister, you bastard."

Obviously frightened, the old woman lashed out wildly. Hildhard timed his dodge poorly. The woman's hand crashed into his groin. With an angry, pain-filled oath, the guard punched even as he doubled over. His fist struck her cheek with a resounding crack. She tumbled backward, into the sewage trough. "Dirty old pig!" Hildhard spat on the struggling woman.

Taziar had always felt a camaraderie with the drunkards and beggars who shared the city streets. Outraged, he tensed. His hand crept toward the hilt of his dagger. Still staggering slightly, Hildhard advanced. The beggar woman cringed with a cat-like hiss. Adlar caught Hildhard's forearm. "Enough. We're late already."

Hildhard glanced from the woman to his companions. Straightening his soggy uniform, he mumbled. "Shouldn't allow trash on the streets." The three guardsmen continued their patrol through the alleyway.

Relief uncoiled Taziar's sweat- and rain-soaked limbs. *My father's men would never have beaten a helpless, old woman.* Recalling the captain's disdainful tales of guards' cruelty in other regiments, Taziar knew his thought a certainty. He paused, watching until the beggar worked her way free of the sewage trough. Turning, he slithered across the rooftop and peered into the parallel road.

The street remained empty. Turning his gaze directly downward, Taziar recognized Moonbear hunched against the wall boards. His massive frame and the strands of yellow hair poking from beneath his hood seemed out of place. Taziar gripped the roof edge and lowered himself over the side. Easily, he found toeholds in the moss between panels. He scrambled to the ground. "This way." He pointed in the direction from which the guards had come. *Shylar claimed the baron had trebled city patrols. We haven't much time.*

Swiftly, Taziar and Moonbear stole along the roadway. At the first crossroad, Taziar returned

to the alley where the guardsmen had mistreated
the beggar woman. He continued in the opposite
direction from the patrol, dodging past cottage
and shop windows. As they walked, the sewage
trough widened, but it still scarcely managed to
contain the torrent of rain. Brown-stained water
sloshed over its sides. Its faint, but ever present,
ammonia smell made Taziar's head ache.

The alley ended abruptly in a circle of shops, as
Taziar knew it would. Sewage water poured from
the end of its trough into a man-made drain hole
half-hidden by the dirt of the roadway. Taziar
knelt. The reek of human excrement gagged him.
Many times in the past, he had considered hiding
in the underground river which carried away
Cullinsberg's wastes, but always before he had
found a less repulsive option. Now, trapped by
daylight and plagued by a reward which precluded
all trust, Taziar grew more desperate. He examined the cascade of foaming water which twined
into the ditch. "Moonbear, do you know what a
sewer is?"

Moonbear shook his head. "No."

"Good." Taziar gulped a lungful of air, caught
the edges of the hole, and swung his body down
into it. Sewage water splashed his side. He released his grip. He fell a short distance, struck
thigh-deep water with bent knees, and resisted his
natural urge to roll to ease the fall. Despite dilu-
tion by rain and stream, the odor crushed down
upon him.

The caverns of the underground river rose to
the height of a tall man, pitted and jagged as a
cave. Current dragged at Taziar. He followed it a
few steps to make room for Moonbear. A rat

swirled past; its paws chopped water madly. Taziar tensed, then bit off an oath. *Damn my shattered nerves, it's only a rat.* Behind him, a splash and a muttered expletive heralded Moonbear's arrival.

Though foul, the reek of human waste soon became the least of Taziar's worries as larger concerns necessitated concentration. Never having traversed the sewer, he did not know where it would lead. Its waterways and branches were unexplored territory. He could only surmise from distance and direction their corresponding location in the town overhead. Taziar focused his full attention on navigating the sewers, precluding conversation. As they traveled, he peered up drains, trying to determine his position in the city. He was grateful for the need to devote all his skill to finding his way through the sewer system, for it left him no time to brood about the incident in Shylar's whorehouse.

As the day progressed, the water rose rapidly. By midday, it had reached the level of Taziar's waist. Taziar judged that he and Moonbear actually passed beneath the walls which enclosed Cullinsberg's barony in the late afternoon. The torrent sucked and swirled about Taziar's chest, prodding him forward. Ahead, the warped sunlight which had seeped down the city sewer drain holes disappeared, and darkness limited vision to arm's length. For as far as he could discern, the cavern roof sloped downward.

Taziar watched water lap faults in the walls, acutely aware of the growing lake of sewage. *If the rain persists, water will fill this cavern. Strong as the current has already become, we may not be able to fight our way back to town. We have no choice but to turn around before the river overtakes us.* Preparing to pivot, Taziar sidestepped. The bottom collapsed beneath his feet. A wave crashed against his ribs, driving him under. Current dragged him deeper.

Taziar clawed to the surface and gulped air before the rushing waters closed over him again. Tossed like flotsam, he grabbed for the wall. Granite scraped skin from his knuckles. He grasped desperately for a handhold, kicking downward at the same time. His toes plowed through muck and struck stone. He wedged his fingers into cavern cracks, clung, and heaved. His head broke water. Slowly, as if climbing, he worked his hands up the wall. The current pounded against his legs, as he pulled himself halfway out of the water.

"Moonbear." Testing his balance, Taziar loosened his hold on the wall. "Moonbear!" His voice echoed through the chamber.

Moonbear's gruff singsong came from some distance behind Taziar. "Are you well?"

As well as a person who nearly drowned in shit can be. Taziar freed one hand and wiped grit from his eyes, unable to suppress the sarcasm in his voice. "Just damned fine." He released his grip, countering the current with shifts in position. Ahead, the sound of running water became the roar of a waterfall. Taziar stared at his macerated fingers, waiting for Moonbear to join him. "I think we've reached the river."

Water sloshed as Moonbear quickened his approach. Light filtered through the shaft that was now visible up ahead, painting gray shadows on the wall. "Less water, more sun."

Moonbear states the obvious, like a child. Taziar stifled a chuckle, recalling his initial trepidation upon viewing Moonbear in the baron's dungeon. Briefly, Taziar examined his companion. Moonbear's sodden cloak clung to his limbs, clearly defining the bulges and crevices of his muscled arms. *He's a simpleminded boy with the body of a blacksmith.* Hand pressed to the algae-slicked wall, Taziar continued through the cavern. Moonbear followed.

The river wound to the right. The cavern grew brighter and the water shallower with every step. Excitement plied Taziar. *I'd give all I have for dry clothes and sunlight.* The thought raised a grunt of realization. *A fair trade, perhaps, as all I have is wet clothing, a dagger, and my kind, if slow-witted, barbarian companion.* He turned a sharp left in the cavernway. Ahead, an iron grate spanned the tunnel. Between its bars, Taziar could see a rushing river bordered by green-leaved, twisted trees. Light poked through breaks in the clouds, highlighting every raindrop.

Frustration wrenched a curse from Taziar. "Aga'arin's inspired madness, will luck always work against us?" He approached the grate, aware they could no longer turn back until well after the rain had stopped completely. Fine stirrings of hunger and the realization they would need to sneak past perimeter patrols made the thought of return an undesirable option. Taziar considered. *Why would Cullinsberg's founders place a blockade across the sewer outlet? To keep fugitives from escaping?* The idea seemed so ludicrous, he discarded it. *In drier times, this underground river must become thin as a grass snake. If not for this grate, an army could enter and attack Cullinsberg without broaching the walls.* Comfortable with his explanation, Taziar moved closer. *To prevent enemies from prying down the grate, men must have installed it from our side. Therefore we can uninstall it.*

Determined, Taziar tapped the grate. The iron shivered. Rust colored his fingers orange. He examined the structure more carefully. Though initially cut square, the grating had grown pocked and bent by years of rushing water. A film of rust covered each bar and the four corner spikes which held the grate in place. Reaching down through the water, Taziar discovered one corner so eroded its spike no longer passed over it. Crossing to the other side, Taziar held the grate for support against the tumbling waters. Leaning over, he gripped the head of the opposite spike and pulled. The rust-pitted metal gave slightly. He jerked up, then suddenly downward. The joint slipped further. Taziar pumped the spike, feeling limestone chip around it. In moments, it fell free in his hands.

Taziar rose, still clutching the spike which ran nearly the length of his forearm. While Moonbear wrapped his thick fingers around the spike in the far corner, Taziar dropped the iron bar and turned his attention to the remaining spike. Seizing its tip, he braced his feet and yanked. Pain seared through his shoulder. The spike remained immobile. "Ach!" Shaking his arm, Taziar glanced toward Moonbear. The barbarian was working his spike free with relative ease.

Taziar gritted his teeth, reminded for the hundredth time of the slightness of his stature in a world which valued strength. He wrapped his fingers about the remaining spike. Grimy water surged about his thighs. He threw his weight backward. The movement jarred agony through his strained muscles. The spike remained as fixed as a boulder.

Moonbear stepped over to help. Eyes half closed from pain, Taziar kneaded his shoulder and waved Moonbear away. He snatched the freed spike from Moonbear. Wedging the tip beneath the head of the remaining spike, he levered downward. A cracking sound echoed through the cavern. The head of the embedded spike dropped into the water with a splash. The grate shifted, now held only by the force of the river.

Relief loosened Taziar's frame, dulling pain to an ache. He watched Moonbear peel the grate downward. The metal fell and lay like an orange-brown rug beneath the waters. Crossing over it, Taziar continued along the river. Twilight haze grazed the shadows at the cave opening. Ahead, rain slanted through the forest, rolling from tear-shaped walnut leaves to the tangle of gooseberries beneath. A low waterfall spilled from the cavern.

Taziar clung to the walls as the current grew stronger. He peered from the cave mouth, pleased to find ledges. A child could climb the rocks which framed the cavern. Stepping to one, he inched around the cascade and lowered himself to the riverbank. Turning, he watched Moonbear traverse the same course and drop to the ground beside him.

Rain pelted Taziar. Too wet to care, he welcomed its freshness after a half day's journey through filth. Joy suffused him. *We're free. Free! And the baron can't know we passed the city walls.* Stooping, he ran his hands through the river, washing away rust and filth. Yet doubts arose quickly to splinter excitement. *I've a debt to pay against a traitor who resides in a city I cannot enter.*

And never having left Cullinsberg before, I've no idea where to go.

As if in answer to Taziar's unspoken question, Moonbear pointed away from Cullinsberg. "North."

"North." Taziar repeated. Accustomed to streets and shops, he found the direction ridiculously vague. "Of course, north. North where?"

Moonbear passed Taziar, gliding into the stand of trees. "Home."

Home. The word tore a hollow in Taziar's consciousness. Though unsure of the reason, he knew a loyalty to Cullinsberg far beyond the patriotism inspired by his father. The walled city was the only world he had known since birth, the world where his parents had lived and died, a world with crisscrossed roadways and well-tended shops ruled by any underground sinner daring enough to thwart the baron's laws. Now, outside, Taziar rediscovered an uncertainty he had not experienced since childhood. His confidence and his obsession with action seemed to fade in an instant, as if the goal which had driven him to take on the impossible for eight years remained, unfinished, within the city limits. The thought of the vast, strange lands beyond the barony which should have seemed an exciting new challenge only made Taziar uncomfortable. Forcefully, he shook water from his fingertips and strode after his companion. He stubbed his toe on a half-buried root. With a startled curse, he dropped to one knee. Swiftly, Moonbear passed from sight.

Rising, Taziar blundered after Moonbear, irritated by his own sudden clumsiness. All his years spent perfecting city stealth had not prepared him for the forest. Dead limbs clawed his ankles. Briars rent holes in his cloak, occasionally scratching skin. Forced to guess his course, he fought through undergrowth. Soon, he'd boxed himself between densely packed oaks and a fallen trunk. Unwilling to turn back, he clambered over the deadfall. Bark splintered beneath his fingernails. Swearing, he stumbled to the ground and watched with annoyance as Moonbear moved on without a rustle, leaving no signs of his passage.

Sweat mingled with the rain on Taziar's limbs. He recalled how, at the time of his mother's death, pride kept him from leaving Cullinsberg to become his uncle's smallest, weakest farmhand. Under ordinary circumstances, the same dignity might have spurred him to try to cover up his inexperience with woodland movement. But seven days in a coma and hours slogging through sewage turned the task into an almost overwhelming labor. Moonbear's natural ability quickly inspired resentment; it reminded Taziar of his own incompetence. Pausing to work wood from beneath his nails with his teeth, he glanced around the forest. Some distance to his right, a faint glow penetrated between tree branches. He trotted toward it. Intertwined limbs ripped a clump of hair from his head. Repeatedly, he twisted his ankles on stones and roots hidden beneath a shallow layer of leaves.

The forest broke suddenly to a packed dirt path muddied by rain and scarred deeply by hoofprints. Puddles filled the ruts in the roadway. Yet, to Taziar, this crude roadway seemed as welcome as dry clothing. He started toward it. From nowhere, a hand gripped his shoulder. Taziar gasped, whirling to face Moonbear. The larger man shook his head. "Road not safe."

Taziar broke free. He pronounced each word with sullen force. "*Forest,* not safe, Moonbear! We need to know if we're being followed." Even Taziar recognized it as a lame excuse, but he knew he could travel more swiftly and comfortably on the road.

Moonbear took no notice of Taziar's outburst. "The road is not safe." He pointed southward. "It leads to Cullinsberg."

Taziar gestured northward. "Then I go this way. If anyone comes by, I'll see or hear them and hide." Taziar's bitterness cut the conversation short. He stepped onto the roadway, heading in the indicated direction. Moonbear disappeared back into the forest.

Alone on the pathway, Taziar became intensely aware of gnawing hunger in his gut. Discretion and disgust had kept him from drinking sewage water, but a half day without water had parched his throat until even the road puddles seemed tempting. He plowed through mud, occasionally glimpsing Moonbear in the tangle of woods.

Evening dragged into night. Taziar's hunger passed from pain to vague queasiness. The trees thinned, then broke to towering fields of wheat. Clearly visible against the background of stalks, Moonbear signaled Taziar closer. "Town ahead. Back in the forest. We'll need to change direction."

"Town?" An image of Cullinsberg's tavern filled Taziar's mind. His gut ached, as if begging a home cooked meal. Cullinsberg's thrifty tavernmaster watered his beer, yet even his goods would seem gratifying. "Ahead then. We've need of warmth, rations, and a good night's rest."

"No!" Moonbear stomped his cloth-shod foot.

Perhaps because of anger, his accent became heavier. "Bad people live in towns."

Taziar glanced down the roadway, cursing wasted time. "We're outside Cullinsberg and the baron's influence. We're tired, soaked, and hungry. For a single bowl of beer, I'd steal Aga'arin's chalice again." He glared, and the day's resentment rushed forth unbidden. "I've purposely never left Cullinsberg before. I'm one of those 'bad people' who live in towns. I'm not proud of it, but I make my money conning and stealing from others. The forest has no others."

Moonbear's voice was barely audible. "My people live in the forest."

Taziar sighed, exasperated. "Moonbear, can I have everything you're carrying?"

Without question, Moonbear reached into his pocket and produced a handful of stone arrowheads. He offered them to Taziar.

Taziar bit his cheeks against a torrent of sarcasm. "I'd own everything your tribe has by midday. That's not much of a challenge."

Moonbear pinched his lips into a pout. He returned the arrowheads to his pocket.

"I'm not going to Sweden. I'm just not interested. If that means we part company, let's at last spend our last night together under the wind- and rain-sparing roof of an inn."

Moonbear's expression was unreadable.

Taziar pulled at his own sodden sleeve. "All right?"

Moonbear forced a grin. "All right."

Having won this small battle, Taziar trotted on down the roadway. Rapidly, they passed ineptly crafted cottages which leaned, groaning, in the rain. Accustomed to Cullinsberg's fortress walls and crowded dwellings, Taziar reached the central square before he even realized he had entered the village. A stone and wood building huddled in the middle of town. Dirt paths similar to the one they traversed radiated from it in a star pattern. Blocked granite steps rose to an iron-embossed door, darkly stained. An ornately-shaped handrail led up the stairway, twisted from strips of tarnished copper. It seemed as if the inhabitants had chosen to bestow all their money on this structure rather than on their own meager dwellings. A man sprawled across the lowest step, dressed in ragged homespun pants and a baggy shirt.

Regretting his promise of good food and lodgings, Taziar approached the stranger. "Excuse me. Could you direct me to an inn?"

The man screwed up his eyes and shook his head. "Heyeh?"

Unable to interpret this reply, Taziar wiped wet palms on his wetter cloak and tried again. "My friend and I need a place to eat and spend the night."

The stranger sat up. His breath reeked of drink. His words slurred together, and an unrecognizable accent blurred his speech nearly to imperceptibility. "Wyneth don't have no place like that." He spat at Moonbear's feet. "Go on in the tavern." He made a throwing motion over his shoulder. "Karl'll probably let you lay before the kitchen fire for work price."

"Thank you." Taziar climbed the stairway with Moonbear close behind. As they approached the door, they could see light streaming beneath it. From beyond came the mingled roar of conversa-

tion, interspersed with laughter. Taziar tripped
the latch and pushed. The door swung open easily
to reveal a paneled common room. To Taziar's
right stood four rectangular tables, splotched with
beer and wine stains. Eight men huddled around
two of the tables which had been pushed together.
Five wore carefully-stitched homespun. The other
three sported matching tunics of tan and black.
Guardsmen. Taziar shivered in the rain. He forced
down welling discomfort. *Wyneth's guardsmen. They've
no reason to harm us.* As if to prove Taziar right,
the men glanced in their direction only briefly,
then continued their conversation.

In the far corner, one of the tables had been
pulled away from the others. A man in black robes
of rich design sat there, his hair and beard the
color of goldenrod. His skin appeared as pale as
Moonbear's. An overlong staff of odd design leaned
against the wall beside him. Its end tapered to a
black-nailed claw which enclosed a highly polished,
green jadestone. He seemed intent on a steaming
plate of food and paid the newcomers no heed.

A voice to Taziar's left startled him. "Come in,
please. Shut the door. We prefer the rain outside."

Taziar flushed, aware of the growing puddle at
his feet. He entered along with Moonbear and
closed the door behind him. He looked toward
the speaker, a lean, aging man who stood behind
a waist high bar. Further along the thick, well-
polished barrier, three men holding tankards snickered with the kind of high pitch indicative of too
much to drink.

Taziar approached the speaker, hoping the long
walk through the rain had washed away the last
clinging odor of sewage. "You're Karl?"

A smile swept the older man's face. "I am. What can I do for you men?" His accent resembled that of the man on the porch steps, but his tone seemed friendly.

"My companion and I need a place to stay the night." Taziar poked Moonbear's arm with his thumb. "We've no money. But we're willing to work."

Karl squinted, examining the pair before him with alarming intensity. Straightening, he shrugged. "Kitchen'll make for cramped sleeping for two, but you're welcome to stay. And I do have a task for you. Come with me." Briskly, he turned and whisked through a doorway behind the bar. Trotting to keep up, Taziar and Moonbear followed him.

Karl led Taziar and Moonbear into a square cut chamber. A huge, stone, cooking fireplace nearly filled one wall. A metal rod within it skewered a chicken. Fat droplets sizzled on the glowing coals beneath it. The aroma of roasting meat and potatoes wafted through the room, reawakening Taziar's hunger. Barrels, crates, and casks lined the opposite wall. Three cockerels hung by their feet from the rafters. Blood parted trails through one's neck feathers, pattering to the table beneath it. Karl stopped before a thick, white door at the far side of the room. "You from Cullinsberg?"

Taziar saw no reason to lie. "Yes."

Karl tripped the latch and ushered Taziar and Moonbear into the night. "I once served in the baron's army."

Taziar's heart quickened. He studied Karl in the moonlight. Gray-streaked hair tumbled to the nape of his neck. Though thin, Karl sported a large frame and thick hands which suggested a previous robustness.

Apparently noticing Taziar's appraisal, Karl shook his head. "Oh, I was big once. I fought years ago, in the barbarian wars." He rubbed his hands together, regarded Moonbear closely, and suddenly seemed uncomfortable. Pointing to a cart and hitch in the yard, he changed the subject. "When my boy, Meier, returns, you can help him unload the beer."

Within the wagon stood a pair of barrels so wide they filled it completely. Taziar estimated each at four times his own meager weight. *Three men together should move them fairly easily.* "Agreed."

Karl turned back toward the kitchen. Taziar followed him. But Moonbear remained, staring out over the pastures and fields of Wyneth. As Karl continued through the kitchen, Taziar paused. "Moonbear?"

Moonbear raised a hand to indicate he heard.

Suspecting Moonbear needed to relieve himself, Taziar smiled. "Come back inside when you're ready."

Moonbear nodded.

Taziar followed Karl back into the tavern. The older man strode to the largest table to take an order. Taziar took a seat before the bar. His stomach felt drawn tight. His throat burned. The raucous calls and laughter of the three soused men to his right quickly became an annoyance. Awaiting Karl and Moonbear, Taziar watched the men at the bar, pondering ways to convince the drunkards to part with some food and drink.

The man nearest Taziar sported a red-brown beard soaked with beer foam. To his right, a burly man giggled like a girl over his half-eaten chicken. The last of the trio was a dark-haired giant of a man who appeared to be the leader. Snatches of boisterous conversation revealed his name to be Willamar.

After a time, Karl retook his position behind the bar. Hoping to obtain a clue to his father's death, Taziar waved him over. "So you fought in the barbarian wars. What were they like?"

Karl leaned across the counter, chin in his palms. "Truth?"

Taziar nodded.

Karl rolled his eyes to meet Taziar's gaze. "Not the glorious, glamorous combat I expected as a young warrior. Those barbarians knew the forest like we knew the insides of our cottages. Not surprising when you realize the woods were their home."

Karl pulled a wet rag from beneath the bar and flicked it across the already spotless counter. "I remember how they seemed to come from nowhere to strike without sound. I lost many friends and comforted a lot of widows. Then I started wondering about the barbarians' widows and orphans. That's when I quit. I took my pay and opened this place. . . ."

Moonbear appeared suddenly from the kitchen doorway. Crossing around the bar, he took a seat beside Taziar.

Taziar confronted his companion. "What took so long?"

Moonbear's shoulders rose and fell. "I carried in the barrels."

The pronouncement struck Taziar momentarily

speechless. The idea of one man hauling the casks seemed impossible.

Wide-eyed, Karl peeked through the kitchen doorway. He turned back to Taziar, shaking his head in bewilderment. "He did it." He indicated Moonbear with a toss of his head. "Convenient companion to have along . . . uh." Karl paused, apparently realizing he had never asked Taziar's name.

Moonbear took the cue. "He's Shadow. He's a thief."

Horror stole Taziar's breath. *Real damned convenient!* He forced a weak smile, hoping Karl would take the revelation as Moonbear's simpleminded rambling.

Karl screwed up his eyes and glanced from Taziar to Moonbear. "Eh? What do you mean?"

Taziar drew breath in defense, but Moonbear spoke first, in the firm, matter-of-fact tone of a proud father. "He takes things from people."

Struggling to salvage his life, Taziar added quickly. "He just means I take money with tricks." He recalled his early days with Cullinsberg's street rogues when his swiftness and agility predisposed him to pickpocketing and sleight of hand. "Do you have a coin?"

Karl's features crinkled in mistrust, but he reached into his pocket and flipped a copper ducat to the counter.

Taziar placed his palm over the coin. "Watch carefully." He shuffled it rapidly from hand to hand, stopped, and worked it between his left second and third fingers. Distracting Karl with a toss of his head, he asked, "Where's the coin?"

Karl indicated Taziar's left hand. Taziar raised

it, revealing nothing beneath, then slipped the ducat into his pocket. He lifted his right hand to show the coin had disappeared.

Karl laughed. "He's right. You are a thief. I don't suppose I'll see my copper again, unless you use it to buy a drink." His gaze swept past Taziar. "Excuse me a moment." Karl produced a glass, filled it with deep purple wine, and strode toward the table of the black-robed Northman.

Pleased by the quick thought and maneuvering which had rescued him from potential disaster, Taziar slapped the ducat down on the bar and awaited Karl's return. Confronting Moonbear, Taziar sought words to explain the conventions of civilization when Willamar's voice interrupted. "Heyoh, Shadow-thief. Know any more tricks?"

Taziar turned. The hefty, dark-haired leader of the drinkers at the bar peered over the heads of his companions and met Taziar's gaze. Seizing the opportunity, Taziar rose and approached. As he passed Willamar's bearded friend, Taziar flicked his hand into the pocket of the man's homespun, tangled his fingers in purse strings, and freed the pouch with a deft twist. He made a subtle gesture to mask the action of slipping it into his own pocket. Faint stirrings of excitement rewarded the theft. *It's been years since I've done any pilfering, but the skill is still there.* Continuing his motion naturally, Taziar took a seat on the far side of Willamar.

Taziar placed his elbow on the counter and faced Willamar. "I also hustle drinks."

Willamar imitated Taziar's position. He leaned closer. "Fine, Shadow-thief. Hustle." The burly man beside him giggled. The bearded man choked on his drink.

Taziar waited for their laughter to fade. "I'll bet a meal and a beer I can take your purse without you realizing it."

Instinctively, Willamar's hand dropped to his pocket. His voice went shrill. "Touch my money and die."

Hoping he had not miscalculated, Taziar answered quickly. "Fine, then. I'll bet meals and drinks for me *and* my friend I can take *his* purse . . ." He gestured at the bearded man. ". . . without *either* of you noticing."

Willamar judged the distance between Taziar and his chosen victim. He chuckled. "I'll take that bet. Give it a try."

The bearded man stiffened. "Hey, you can't . . ."

Grinning wickedly, Taziar displayed the bearded man's purse. The man swore. He snatched back his property. Willamar doubled over with laughter. His fat friend's belly heaved, emitting rumbling chortles. As Karl returned to the bar, Willamar waved him over. "Feed Shadow and his friend on me."

Having obtained dinner, Taziar saw no further reason to continue petty, conmen's antics. He returned to his seat beside Moonbear. Karl headed into the kitchen and reemerged with two plates, each with half a chicken and several small potatoes smothered with thin, yellow gravy. Wisps of smoke curled toward the ceiling. Karl placed the dinners before Taziar and Moonbear. "Enjoy. Willamar must have sold a good crop to have become so generous." He nodded toward the dark-haired leader, then hunkered closer to Taziar's ear. "That or he's drunker than he thinks." He winked. He went to the kitchen and brought two bowls filled with froth-capped beer.

Food and drink had never tasted so good to Taziar. In his mouth, the fowl seemed to turn into the finest fried beefsteak. The beer eased the pain in his throat. Oblivious to every other thing in the common room, he bolted the meal. Then, feeling bloated but happy, he leaned back in his chair.

The bearded man approached Taziar. Freeing his purse, he dumped three silver ducats to the countertop. "Yours, all of it, if you can steal anything from the Norseman." He inclined his head toward the lone, blond patron in the corner.

Taziar frowned, aware several silver coins must seem a fortune to a farmer in a town as small as Wyneth. But Taziar had given larger sums to orphans on Cullinsberg's streets. "I just hustle meals. I'm not for hire."

With a growl of disgust, Karl shoved the ducats at the bearded man. "Stop it, Tabbert! I'll not have you sending a man to die for sport." He made a motion toward the door. "Get out of here."

Mumbling veiled apologies, Tabbert reached for his coins. But Karl's words had turned the bet into a challenge. Despite attempts to hold curiosity in check, Taziar's interest sparked at the thought of a theft deemed impossible by an ex-warrior who must have served under Taziar's father. "Wait." He caught Tabbert's arm. "Who is this Norseman?"

Karl glowered at Tabbert. "A stranger. Calls himself Mordath. I don't know who he is, but he claims he's Dragonrank."

The word meant nothing to Taziar. "Dragonrank?"

"Dragonrank," said Tabbert, as if repeating the word could serve as clarification.

Karl tapped his fingers against the bar. "Dragon-ranks are just mothers' stories, sorcerers from the north who supposedly steal away bad children and can create or destroy at will. But this mad Norseman really believes he's Dragonrank. Stay away." Karl trotted off to fill another order.

Taziar paused, knowing it was best to heed Karl's warning, yet enticed by the opportunity to perform against steep odds. Knowing himself too well, he sighed. "I'll take your bet." Committed now, Taziar turned. Mordath sat with the wine glass pressed to his lips, his attention seemingly unfocused. His posture was that of a man withdrawn into some private reverie. His hands looked as smooth as a princess'. The jadestone at the tip of his staff appeared to flicker and pulse in the candlelight.

Taziar's heart pounded in the familiar slow cadence which came whenever he faced a task of such immensity. His restlessness returned; for an instant, time seemed to reverse and he stood before his father's corpse. Then, shrugging with impatience at his lapse, Taziar put aside all memory of the past he could not change. For the duration of the attempted theft, excitement would whip him to a frenzied intensity which would preclude all extraneous thoughts.

Taziar threaded around chairs and tables, approaching Mordath with a swaggering gait. The Norseman ignored him, apparently absorbed in the bouquet of his wine. Arriving at the corner table, Taziar hooked a chair with his foot, thrust it backward betweeen his legs, and leaned across the carven rail of its back. "Mind if I join you?"

Mordath raised his head with the slow deliberateness of a baron. His eyes glimmered, blue-green and as sharp as a house cat's. His accent echoed Moonbear's, but his words sounded more crisp and refined. "Would you have me tell your future?"

The question was unexpected. Taziar shifted in his chair, trying to look nonchalant. "If you'd like." Beneath the table, his fingers crept toward the other man.

Mordath's face locked in an expressionless pall. The hand on his glass made circles, sloshing the last mouthful of wine. He made an arching gesture with his other arm.

Taziar's hand skittered from the fox fur-lined trim of Mordath's robe to the corner of a pocket. He edged his fingers inside and came upon a smoothed, rectangular gemstone.

A sibilant quality entered Mordath's voice. "I see a sudden, violent death at the whim of an irate Dragonrank sorcerer."

Taziar winced, hoping the Norseman's rage was channeled at him merely because of his presence rather than due to awareness of the theft. A sharp burst of adrenaline made Taziar's hand shake, hampering his effort to grip the stone.

Mordath's fist crashed against the tabletop. "Witless servant! Leave before I set you and this broken-down box of timber to flame."

Taziar recoiled, using the movement to flick the stone into his palm. He slipped it in his breast pocket, disguising the motion by raising both hands in a gesture of surrender. "Forgive me." He stood hurriedly. "I didn't mean to anger you."

Mordath's feline eyes narrowed. His gaze focused beyond Taziar. He raised his arm with the bold commitment of a dancer.

From habit, Taziar retreated past the range of a

physical blow. The Norseman's movement seemed eerily unnatural. *Could this man really be a sorcerer?* The very idea seemed ludicrous, yet doubt clung in Taziar's mind. His eyes were trained on the uplifted hand.

Suddenly, Mordath's thumb and middle digit pressed together and then separated with a distinctive snap. His forefinger beckoned. From the periphery of his vision, Taziar glimpsed Karl approaching, wine bottle in hand.

Mordath only wants a drink. The realization made Taziar feel foolish. Sweat congealed on his limbs. He started back toward Willamar at a confident trot. Once at the bar, he dropped into the chair.

Like vultures, the drinkers surrounded Taziar. Tabbert hissed. "Did you take something?"

Briefly, Taziar glanced over his shoulder. Mordath sipped at his freshly-filled wine glass, head tilted toward the ceiling. Karl was bustling toward the bar. "Yes. I took . . ." He paused dramatically. ". . . abuse."

Willamar loosed a guttural noise. His fat companion drew a handful of coins from his pocket and reached toward Tabbert, obviously paying a private wager on Taziar's presumed failure.

Quick as fire, Taziar hooked the fat man's sleeve. "I also took this." He retrieved the gemstone and tossed it casually to the countertop. It was a jade, milky green and intricately cut and shaped to resemble a faceted diamond, twin to the stone which graced the clawed tip of Mordath's staff. An oil lamp behind the bar carved shadows on its flattened surfaces. Abruptly, light spread like a spider along each edge, intensified to glaring white, and exploded in a flash as brilliant as lightning.

Taziar leaped to his feet. Willamar's chair tumbled to the floor. Oblivious to the shocked gasps of his companions, Taziar glanced across the common room. Mordath rose. His eyes wrenched open as wide as unshuttered beacons, and the object of his scrutiny was obviously the jadestone on the bar.

Words failed Taziar. The quick wit which had rescued him from violence in the past seemed to have abandoned him completely. He clamped a damp palm over the stone and whisked it into a pocket. The effort was ill-spent. There could be no doubt Mordath had seen it.

Mordath's hand drifted to his violated pocket. His lips oozed into a smile. His mouth writhed open in soundless laughter. With the calm manner of a courtier, he tossed down the last mouthful of wine and scattered several oddly-shaped, gold coins on the table. Disinterested in the worried stares of everyone present, he strode across the room, through the door, and out into the night. The click of the latch echoed loudly in the oppressive silence of the common room.

Taziar remained still, flushed with disbelief. The tension in the tavern grew unbearable. Willamar's veined fist gripped the bar. Tabbert's lips pursed in alarm. Suddenly, Karl sprang forward. He tore at a fold in Taziar's cloak, and his unbridled curses shattered the stillness with a cyclone's force.

Anxiety and uncertainty masked most of Karl's words. Taziar identified blasphemies and insults interspersed between a fluttering of "I told you's." Unable to concentrate on the blustering barkeep, Taziar turned his attention to the occupants of the tavern. The largest table's occupants had dwindled to two, neither wearing the tan and black tunics Taziar had noticed on first entering the common room.

From some distance came the growing cadence of hoofbeats. *Soldiers?* Taziar felt gooseflesh prickle his skin. *A village this small couldn't afford a mounted army.* Karl's admonishments flowed past him like unintelligible music. Something just didn't make sense. *Would Wynethian guards summon aid from Cullinsberg?* Taziar spoke softly, but his urgency transcended Karl's tirade. "How long ago did the guardsmen leave?"

Karl released Taziar. "Huh-eh? Are you listening to me?"

Taziar declined to answer. "How long ago did the guardsmen leave here?"

"Guardsmen?" Karl shook his head. "You mean the men in the uniforms?"

Taziar nodded.

Though his anger had not fully died down, Karl managed a weak smile. "Tax collectors from Cullinsberg. Wyneth's far too small for soldiers. The baron would never let one of his farm holdings have its own army."

"Cullinsberg . . . holding?"

Realizing he had not answered Taziar's question, Karl finished. "They left long ago, while you were winning dinner from Willamar."

Long enough to have reached Cullinsberg and returned. Taziar berated his carelessness with silent curses. The hoofbeats in the town square were unmistakable now. Lantern light swam through the dusty window. "I think it's time we departed." He started toward the exit.

The door crashed open suddenly. Six men stood

in the portal, dressed in the crisp red and black of Cullinsberg's army. Even as Taziar recognized his peril, the commander raised his arm and pointed directly at Moonbear.

CHAPTER 6

The Kielwald

"Not every man is so great a coward as he thinks he is . . ."

—*Robert Louis Stevenson,*
The Master of Ballantrae

In the portal of Karl's common room, the commander of the five Cullinsberg soldiers made a sweeping gesture. In response, his men advanced on Moonbear. Crouched in expectation, the barbarian retreated, eyes locked on the pinched hands beneath the guards' red cuffs. Suddenly wordless and solemn, Karl slipped back behind his bar, studying the guardsmen and their quarry in the guttering swirl of candlelight. The remaining Wynethians straggled to the relative safety of the room's center.

Recalling the doorway into Karl's kitchen which led outside, Taziar edged around the bar with deliberate slowness designed to mask his movement. His heart raced. Memories of guards' tortures sent waves of pain through his limbs. The urge to slip away became an all-consuming passion. *Apparently they want Moonbear. I'm no help to him in a fight. No need for both of us to die.*

The guards clustered in on Moonbear in tight formation. The two in front kept their weapons sheathed. Behind them, their three companions clutched swords, angling to block Moonbear's escape. The commander hung back. He called an order, and his men stopped, a grim, black semicircle of threat. Moonbear continued his steady backward motion until his heel touched the wall. He remained there, poised and restless as a coiled spring.

The commander addressed Moonbear. "Be still, barbarian. We've no wish to harm you. You can't stand against all of us."

Moonbear's calm naïveté disappeared. His brows bunched into a defiant glare. His singsong accent added a mocking quality to his reply. "I shall not be caged again. Many of your men will fall before me. The survivors can drag my corpse back to your baron."

Moonbear's bold oratory wrung shame through Taziar. He stopped his slow, careful retreat. A sense of loyalty warred with his instinct to escape, igniting an ancient memory of his father's words: *The only true sin is cowardice, that limitless fear which allows a man to forsake his fellows in combat.* Taziar swallowed as the guards shuffled forward. *I still owe Moonbear my life. Abandoning him now would make me as contemptible as Ilyrian.* Aware that his presence in battle would only hamper Moonbear, Taziar fingered his dagger, hoping for an opportunity when his intervention might tip the odds toward Moonbear.

The guards closed. With the caution of lion

trainers, the unarmed soldiers reached for Moonbear's arms. Without warning, Moonbear kicked. The side of his foot smashed into a guardsman's knee. The crack of impact shattered the silence. The injured man screamed and crumpled to the floor.

Moonbear continued his motion. His fist crashed against the other guard's head. The man staggered. Moonbear seized the dazed guardsman by an arm and whisked him inward. The barbarian gripped the man like a shield. The swordsmen hesitated. Their commander shouted from his position beyond the battle. Moonbear stepped forward. He hurled the stunned guard toward the naked sword of one of his fellows. The blade caught the unarmed guard in the stomach and ran him through. The wielder cried out in surprise. Momentum toppled man and corpse to the hard stone floor, and Moonbear whirled to face his last two assailants.

The splash of blood recalled the memory of Taziar's mother's death. Nausea slid through his gut. The crafted hilt of his dagger bit into his palm.

One of the two remaining soldiers rushed Moonbear. His sword cut gleaming arcs through the air. Though unarmed, Moonbear held his ground. Taziar freed his dagger, hoping a well-aimed throw could stop the guard's strike before it landed. Abruptly, Moonbear lashed out with his arm. The back of his wrist beat the flat of the swordsman's blade, knocking it aside. The guard's momentum carried him off balance. A blow from Moonbear's fist knocked the man sprawling. Moonbear wrenched the sword from the soldier's hand. Flicking the blade into an offensive position, the barbarian bore down on his last opponent.

The commander uttered a curse. His remaining charge crouched, understandably wary. With slow backsteps, he drew Moonbear forward, buying time for his dazed and injured companions to rejoin the fight. Taziar growled a silent oath, aware Moonbear's battle was again about to become many against one. Time seemed to slow; seconds spanned eternity. A candle on the counter fizzled to a trail of smoke. Taziar glanced toward the commander and noticed, with alarm, that the man was returning his gaze. Steel chimed from Moonbear's direction, and Taziar suddenly became aware of his own peril. The commander started around Karl's bar. Still clutching his knife, Taziar bolted for the kitchen.

The hearth fire had dwindled to a dappled pattern of spent coals and faintly-glowing, orange bricks. Shadows splashed the painted white of the outer door. Taziar sprinted for it. Behind, he heard the pursuing slap of the commander's boots. A gruff voice screamed his name like an order. "Taziar!"

Taziar reached the door. He curled his fingers around its latch, cursing the seconds its opening cost him. Pulling the panel inward, he sprang for the yard. But as he moved, one of the commander's hands whipped over Taziar's shoulder and closed on his chin, dragging the maneuver short. Fingers gouged Taziar's face. He surged forward, attempting to tear free. The soldier's grip held. He wrenched Taziar backward. Taziar slipped, twisting as he fell. The dagger jarred from his fist and spun, flickering, into darkness. He landed on his side. A kick from the commander sprawled Taziar supine. He tensed to rise. The commander's sword hissed from its sheath, and he placed the blade at Taziar's throat. "Be still, Medakan thief. My orders read to bring the barbarian alive. You . . ." His voice went dry with contempt. "You, I can carve into steaks if I wish."

Taziar's mind raced. Moonbear's battle sounded heated; surely some time would pass before the barbarian could tend to anything but his own defense. Taziar's gaze swept every quarter of the room. Barely within reach of his left hand, his dagger lay beneath Karl's blood-spattered butchering table. "Steaks," Taziar said, hoping to distract the guard, with idle conversation, from the steady inching of his fingers toward the knife. "Has Cullinsberg's baron turned cannibal?"

The commander sneered. "Who said anything about *people* eating you? These woods have foxes, bears, and feral lions who would love fresh thief meat, even from one so small and bony."

Taziar's hand snaked toward the dagger, though he was intensely aware of the constant pressure of steel at his neck. "Kill me then, soldier. But the baron will never know why I stole Aga'arin's chalice nor the names of my accomplices." His fingers touched the sharpened edge of the knife blade.

Suddenly, the guard shifted. His foot came down hard on Taziar's groping fingers. With the toe of his other boot, he back-kicked the dagger across the room. "Nice try, weasel," he hissed. "Now I can't risk bringing you in alive." He raised his sword. His lips twisted in a grimace of contempt.

"Wait!" screamed Taziar, trying to stall. The crash of steel in the common room seemed distant and unreal. His head ached, filled with images: his mother, condemned by the name of her accused husband, pleading for understanding from neighbors who'd once served as friends; his father's eyes, demanding vengeance; Moonbear asking nothing yet deserving a fierce loyalty Taziar had no power to provide. Burdened by promises, Taziar dared not believe he would shed his last blood, like a butchered hog, on a kitchen floor.

The commander's sword carved downward, colored fire red by the last remnants of hearthlight. A sudden slap resounded through the room. The commander crumpled. His sword struck the floor with a ring of sound. Shocked, Taziar lurched to his feet and confronted Karl's weathered features. The tavern master clutched a huge wooden baking paddle, streaked with guard's blood.

"Karl?" Taziar shook his head, wondering if he might become the ex-warrior's next target. "Why?"

Weak shards of moonlight from the open door etched Karl's harried-looking face into a mass of wrinkles. "Your name. You're Captain Taziar Medakan's son?"

Accustomed to jeers since the malicious gossip and lies which had accompanied his father's death, Taziar nodded carefully.

Karl lowered his makeshift weapon. "No resemblance. But your voice is the same. And you have your father's damnable courage."

Taziar flushed scarlet, feeling guiltily undeserving of Karl's praise.

Karl inclined his head toward the door and tangled black and gray hair fell across his cheek. "I owed Taz my life many times. Now my debt is paid. Please, go now."

Taziar required no prodding. Suppressing the urge to waste time thanking Karl, he scrambled from the kitchen into the semidarkness of a thieves' moon. Grasses prickled between the bindings of his sandals. Night air chilled through his drying tunic. Wind rattled against the hulking shadow of the emptied beer wagon. Concerned for Moonbear, yet bound by Karl's request, Taziar did not reenter the common room but crossed to its front. There he discovered half a dozen of Cullinsberg's striped zebra steeds bridle-tied to the copper handrails. He freed them all. Catching the reins of two, he waited, alone save for the crisp chorus of insects in the village square.

Suddenly Moonbear's mountainous figure appeared in Karl's doorway, clutching a sword in each fist. Transferring both sets of reins to the same hand, Taziar waved urgently. Familiar with Cullinsberg and its soldiers, he knew scant time would pass before these six were missed and sought. "Moonbear!"

Moonbear shuffled toward Taziar through the darkness. Impatiently, Taziar waited until his companion reached the last stair. "Here!" He tossed one pair of narrow, leather reins and led his own mount into the roadway.

Moonbear made no effort to catch the reins. They swung in a short arc, slapping the horse's black-barred neck. The beast snorted and pranced sideways, twisting its head toward Moonbear contemptuously. Taziar caught the flapping reins. He slapped them into Moonbear's thick hand. "Get on!"

Moonbear stared from the braided leather in his fist to the striped steed. Suddenly, he raised his head. "Many horses approaching from the south."

Taziar swore. *The men Moonbear fought must have been the gate guard sent only to detain us until the army could mobilize. But why send so many after so few?* Devoid of a logical answer, Taziar turned his attention to escape. Flipping the reins to their correct position on the horse's neck, he vaulted to its back. Moonbear just stood there, still studying his zebra steed.

Now Taziar, too, heard the pounding hoofbeats of the pursuing army. "Aga'arin's blood, Moonbear. Have you gone daft? Mount up." Taziar reined in his steed, fearing Moonbear might have sustained a skull injury in the battle.

The hoofbeats grew louder. Moonbear dove. He came down heavily on his stomach across the horse's withers. Breath rushed from him. Taziar cringed in sympathy as Moonbear scrambled into place with uncharacteristic awkwardness. Waiting only until Moonbear wound a hand in the beast's smoky mane, Taziar kicked his own horse into a gallop. From habit, Moonbear's mount followed.

At Taziar's prompting, the zebra steeds charged down the wet ribbon of roadway. Their hoofs chewed into the surface, flinging mudballs in their wake. Taziar hunkered flat to his horse's neck, avoiding the resistance of wind and falling comfortably into the swaying rhythm of the run. From behind came a long string of speech in a Northern tongue. Moonbear sounded distressed.

Sitting upright, Taziar passed both reins to one hand and swiveled to face Moonbear. The barbarian's knuckles were blanched white; the horse's mane striped his fingers like ink. Each galloping step hurled him up from his seat. Overcompensating, Moonbear would try to gain his position, only to slide across the opposite flank. Taziar loosed his reins and gave his horse its head, fascinated by Moonbear's antics. The barbarian seemed as clumsy as a toddler learning to dance.

The looming darkness of the Kielwald Forest on either side seemed to crush in on Taziar and Moonbear. The thieves' moon limited vision to fingerbreadths of roadway. Moonbear's horse sidled to avoid a puddle. With a sharp cry of surprise, Moonbear tumbled. He crashed to the ground and rolled, a handful of mane still clenched in his fist. The zebra steed raced onward.

Taziar reined in his mount. Its hoofs skidded through the soft muck, then it slowed to a walk. Taziar drew it in a tight circle back to Moonbear. The barbarian scrambled to his feet as dirt-covered as an ancient statue. His hair hung in brown clumps. Concern overcame Taziar's urge to laugh. "Are you hurt?"

Without returning Taziar's gaze, Moonbear shook his head. "Hoofbeats from both directions. Into the woods, quickly!" Moonbear disappeared between the trunks.

Taziar hesitated, reluctant to sacrifice the horse's speed. *As if it will do me much good when I'm trapped between two guard forces and executed for thievery.* Taziar dismounted. Catching the bridle, he directed his steed northward. A slap on its rump followed by a wild waving of Taziar's arms sent the beast skittering after its fellow.

Moonbear reappeared, peering out from the woods. "Follow me closely."

Taziar nodded. Knowing that on his own he

could not negotiate the woodlands with the necessary speed, he wound his hands in Moonbear's cloak and pressed his head against the barbarian's back. The damp, muddy folds of cloth smothered his reply. "Go." Like wind rustling through the treetops, Moonbear entered the tangle of trees and vines. Betraying none of the ineptness he showed on horseback, he threaded through the brush with the agility of a forest animal. Though feeling uncomfortably close to Moonbear, Taziar hung on tenaciously, devoting his attention to the placement of his own sandaled feet. With each step, he vowed to learn to traverse the forest with Moonbear's animal stealth.

After a time, the darkness and Moonbear's constant jog became familiar to Taziar. Still weak from his recent experiences, he trailed Moonbear like a man in dream. Hours passed in a cold haze. Then Moonbear's pace slowed to a walk. He plowed through a copse of fir beneath a web of oak boughs which obscured the sky. Crouching beside a sheltering deadfall, Moonbear spoke. "We sleep now."

Taziar dropped to the ground beside Moonbear. He yawned. His eyelids felt weighted and his limbs unusually heavy. "No argument." He curled into a ball. Fallen branches gouged through his tunic and into flesh. Cursing, he cleared a spot on the forest floor and sprawled across it. Taziar squeezed his eyes shut, craving sleep yet hyperalert. He could feel his heart beating, rapid and thready.

Taziar rolled to his side, seeking the most comfortable position. Thought crowded in, replaying the events of the previous day: the pervading stench of Cullinsberg's sewage, the commander's sword raised for its killing strike, lives spilled like water

in Wyneth's common room. His uneasiness intensified. Sleep hovered, a distant compulsion.

A noise broke the stillness, a series of whirring
barks. Taziar leaped to a crouch, heart pounding.
An answering chorus sounded from nearby. "What's
that?" he whispered.

Moonbear snickered. "Foxes bickering over territory. They are no danger to us. Go to sleep."

Taziar lay down, certain every normal woodland sound would startle him awake. "I wish I
could."

Mooonbear rolled toward Taziar. "What's wrong?"

Taziar shook his head. "Strange place. And too
many things to think about." He sighed. "Moonbear,
why is the baron willing to empty his treasury to
get you back in his dungeon?" He met Moonbear's
gray-eyed stare, expecting a noncommittal answer.

"He knows my people will pay with gold for my
safe return."

Surprised by the directness of Moonbear's explanation, Taziar sat. "More than five thousand
weight?"

Moonbear shrugged. "Whatever he asks. Our
fathers have blessed our rivers with enough of the
yellow metal to meet our needs. Conquests have
gleaned still larger amounts. We use it to conse-
crate tombs, but we've plenty extra." Moonbear
leaned on one elbow, propping his head on his
palm. "My people care more for my life than my
. . . *dekorasgrav*." He struggled to define the foreign concept. ". . . my grave gold."

Taziar gnawed at a thumb callus, envisioning
streams clotted with melted gold. "So, all of your
people have a death fund which can become
ransom?"

Moonbear considered Taziar's odd word choice briefly. "No, not all. Only royalty."

"Only royalty." Slowed by exhaustion, Taziar took several seconds to make the obvious connection. "You? You're royalty?"

Yawning, Moonbear nodded. "I am the prince."

The heavy burden of fatigue lifted slightly. Taziar leaned forward. "Why didn't you tell me?"

Again, the foxes yipped an exchange. Moonbear waited until the din subsided. "What difference would it make?"

Moonbear's news and his calm nonchalance shocked Taziar. "What difference would it make!" He pondered his own outburst. *We're trapped in the forest; what difference* would *it make?*

Moonbear answered his own echoed question. "None. The baron already knows my title. It could only change the way you act toward me. I don't want that."

Amused by the irony of their union, Taziar loosed a snorting laugh. "A noble and a thief escaping together." He finished softly. "What a disgrace."

Moonbear's face folded into angry creases. "Cullinsberg's baron is cruel, but that is no reason to condemn all royalty. You did not find me a disgrace when I fought the guards in Wyneth."

"Aga'arin's pompous followers!" Taziar threw up his hands in disbelief. "Moonbear, I meant me. I'm the disgrace. I'm a thief."

Moonbear remained sullenly silent.

Taziar's tirade gained volume. "Are you stupid? Can't you understand? I take things. I'm not trying to mislead you. I owe you the truth. I steal. People pay me to take possessions from others."

Moonbear relaxed. "Good."

"Good?" Taziar realized he was shouting and lowered his voice. "Not good, Moonbear. I'm bad." He stared at the black expanse of sky as uncomfortable as a parent explaining sex. "I take things . . ."

Moonbear interrupted, ". . . from men who don't need them and give them to those who do. Anyone who does not make himself my enemy is my friend. If my friend needed something I had, I would give it to him. If I see my friend drowning, I pull him free. Things like this are normal, Shadow." Moonbear sat up straight with his back against a fallen log. "It's not natural for too many animals to live in one place. The foxes fight for territory. When the forest fills with deer, many must die for lack of food. When too many people dwell crushed together like ants, they become violent. Cullinsberg needs thieves like you to restore honesty and kindness."

Taziar rammed his hands into his pockets. "I can't believe you just used the words 'thief' and 'honesty' in the same sentence. Listen, Moonbear. I want to accept your admiration graciously, but my conscience won't let me. I don't steal because I'm nice. I do it for money."

Moonbear laced his fingers. He spoke accusingly, as if he had caught Taziar in a lie. "I talked with Shy Lark. You give that money to people who need it."

Taziar lowered his head and confessed. "All right. I care little for the money. But I don't steal for lofty or moral reasons either. I simply seek the thrill." He considered, trying to put the concept into words. "I'm very much like that drunkard on the steps of Wyneth's tavern. But my drink is a good challenge." Embarrassed by his own revelation, Taziar avoided Moonbear's gaze.

"So? My people hunt for food. Yet some trade other chores for more time in the field. They find it exciting." Moonbear tapped Taziar's foot reassuringly. "They bring us dinner. Their motivations do not concern me. It's no disgrace to enjoy what you do."

Taziar lay back down on his cleared patch of forest floor, contemplating his companion's words. Though far from the only home he knew, with no specific destination, and plagued by a vow of vengeance which filled him with restlessness, Taziar found Moonbear's comments soothing. *I've misjudged him. He's not slow-witted, just naive. A city society would crush him. If in no other way, I can pay him back for my life by seeing to it that he returns to his people.* Taziar watched Moonbear settle into a comfortable sleeping position. "Moon, I'm sorry I didn't help you fight the guards in Wyneth. I guess I'm accustomed to avoiding those situations."

Moonbear's voice was a sleepy mumble. "You would have gotten in my way. You're not a warrior."

Taziar bit his lower lip. "In a way I am. My father taught me the basic maneuvers. I wish I'd taken his lessons more seriously." Taziar recalled his feelings of inadequacy whenever he tried to swing a heavy blade and the dull dissatisfaction which showed in his father's eyes because Taziar would rather climb trees than hurl daggers into their trunks. "If you'll sword-train me, I'll show you how to ride a horse."

"Good. The swords I took from the guards will get used." Moonbear chuckled. "I have never sat on a beast before. The towns outside our forest have ponies, but they are too small for anything except packs. And I have not seen any striped animal larger than a badger."

Taziar smiled. "The zebra steeds are just normal horses bred for color. The baron thinks their hides blend better with the forest shadows, and the pattern prevents disputes about ownership. All of the ugly animals belong to his army."

Moonbear whispered. "Ugly animals for ugly warriors."

Taziar smiled. He watched as exhaustion gradually overtook Moonbear. But for Taziar, sleep remained elusive. He slipped his hand into his pocket and stroked the smoothed surfaces of Mordath's jadestone. *Even those citizens with unbridled faith in gods do not believe the myths of magic beyond the Kattegat Sea.* Yet Mordath's strangeness raised doubts. No trick of light and shadow could have caused the flash of the gemstone in Karl's tavern. *What would make this stone so terrible a man who believes himself a powerful sorcerer would wish to be free of it?* Taziar had no answer, but he felt an overpowering compulsion to keep the jadestone. Its finely polished edges seemed to promise success and reinforced his decision to head north with Moonbear.

As Taziar hovered near sleep, his mind conjured the image of a woman. Wind pushed her short, blonde ringlets back from a beautiful face. Her blue eyes beckoned. Her mouth was soft with a laughter which filled Taziar's dreams. He slept deeply, oblivious to the staccato yaps of hunting hounds which gradually replaced the smooth, fluent music of the foxes.

CHAPTER 7

The Bounty Hunter

"A stoic of the woods—a man without a tear."
—Thomas Campbell

The morning sun rose over the Kielwald; its beams reflected like emeralds from raindrops on the aspen leaves. In the forest south of Cullinsberg, the woodsman, Aird Moor, stacked knots of rotten oak on the fire in his stone hearth. He placed each log with practiced care, knowing it would continue to smolder until his return that evening. Smoke billowed out from the blaze into the confines of his one-room cabin. A wolf spider raced frantically from a crack in the burning wood. Seeing no purpose in its death, Aird Moor leaned a stick against the log. The spider scampered down it and disappeared into the moss-chinked wall. Aird Moor kicked the twig into the fire. "A second chance is a rare thing no one deserves. I hope you appreciate it."

Wind ruffled the skin door of Aird Moor's cabin, admitting the sun in undulating bands. Light sheened from the off-white surface of the antlers which supported his bow and quiver. Won from a red deer stag, the rack served as Aird Moor's only furniture except for his fur bedding by the fire and a rough wooden table. Disdainful of possessions he could not easily carry or replace, Aird Moor's wanderlust kept his furnishings simple and his social encounters brief.

Stepping over the sword by his bedside, Aird Moor retrieved his bow. He strapped the quiver across his back and examined the bow for wear. Satisfied with its condition, he strung the weapon and slipped through the cabin door into the surrounding glade. A squirrel bolted from the clearing. It scrambled into a tree and watched Aird Moor in silence. Saplings bowed in unison; their taller fathers stood firm, unswayed by the breezes which rattled through their branches. Aird Moor's buckskin hunting shirt absorbed the morning warmth. Bow in hand, he jogged across the meadow to the trail which led to the thickly-forested hills to the south.

Once on the path, Aird Moor slipped into the habitual stealth of a predator. He walked into the wind. He paused to observe and listen between steps. His senses sifted purposeful movement from the intermittent effects of the breezes. Behind him, he heard the sudden whir of a flushed grouse. Uncertain as to what had frightened the bird so close to his cabin, Aird Moor eased against the base of an uprooted tree.

In the glade, the squirrel chattered excitedly, warning of a less than subtle intruder. *Surely a man. No animal would move clumsily enough to upset it.* Aird Moor knew he possessed nothing in his cabin worth stealing. Unhurriedly, he worked his way beyond sight and sound of the clearing. He followed a stream bed to the far side of the meadow and positioned for a downwind approach. Beneath a tangle of blackberry bushes at the northern edge, he hunched in the gulley, listening.

A horse snorted and pawed the ground impatiently. Aird Moor raked fingers through his close-cropped, auburn hair. He retrieved a knife from the pocket of his buckskins, unsheathed it, and quietly and deliberately cleared a shooting path through the vines. An arrow pressed to his bow, he raised his head and peered into the clearing.

The horse was a zebra steed tied to a tree trunk by the reins of its bridle, its gray and black barring unmistakable. Before the door to Aird Moor's cabin, a man in black and red poked the hanging skin door. Aird Moor snorted. *Cullinsberg guard. I should have guessed by his ineptness.* The discovery revived memories of Aird Moor's time served in the baron's army. *If we'd crashed through the forest with his lack of caution, the barbarians would have butchered us like cows.*

Aird Moor nocked the arrow and aimed it through his cleared fire line. "Turn slowly."

The guard's muscles knotted beneath the linen of his coat. He whirled. His gaze flitted across the brush, unfocused. His hand fell to his sword hilt. "Who are you? Show yourself."

Disgusted by the guard's recklessness, Aird Moor remained still. "You're in no position to make demands."

The Cullinsbergen's eyes swept the clearing, seeking the source of Aird Moor's voice. "Show yourself. I like to see the people I talk with."

"Very well." Aird Moor stepped from the blackberries, holding his arrow in place with a finger looped over its shaft. "But your enemies won't always grant you this courtesy. What do you want? I don't take well to uncoordinated children stumbling through my forest."

The guardsman's face flushed scarlet with offense. "I'm a soldier, trained to excellence by Captain Salik Kanathul."

"Then Salik has become an idiot. If he'd taught you properly, I wouldn't be standing here with an arrow pointed at your chest. Now, why have you come?"

The guardsman glared. Apparently finding further argument futile, he addressed Aird Moor's question. "I came seeking Aird Moor, the bounty hunter." He shifted his hand from his hilt to a less threatening posture.

Aird Moor lowered his bow. "You found me."

The zebra steed tore at the ground with a hoof. The guard smiled weakly. "The baron wishes to hire you."

Aird Moor scratched through the curled, wiry hair of his beard. "For whom?"

The soldier fidgeted. "A couple of prisoners escaped from the dungeons a week ago. One's a local thief, a black-haired, blue-eyed, skinny, little snake about this tall." He indicated a level just beneath Aird Moor's chin. "The baron doesn't care in what condition you bring him in. He's only worth a fraction of your bounty. His companion . . ."

The guardsman reached his arm as far as it would stretch. "Yellow-haired barbarian. He's fierce."

Aird Moor studied the guardsman's shadow-streaked face in the thin light of morning. "How fierce?"

"Six of our men cornered him in Wyneth's tavern. He left four dead and two injured."

That's fierce. Aird Moor considered. "I don't work cheaply."

The guardsman's mouth flicked into a smile, as if he found the statement particularly humorous. "The baron's ready to pay four thousand gold weight for the barbarian and one thousand for the thief. But you'll get no money if the barbarian's killed."

The sum struck Aird Moor momentarily speechless. A vision of his beloved Inge filled his mind. Her blonde cascade of hair danced in Norway's autumn breeze; a heavy, bearskin robe disguised the graceful curves Aird Moor knew so well. Five years ago, he had asked for her hand in marriage. Her father's reply still rumbled through his thoughts, sour as mocking laughter. "My son is Dragonrank and my uncle a jarl. My family is blessed. I will not wed my only daughter to an impoverished foreigner. Begone! I forbid you to see her again." And, though Aird Moor had spoken of love and escape, Inge dared not defy her father's decree. Now, in his familiar clearing in the Kielwald Wilderness, Aird Moor felt hope displace the bitterness his memories inspired. *With five thousand weight in gold, her father must accept me.* But he also realized the baron would not offer such a staggering reward for a simple quest. "This barbarian bested an entire patrol, and the baron expects me to bring him in alive?"

The soldier shrugged. "You have to earn five thousand weight of gold. Salik has a division of our army tracking them now. If you can deliver the prisoners directly to him, you'll still get your bounty."

Aird Moor plucked at his mustache, suspecting treachery. *If I give the fugitives to Salik, what would keep him from claiming their capture? If I turn them over to the captain, I'll need many witnesses and some assurances.* "Tell your baron I'll take his offer. But if I deliver the barbarian to Salik, he'd best be carrying my bounty. I'll not have my payment delayed."

The Cullinsbergen started toward his horse. He made a noncommittal gesture, indicating that Aird Moor's request was beyond his authority to grant.

"Where are they now?"

The guardsman freed his zebra steed and snapped the reins over the horse's ears. "In the Kielwald, probably not far northwest of Wyneth. Our army's close behind with hounds. We may not need you."

Aird Moor laughed. "You'll need me. Crashing through the forest like a cattle herd, your men won't get within arrow shot of a barbarian." He watched the guardsman mount his oddly-colored horse. "Soldier."

The guardsman reined his steed.

Aird Moor rubbed his weathered hand across his brow. "Next time you or one of your fellows enters my glade, he'd best do so without disturbing the game." He raised his bow to remind the man how narrowly he had escaped death.

Without replying, the guardsman rode into the forest.

Aird Moor walked to his cabin to retrieve his sword. It seemed strange to accept a mission of blood to regain the love he had lost so long ago in

Norway. But, during his ten years of warring against barbarians, killing and hunting men had become routine. After a decade steeped in blood and death, returning to the mundanity of Cullinsberg to brag about the war and its atrocities had seemed a farce. Instead, he'd traveled extensively, seeking a peace he found only by settling in the same woodlands which had served as the battlefield. "Good hunting," he murmured to himself.

Aird Moor arrived in Wyneth near midday. He walked in silence, feeling conspicuous among open village roadways and pastures. Unlike Taziar, Aird Moor found no security in the sight of Karl's neatly-painted tavern with its copper railway. Approaching it, he tripped the latch and entered the common room.

Dressed in buckskin from his coarse shirt to the boots on his feet and equipped with bow and sword, Aird Moor seemed out of place among the Wynethian farmers. Though aware of the presence of three other customers, he did not trouble himself to glance at them but walked directly to the bar and took a seat.

A pock-faced adolescent with wild, dark hair confronted him from the working side of the bar. "Drink, sir?"

Aird Moor pinched leaf mold from the lining of his empty pocket. "No, not now. Is Karl in?" Nine years had passed since Karl and Aird Moor shared time in the baron's army, but allies made in combat are not soon forgotten.

The youngster shook his head. "No, sir. Karl's out buying beer."

Aird Moor scowled. "When will he return?"

"Not until nightfall."

Aware of the distance a barbarian could cover by evening, Aird Moor tapped his fingers impatiently against the countertop. "Did you see the fight last night?"

The youngster gnawed his thumbnail nervously. "No. Karl worked alone."

"Do you recognize anyone who might have been here?" Aird Moor made a sweeping gesture encompassing every man in the room.

The adolescent examined his patrons. He pointed to a table in the farthest corner. "Just the Norseman, sir."

Aird Moor glanced in the indicated direction. A man sat alone, hunched over a glass of fine wine. His white blond hair fell to the small of his back, as well-tended as a woman's. A closely-cropped beard masculinized features familiar to Aird Moor. *Mordath?* Aird Moor shook his head, shocked to find Inge's brother so far from his Northern home. "Thank you." Aird Moor dismissed the barboy. He hesitated, uncertain whether he wished to speak with Mordath. He had never cared for Mordath's manner; the sorcerer had always acted blatantly scornful of Aird Moor's presence around his sister. But as far as Aird Moor knew, active hostilities had never arisen between them. *The gods alone know what business he has in this part of the world. But I did come for information. I can weather his glares for the price of knowledge. And maybe he can tell me of Inge.* With that thought, Aird Moor strode to Mordath's table.

Mordath stared into his drink with an intensity which Aird Moor suspected was an act. The sorcerer waited until Aird Moor sat across the table, then raised his head with regal disdain. He studied the woodsman in the crisp afternoon sunshine. His pale eyebrows arched in recognition. His mouth set in a grim line of interest. "You." He stretched a long-nailed finger toward Aird Moor's chest. "You've come to me."

Mordath's affectations amused Aird Moor. He smiled. "Not intentionally. Wyneth is the last place I'd search for a sorcerer. What are you doing here?"

Mordath remained leaning forward, hands balled on the table before him. "I came for you."

"For me?" Brazenly, Aird Moor chuckled. "You could have waited in this tavern until Ragnarok. You know I live in the forest. So does anyone you might have asked."

Mordath's lips twitched upward. "Ah, but you're here now, hunter." His palm curled back to the body of his wine glass. "I knew the precise location of your hovel in the Kielwald. This past year, I gained the ability to track magically." He inclined his head to indicate the jade-tipped dragonstaff. "Meanwhile, I had Dragonrank business to attend in town."

Aird Moor snorted. "You always were a bad liar. The handful of people south of the Kattegat who have heard of Dragonrank or sorcerers believe in them only as beggar's tales. What business could you have in a farm town?"

Mordath's long fingernails clicked against his glass like windblown branches. "That's none of your affair. I wish to meet with you for unrelated reasons."

Aware of his advantage, Aird Moor considered whether to bother dragging the information out of Mordath. The mage would come this far only from desperation; apparently he needed Aird Moor. And the Dragonrank training, which required those studying the magical arts to spend eleven months of the year on the school's grounds, spawned sorcerers with no concept of social interaction. For all his self-important power, Mordath was as manipulable as a child.

Mordath continued, obviously mistaking Aird Moor's hesitation for acquiescence. "For two years after you left Norway, I wasted my month vacations tracking you. Had I found you, I would have slain you."

Aird Moor shrugged unsympathetically. "If you spent more time in the woods and less in class, you wouldn't have so much difficulty trailing me." He considered. "You're neither the first nor last man to try to kill me. But why would you wish me dead?"

"I don't anymore." Mordath explained. "At the time, I hated you for what you did to my sister . . . and my nephew."

Surprise crushed down upon Aird Moor, and he lost the urge to parry insults. "There was a child?" He fidgeted in the chair, suddenly uncomfortable. "I—I didn't know. Is there anything I can do?"

Mordath lifted his glass to his lips and swallowed. "Yes." He lowered his drink. "That's why I'm here. You tainted Inge, spoiled her bloodline so none of our men would have her, save one."

"Which one?" Aird Moor whispered, unable to shake the sudden despair of his loss.

"His name is Brandr. He's a pirate and a scoundrel who spends his days raping and plundering, then brings his concubines home to live with Inge. She's miserable. And the boy, four years old and already as dirty and foul-mouthed as his mother's husband."

Anger swept through Aird Moor.

Repeatedly, Mordath's fists clenched and loosened on the tabletop. "I want you to kill Brandr."

Suspicious, Aird Moor went cautious. "Why come to me? Surely you have the power to slay him, Dragonrank. And even Norway must have assassins for hire."

Mordath took a great gulp of air and loosed it in a sigh of blatant exasperation. "Brandr is a soldier. For me to kill him would require magic. Dragonrank mages are rare, even in Norway. Every citizen of Narvik would know *I* murdered him, and I've no wish to become a fugitive. As to your other foolish statement, Aird Moor, I spend eleven months of every year on the Dragonrank grounds where there is no contact with visitors. What would I know of finding or hiring assassins? I came to you because you love Inge. It's a fair trade, I think. Brandr's life for Inge's happiness."

Aird Moor frowned, too familiar with Northern culture to believe Inge's father would reconsider the advances of a foreigner even after Brandr's death. "And once I've slain Brandr? You'll help me marry Inge?"

Mordath shrugged. "I won't oppose you, but I can't speak for my father. He has a strong will. He would rather see Inge with a man like Brandr than living in poverty with a forester."

Realizing that five thousand weight in gold could barter better than words, Aird Moor returned to his initial purpose. "I'll consider your offer, but

I've another job to finish first. I need information. Did you witness the odd goings-on here last night?"

"Some," replied Mordath. "I left before the battle."

"No matter." Aird Moor leaned across the table. "I just need some idea of direction." He met Mordath's emerald green stare. "Did the barbarian or his scrawny companion say anything about destination?"

"Barbarian?" Mordath massaged his knuckles through his beard. "Do you mean the Northman? He was no barbarian. He spoke little, but when he did, he used your tongue fluently. And his accent was Swedish." His eyes crinkled in thought. "Of course, Sweden does have barbarians. No relation to your Danwaldians, I don't believe."

Aird Moor's brows knitted with interest. "North then. Calrmar Port is the only city I know with transport ships which cross the Kattegat." He looked to the Norse mage for confirmation, but Mordath seemed suddenly agitated.

Mordath's feline eyes went deadly direct. "North," he repeated, his earlier composure broken. "You think they're headed north." It was a statement, not a question.

Alert to Mordath's abrupt change in temperament, Aird Moor replied. "You as much as told me so. Tribal bonds would draw a barbarian home."

Mordath caught the edge of the table, nodding agreement. "But I didn't know he was a barbarian until now. I . . . will help you find them."

"No," said Aird Moor. His tone was soft, but his hostility unmistakable. *I work alone. I don't make errors, and I'd become one of Karana's damned before I'd die for someone else's blunder.*

"No?" Mordath paused, apparently confused. "Are you stupid? I'm Dragonrank. Have you forgotten my tracking spell? With a little effort and will, I could tell you the barbarian's exact location."

Aird Moor scowled, recognizing the value of Mordath's power yet unwilling to sacrifice his solitude. Mordath's arrogance and social incompetence might cause more difficulties than his magic could solve. "What stake do you have in my manhunt?"

Mordath's aura of contempt returned. He seized his staff and flicked it around so its clawed end rested on the tabletop. "I'm seeking a jadestone like this one. The thief stole it from me." Apparently thinking Aird Moor feared for his bounty, Mordath continued. "It's worth a scant handful of silver. Your reward, their lives, and anything else they might carry belongs to you."

Caution goaded Aird Moor to question further. "If you want the jadestone back, why don't you track it, transport yourself, and retrieve it? Why do you need me?"

Mordath hesitated, as if weighing his alternatives. "I can't locate the gem, nor the person who carries it. The best I can do is find the Swede and hope the little weasel is with him." He folded his arms across his chest. His eyes narrowed. "The magics of transport and murder would weaken my life energy. If my killing spells missed either target, I would be forced to fight, draining further power." Mordath shrugged. He continued with glaring honesty. "You're a soldier. Why should I risk having to battle with the barbarian?"

One question still plagued Aird Moor. "If you

knew the thief took your gem, why didn't you get it back before they left town?"

Impatience grated through Mordath's answer. "I mistook them for local peasantry, a small-time pickpocket and a Swede who chose to live in the west. The jadestone is of no use to me. I came to Cullinsberg to rid myself of it." He clapped his palms to his chin in disgust. "Had I known they headed north . . ." He broke off.

"What's so special about this gem?"

Mordath waved off Aird Moor's question. "I don't wish to speak of it."

"But you will." Aird Moor pressed. "I don't perform any task without all the knowledge available."

Mordath said nothing.

Aird Moor shrugged. "Very well. When I find the thief and retrieve your gemstone. I'll seek out another Dragonrank mage to explain its value."

Amusement crossed Mordath's features. "You're bluffing, Aird Moor. You'll never find a Dragonrank."

Tiring of the game, Aird Moor stood. "I'll find one, even if I have to go to the front gate of the Dragonrank School to do it. Good day, Mordath."

"Wait." Mordath's word was a menacing command.

Aird Moor raised his eyebrows to indicate interest.

"There's nothing about the gem you need to know." Mordath tapped the jade in his staff. "The rankstones serve as an indication of experience and a means to store power. Each stone is designed to hold a maximum of all of its wielder's . . . stamina, his "life aura" as we call it. The stolen jade contains nearly all the magic, thus the life force, of another mage. If I destroyed it, I would instantly kill its owner, an action forbidden to me by Dragonrank law."

"So, why did you wish to be rid of it?" asked Aird Moor. "And now that you are, why do you want it back?"

Mordath scowled with scornful impatience. "We're wasting time."

Aird Moor sat down again. "Then finish quickly. Time is of less importance than information. I'm not leaving until you've answered my questions. You're the one delaying this mission with useless conversation."

Mordath's demeanor went hard as flint. His hands gripped the sides of the chair, as he fought a private battle between addressing Aird Moor's statement and storming from the tavern. At length, need won out over pride. He settled back into his chair and continued. "The spell which holds the other sorcerer's life aura also draws magic into the jadestone. The gem weakens any other Dragonrank who carries it. I came to find you, but I hoped I could lose the cursed, power-stealing stone in Cullinsberg's den of bandits. Now you tell me the thief is headed directly for the owner of the jadestone, the one person who could reclaim its powers."

Aird Moor pondered Mordath's words. The story seemed too strange to be a lie. Mordath's reticence appeared logical. *He is probably not fully free to disclose the Dragonrank teachings, and he might well fear I would double cross him and sell the gem to its owner.* Aware the Jaderank Dragonmage whose essence occupied the stone could become his most difficult rival, Aird Moor realized he needed a sorcerer's aid. Yet, still disliking ties and loyalties, he agreed with reluctance. "All right, Mordath. We work together. But I make all the decisions."

Mordath nodded his acceptance, and Aird Moor pressed forward for a whispered conference.

The sun arched over the Kielwald and began its gradual descent. It peeked through breaks and tears in the woven interlay of branches. Cullinsberg's patrol of twenty mounted cavalry and thirty foot soldiers reclined, savoring the final remnants of their midday meal. Set apart from the others, Ilyrian sat beside Captain Salik Kanathul. The guardsman ate in contented silence. The prime minister plotted.

Salik's too honest for bribery and not quite stupid enough to control. Ilyrian gnawed a handful of smoked venison. *If we haul the barbarian prince back to Cullinsberg alive, Baron Dietrich will become a wealthy man. We're just hirelings performing our duties; we'll see none of that gold.*

Ilyrian lost interest in his food. He set the meat aside. *The baron can't afford to let the barbarian escape. Not only would he lose vast sums in ransom, he would risk the wrath of the entire tribe. Once their prince came safely back among them, the barbarians could attack the barony. By the desperation of his bounty and the intensity of our hunt, Baron Dietrich must fear his men could lose such a battle.* The thought made Ilyrian grin. *I have a third option, the most pleasing of all. Somehow, I must see to it the barbarian prince is slain by Cullinsbergen warriors in the baron's name. That would assure a war.* Ilyrian smiled, considering the results of his decision. *The citizens of Cullinsberg are still bitter over the last barbarian war; their sons and husbands died for no gains in gold, power, or territory.*

*With the proper motivation, the Cullinsberg citizenry
could be swayed to oust their baron. And, while barbarians and Cullinsbergens kill one another, I will haul
away the barbarians' gold and become the richest man
in the realm. Who could better replace Baron Dietrich
than the wealthy prime minister who was brave enough
to lead his soldiers into battle?*

Wicked joy suffused Ilyrian. So far, the Shadow
Climber, the baron, and Cullinsberg's former supreme commander had played into his hands like
pawns on a chessboard. The escape had been un-
foreseen, but it, too, might work to Ilyrian's advantage. He recalled the careful, patient planning
which had brought him to his current position:
the forged reports which led to Captain Taziar's
hanging; the well-paid messenger who'd implicated
the captain, then conveniently died after the trial
from a "self-inflicted" drug overdose; the brilliant
revelation which brought the Shadow Climber to
justice and confirmed Ilyrian as prime minister.
There remained only one last step. *I must gain
control of the army, force their hand against the baron,
and take his position myself.*

Suddenly light flared in the center of Ilyrian's
and Salik's camp. Both men leaped to their feet.
The captain's sword rasped from its sheath. The
radiance stained his steel blade in a series of blacks
and greens. Stunned beyond action, Ilyrian stared
as the sorceries faded and a man appeared in the
dispersing glow. His hair hung in a neatly-tended,
blond cascade. His long, slender fingers gripped a
staff; its end tapered to a huge, black-nailed claw
which clutched a faceted, milky green stone.

The mage indicated Salik with his free hand.

"Sheathe your weapon! If I wished to kill you, I would have done so already."

Salik obeyed with obvious reluctance. His fist remained poised near his hilt.

Apparently satisfied, the sorcerer continued. "I am Mordath, Dragonrank of Jadeclaw. I have come to aid your task."

Ilyrian stared, not quite willing to accept the reality of Dragonrank legends, yet struck by an entrance too grand to deny. More accustomed to verbal diplomacy than Salik, Ilyrian recovered his tongue more quickly. "We are honored by your presence."

Salik added, "Indeed. We would find your help invaluable. Unfortunately, we've no money to pay."

Ilyrian winced, wishing Salik would leave politics and negotiations to him.

Mordath pursed his lips with calm indulgence. "I don't want your gold. I'm working for another, though our purposes are the same."

Accustomed to his own use of betrayal and treachery, Ilyrian grew suspicious. He phrased his query delicately. "The value of your skills is unquestionable. What can we do to make your task easier?" Ilyrian waited, certain the sorcerer's reply would reveal his true motive.

Mordath smiled, perhaps reading Ilyrian's intention through the cautious construction of his question. "My . . . um . . . employer will divert the men you seek toward Hawk Rock. He said you would know where that is." He studied Ilyrian and Salik as if seeking confirmation.

Ilyrian nodded, pleased at this opportunity to capture Moonbear yet concerned that the presence of Mordath and his partner might impede his plan to slay the barbarian. "We know of it. Should we pull in the hounds and head toward Hawk Rock?"

Mordath repied with emphatic swiftness. "No! You must continue your chase and more quickly now. Drive the barbarian and the thief toward the Kolding Hills without rest. Make them careless. Otherwise, Aird Moor will never find them . . ."

"Aird Moor!" Ilyrian's exclamation was startled from him. The name jarred a scene from memory. Ilyrian stood on the wide street before the baron's castle, his thoughts warm with the impending success of his treacherous intrigues against Captain Taziar Medakan.

"You!" Aird Moor's voice ground through Ilyrian's reverie, heavy with threat.

"Aird Moor?" Ilyrian's reply was a quiet monotone, free of guilt. Cautious as a cat, he turned, shocked to discover the bowman stood within arm's length. Ilyrian took a startled step back.

Aird Moor's face crinkled with fury; his eyes went dark and unforgiving. "I know what you did, you lying, stinking, hell-damned vulture! And you're going to confess to the baron." He lunged, quick as a striking cobra.

Ilyrian loosed a small scream of surprise. He flung up an arm to protect his face. Aird Moor's fist smashed into his nose, drawing blood. Ilyrian lurched away. A second blow thudded into his cheek, sending his consciousness swimming. From the periphery of his vision, he saw the off-duty guards rushing toward them from the field grounds. He fended off Aird Moor's third strike, then caught the bowman's wrist. Aird Moor twisted, and both men crashed to the street.

Enmeshed in memory, Ilyrian recalled how the flat of Aird Moor's hand battered his skull. Ilyrian's forehead struck the road. Head ringing, he writhed free. Blood dripped to the street. He spun toward Aird Moor. The bowman's fingers skittered forward and locked on Ilyrian's throat. He dragged the nobleman to his feet. "Admit it, you bastard!" Aird Moor hissed. "You invented those charges against Taz." His nails gouged Ilyrian's neck. "Say it!"

Oblivious to the presence of Mordath and Salik, Ilyrian followed the painful progression of images in his mind. He recalled how the soldiers arrived to give him aid even as Aird Moor forced a gasped confession. "I invented those charges against Taz."

Aird Moor's fingers dug deeper. "You bribed the messenger to mislead Taz."

Ilyrian stared at Aird Moor through a ragged veil of darkness. Sweat doused his body, and he knew real fear. "I did," he panted, his breath a thin whistle.

Then suddenly the guardsmen came to his rescue. Three pulled Aird Moor, flailing and cursing, from Ilyrian. A fourth supported the nobleman's sagging form. "You're all right now." Ilyrian rubbed at his bruised throat. He passed a hand across his face, and his palm was suddenly streaked with red.

The task of dragging Aird Moor to the castle required six men. Ilyrian heard the bowman's righteous screams. "You traitors, let me go! He betrayed our captain! You heard him! He admitted it!" His angered cries faded into the distance.

One of the soldiers cleared his throat. "Will you press charges?"

Ilyrian shook his head, not wishing the matter
to go to trial. Though the guardsmen would tes-
tify that his confession was obtained under duress,
he had no wish to allow Aird Moor's knowledge to
halt Captain Taziar's execution nor bring Ilyrian's
innocence into question. "No. He served with Taz
a long time. It's hard to accept deceit from a
commander who was also a friend. Aird Moor
needed someone else to blame. For whatever reason, he chose me." He smeared blood from his
palm to his sleeve. "For my own safety, I would
ask that you keep Aird Moor locked up until after
the captain's trial."

Now, standing in camp in the Kielwald Forest,
Ilyrian realized he did not wish to face Aird Moor
again. *Aird Moor, too, must die.* And Ilyrian knew
he would need Mordath's cooperation to accom-
plish such a feat. Without the sorcerer's assistance,
the woodsman would prove too powerful an
opponent.

These thoughts flashed through Ilyrian's mind
within seconds. Memory broke to reality. Salik
and Mordath stared at Ilyrian with questioning
intensity. Unnerved by their scrutiny, he sought
words to explain his heated repetition of Aird
Moor's name. He met Mordath's gaze. "Forgive
me. Is Aird Moor your friend?" He waited, aware
success or failure of his desires might rest upon
Mordath's answer.

"By Thor, no. We're just men with a common
goal." Mordath thumped the steel-tipped base of
his dragonstaff in the dirt to punctuate his reply.
"If you know something important about Aird
Moor, speak it."

A note of hostility and uncertainty in Mordath's

voice sparked a thrill through Ilyrian. He played this new advantage. "I'm surprised a man with your talents would weather the company of one so deceitful. Dare you trust him?"

"Trust?" Mordath went pensive. "I have abilities beyond your understanding. But I judge character as any other man." Braced against his staff, he leaned toward Ilyrian. "What do you know about Aird Moor?"

Ilyrian suppressed a smile, aware he had won Mordath's attention. "We served together in the barbarian wars." With practiced ease, Ilyrian spouted lies. "Aird Moor would find excuses to remain at camp or in the barracks while we fought battles or tended watches. On our return, we would notice things missing: a few silvers, a trinket." Ilyrian shrugged. "We never proved anything, of course. But I saw him steal jewelry from the dead, ours as well as the enemy. The few times we plundered villages, he was quick to rape, sometimes boys as well as those dirty, barbarian women." For effect, Ilyrian concluded with a description of himself which he had once overheard his father say to Ilyrian's eldest brother. "For a handful of gold ducats, the man would slaughter his mother, and falsehoods slip from his tongue as glibly as truth."

Mordath's eyes glimmered. He turned his gaze to Salik. "Is this true?"

Ilyrian held his breath. As second in command, Salik had led a different regiment in the barbarian wars and could have had few dealing with the bounty hunter.

Salik's thin face puckered in a grimace. His reply was brusque. "I don't know, but it wouldn't surprise me. Aird Moor undermines my authority and bad mouths my men." He shrugged. "The baron seemed certain he could track the prisoners. It's not my place to argue."

Ilyrian realized Salik had known about Aird Moor's hiring and bit back an oath. He had worked and cheated his way to his position as prime minister, yet he was unaware of this important decision. He quelled rising resentment with effort. For now, Salik's silence would pass unpunished. The attainment of Mordath's good will precluded irritation.

As the three men talked, the speech of guardsmen in the surrounding camps intensified from exchanges snatched between bites of meat to the steady hum of conversation. In their growing impatience, some of the men began sparring. The crash of swords punctuated their voices.

"Forgive me." Salik said to Mordath. "You suggested we move quickly. I'll rally my men. And I assume you'll need a horse, lord Dragonrank?" He waited until the sorcerer answered with a nod, then trotted toward his troops.

Mordath lowered himself to the ground. "Aird Moor also asked that you have his bounty with you at Hawk Rock."

Ilyrian stared, fighting the urge to laugh. *Does Aird Moor expect an army patrol to bring enough extra horses to carry five thousand weight in gold?* Ilyrian sat across from Mordath, immediately thinking of a means to capitalize on the mage's apparent ignorance. "I know this is none of my affair, but how much of his bounty has Aird Moor offered you?"

Mordath drew his knees to his chest. "I'll get none of it. I've too much power to concern myself with money."

"Mmmm." Ilyrian nodded agreeably. "Although . . ." He studied Mordath's face for clues to his disposition. "Even a master magician would have uses for a half share of five thousand weight in gold."

Mordath's eyes went wide with curiosity. "Five thousand?"

"That's the bounty."

Mordath stroked the smoothed edge of his dragonstaff, saying nothing.

Afraid to lose Mordath's attention, Ilyrian continued. "Of course, if I could claim the reward, I would share it with you. But, in fact, I know a means to attain enough gold to make the bounty seem a mere pittance. Interested?"

Mordath frowned. "Perhaps. Explain."

With delicate care, Ilyrian wove his web of deceit. He described the barbarian's vast wealth and Moonbear's importance to his tribe and the barony. He concluded with the necessity for Moonbear's, Taziar's, and Aird Moor's deaths. Then, while Mordath calmly considered his options, Ilyrian waited in strained silence.

Graceful as a house cat, Mordath rose. "Can you promise me one more murder? A Norse pirate by the name of Brandr?"

Ilyrian smiled. "Easily arranged."

"I'm interested," Mordath said.

CHAPTER 8

The Hunted

"Every cradle asks us 'Whence?' and every coffin 'Whither?' The poor barbarian, weeping above his dead, can answer these questions as intelligently as the robed priest of the most authentic creed."
— Robert Green Ingersoll,
Address at a child's grave

Oblivious to Ilyrian's designs against his life, Taziar Medakan slipped through the undergrowth and debris of the Kielwald Forest. Long ago, he had sacrificed attempts at stealth in favor of speed. More recently, fatigue had forced him to just concentrate on continuing to move through stands of beech, oak and chestnut. Nothing seemed to change. Trees blurred to more trees. No longer did he see beauty in the forest or derive pleasure from birdsongs. Moonbear's frequent disappearances to scout or pick the wild berries which had sustained them through the day ceased to concern Taziar. Memories of gang fellows and exhilarating thefts obsessed him. *And I can't ever return home.*

Sadness enveloped Taziar. A city child from

birth, he had never learned to appreciate the true wonders of the forest. Ilyrian's deceit and his own love of action had wrenched him suddenly and cruelly from the only world he knew: his life, his loves, and his friends. He wondered how Shylar fared now and hoped his presence and the guard Moonbear had killed had not gotten her into trouble. He smiled at his own concern. Shylar had spent too many years aiding the underground to become a casualty of the baron's manhunt.

Engrossed in thought, Taziar did not realize he was once again alone nor that he had passed through clustered pine and into a clearing. A crackle of branches to his right startled him. He turned. A man emerged from the brush. He towered over Taziar, his arms thick as fence posts. His hair hung in wild disarray. His eyes fixed on Taziar, blue and demanding. He clutched a spear, its tip angled at Taziar's chest.

Taziar recoiled with a surprised gasp. He held his hands outstretched and away from his swordhilt, indicating surrender. He backstepped; the movement nearly impaled him on another spear behind him. He whirled to face a man enough like the first to be a brother. Taziar cried out in alarm. Even as he turned to run, eight more spearmen stepped from the forest, trapping him in the clearing. *Guardsmen?* Taziar shook his head in disbelief. People in the countries surrounding Cullinsberg sported dark hair and features, yet these woodland soldiers all seemed fair and blond. And spears had never proved a popular weapon in Cullinsberg's army.

A muscular redhead jabbed his spear toward Taziar and spoke in a strange language with a heavy accent reminiscent of Moonbear's. The circle closed. Taziar tasted sweat. He shook his head to indicate he did not understand. "My name is Taziar Medakan. I mean you no harm." Lacking skill with a sword and surrounded by warriors, Taziar realized the absurdity of his reassurances.

The spearmen shifted and whispered to one another. Momentarily, Taziar suspected they would laugh at his name as Moonbear had in Shylar's tavern. The thought reminded him of his companion's absence. "Moonbear? Moonbear!"

From beyond the tightening ring of soldiers, Moonbear's gruff reply was unintelligible to Taziar. But the spearmen turned at the sound of the barbarian's voice. "Manebjorn." The word swept through their ranks like an echo. Several of the spearmen dropped to their knees.

Taziar read anger in Moonbear's next utterance. As one, the warriors leaped to their feet and rushed down upon the Swedish barbarian. Helpless against men in such numbers, Taziar feared for Moonbear's life. But the first man who reached him dropped his spear and embraced Moonbear. The others pressed around the two men, chattering excitedly.

No longer endangered, Taziar waited with patient curiosity until the reunion amenities were finished. Moonbear pushed past his friends to Taziar's side. Still speaking the Northern tongue, Moonbear made an introduction in which he called Taziar by a name which sounded uncomfortably like "sugar." He then addressed his companion. "These are my Danish cousins. We have entered the forests your people would call the Danwald

Wilderness. My cousins have invited us to their camp for supper and a story."

Taziar thought, *some friendly invite*. His gut ached with a hunger berries could not satisfy, but caution overshadowed his desire for food. "I appreciate their kindness and the fact that they chose to let me live. But do we have time to spare for tales?"

"We are safe with Deerrunner's tribe. And we would insult them if we refused."

Taziar studied the fur-clad, hardened barbarians and decided offending them would not be wise. "Then I guess we join them with pleasure."

Moonbear communicated their acceptance. The Danwaldian barbarians funneled into the woods, sweeping Taziar and Moonbear along with them.

"What was that name you called me?" Taziar questioned as they walked.

"Skygge." Moonbear spelled it out for Taziar, but he still pronounced it like "sugar." "It means shadow."

Taziar went silent, surprised Moonbear could read. Although both of Taziar's occupations required such knowledge, few of Cullinsberg's citizenry could master printing more complicated than a tavern sign. Again, Taziar realized how guards' stories of barbarians and his own early judgment of Moonbear's intelligence still influenced his opinion.

The spearmen led Taziar and Moonbear along narrow trails and through brush which seemed impenetrable. The barbarians traversed the densest copses with animal grace and quietness. Despite a day of practice, Taziar still felt as awkward as a zebra steed in comparison. He dogged Moonbear's steps, but branches jabbed like daggers; brambles tore through the linen of his cloak and scratched welts into his back.

Soon, the aroma of roasting meat and potatoes intermingled with smells less familiar to Taziar. The barbarian warriors entered camp in a clearing ringed with pine. In its center, half a dozen golden-haired women tended a huge cooking pit. Nearby, several others hacked roots, stems, and nuts with curved, copper knives. Children of varying ages scurried about the camp. The older males sparred under the watchful eye of a wizened, white-haired man who seemed unusually spry for his years. Other warriors guarded the perimeter, but they left their posts as Moonbear entered the camp.

Moonbear inclined his head toward the elderly swordmaster. "That is Prince Deerrunner. I have matters to discuss with him and his men. You wait here." He motioned toward the fire.

Taziar watched Deerrunner jog toward them. *Prince?* He tossed his head in disbelief. *Their king must be ancient.* Obediently, Taziar wandered to the indicated position while the warriors converged on Moonbear. Even as Taziar started to hunker down, he found himself surrounded by children.

Surprised by the youngsters' boldness, Taziar remained standing while they poked and prodded his clothing. A girl seized his hand and traced the calluses gained from years of climbing, which must seem oddly placed to children accustomed to warriors. A boy no older than ten positioned himself beside Taziar. Apparently noticing that their friend stood as tall as the foreigner, the children giggled. Embarrassed by their laughter, Taziar sat in the dirt. Immediately, a toddler climbed into his lap, and the youngsters squatted around him.

Feeling obligated to entertain, Taziar spoke. "Hello. I'm ... um ..." He tried to imitate Moonbear's singsong pronunciation. "... Shee-ooger."

The children broke into laughter. The toddler giggled so hard, she fell from Taziar's lap.

Taziar flushed, hoping he had not called himself something obscene. Seeking a means to distract his overappreciative audience, he thrust his hands into his pockets. His fingers closed about Mordath's jadestone. He whisked it into his palm. Immediately, his mind filled with images of the blonde woman who had haunted his dreams the previous night. Her beauty aroused curiosity and interest, obscuring the question of why her image suddenly had appeared in his mind. Some trick of magic allowed the vision to remain in Taziar's thoughts until it faded gradually to gray. Abruptly, Taziar realized displaying a sorcerer's toy before a tribe of barbarian warriors might not be prudent. He flicked the stone into his sleeve.

The toddler squealed excitedly. She caught Taziar's hand and turned it questioningly. The youngsters all started talking simultaneously. Realizing his sleight of hand had not gone unnoticed, Taziar palmed the jade. Placing his hand on the toddler, he pretended to retrieve the green stone from the folds of her sewn skin garment.

The children clapped delightedly. Shouting praises Taziar could not understand, they urged him to continue. Repeatedly, the thief made the gemstone disappear. Each time, he would reclaim it from a different child and a new location: once an eye, then an ear, then a foot. At last, tiring of the game, he pressed the jadestone back into his pocket. He looked past the children to the warriors who still conversed in a huddle.

A gruff command from one of the women by the cook fire dispersed the children. The women crushed in on Taziar. Several sat before him, offering handfuls of berries, roots, or nutmeats. Others crouched beside him, examining the fabric of his worn and tattered cloak. One raked her fingers through his fine, black hair.

Not wanting to offend them, Taziar accepted several chestnuts. The woman from whom he took them cried out in triumph. The others pressed closer. Suddenly, Taziar realized they were competing for his attention, as if the regard of a stranger somehow raised each woman's status above the others. Bombarded with food and embraces, Taziar tried valiantly to divide his interest equally.

Small and thin, shamed by his father's presumed cowardice, Taziar had never found a woman of his own. But Shylar encouraged her girls to bed Taziar in exchange for his generosity. Now, weeks from his last sexual encounter, he found the barbarians' caresses exciting. He felt a tingling sensation in his groin. Before he could think of fighting it, he had an erection.

Taziar winced and crossed his legs, mortified at his own arousal. "Moonbear?" he called feebly. He glanced toward the men, distressingly aware of the brawny forms of the women's husbands. *I'm dead*. Feigning excessive interest in the proffered food, Taziar shifted uncomfortably and wished he knew how to say "homosexual" in the Northern tongue.

While Taziar struggled with the consequences of the women's kindness, the warriors' meeting broke. The men headed toward the central camp-fire. The large redhead Taziar had thought was their captain shouted at a woman to Taziar's right. She caught the Cullinsbergen's arm and called back to the barbarian. In response, the man strode toward them.

Taziar disentangled himself from the women and struggled to his feet. Concerned for his life, he unsuccessfully sought to find Moonbear among the crowd of returning warriors. His skin prickled with apprehension. He realized he was shaking.

The warrior marched closer. Taziar said nothing, aware he had no words to defend himself from the other men. The women moved aside or walked to the cooking pit. Only the one who had instigated the conflict remained. The redhead stopped and studied Taziar in the shadow-dappled afternoon sunlight. He raised a hand the size of a guard lion's paw and swung at Taziar.

Surprised by the boldness of the barbarian's attack, Taziar sprang away. The blow caught him across the arm. Off balance, he staggered. He tensed to flee. But the barbarians' laughter and a firm hand clapped to his shoulder filled Taziar with relief. The redhead addressed him in a loud but sociable voice. Taziar realized the backslap had not been an assault but a show of companion-ship from a man accustomed to more solid friends.

Taziar managed a weak smile. For lack of a better reply to the red-haired barbarian's unrecognizable statement, he said simply, "Thank you."

The barbarian and his woman trotted toward the cooking fire. Taziar watched them with such intensity, he did not notice Moonbear's presence until the barbarian spoke. "Flamehair told you 'women only cause trouble.' "

Taziar turned to Moonbear. Though not yet ready to generalize, in the current situation Taziar could only agree with the assessment. "Flamehair has a point." He noticed his friend held a huge chunk of meat, too big for one man's supper. "Hungry?"

Moonbear waved Taziar to the ground and sat beside him. He tore the steak into two nearly equal portions and passed half to Taziar. "Eat well. This may be our last good meal for some time."

The roots and berries Taziar had consumed during his encounter with the Danish women had taken the edge from his hunger, but he accepted the meat from Moonbear. Warm grease dripped from his fingers. Following Moonbear's cue, he took a bite. It tasted much like pork, but the absence of sinew and gristle made it remarkably tender. Taziar swallowed. "What sort of animal is this?"

Moonbear gulped his own mouthful before replying. "It is bear."

Taziar continued eating. Around the clearing, barbarian men and women reclined in couples and groups, each with his own piece of meat. The females took turns offering raw or roasted roots, stems, berries, and nuts. "Are these people always so friendly?"

Moonbear stopped one of the wandering women and speared potatoes for himself and Taziar. "They know you are my friend. It's important to them that you like them."

Taziar wiped his fingers on an edge of his cloak. "Please, assure them I do. And let them know I appreciate their efforts."

Prince Deerrunner rose from his meal and crossed to the front of the camp. He raised his arm, and conversation ceased. Moonbear whispered. "Hush now. Deerrunner will tell a tale."

Hugging food to their bellies, the children threaded toward Deerrunner and took seats before him. The adults turned to face him. Even Moonbear ate with rapt attention to the prince. And, while Taziar found Deerrunner's inflections interesting, he could not comprehend a word of the story. The scene revived images of Cullinsberg's old beggar who would sit on the alehouse stairs and tell vivid accounts for a few coppers or the price of a beer. In his early days on the streets, Taziar and his gang companions would rob the peasants who stood listening. On a good day, Taziar would glean enough copper and silver to buy his dinner and pay the beggar what his stories were really worth.

As Deerrunner's story unfurled, Taziar finished his meal. Memories of Cullinsberg reminded him once again that he could never return home. The events of the last few days replayed through his thoughts, and images of the battle in Karl's tavern appeared to him in detail. *I still can't believe I watched while Moonbear could have died.* Guilt prickled the edges of his consciousness. He suppressed his urge to mentally defend his actions. *I do know how to fight. My father taught me to protect Mother in his absence. Surely I could hold my own, at least against a single opponent.*

Taziar pictured himself engaged in battle with a uniformed member of the baron's army. Immediately, an image formed of his mother's body, bloodsmeared, dead at her son's own hand. The bear meat churned in Taziar's gut. He felt nauseated. He knew it was not his own death he feared; too many times in the course of his thefts, his demise had seemed a certainty. But his conscience would not allow him to take another's life.

Restless, Taziar whispered. "Would I offend Deerrunner if I found a quiet corner to practice sword forms until he finishes?"

Moonbear never shifted his gaze from the Danish prince. "No one will mind."

Taziar rose and trotted to the far border of the clearing. He unsheathed his sword. Its steel appeared gray as ash amid the shadows of the trees. Attempting to recall his father's myriad instructions, he executed a simple kata. The action flowed smoothly, without need of conscious thought. *Too easy.* Taziar knew whenever a maneuver felt comfortable, he had made a mistake. The elder Medakan had complained most frequently that Taziar dropped his right shoulder on the strike. He repositioned and tried again. Though less satisfying, the maneuver felt correct.

For a time, Taziar continued his practice. But Moonbear's arrival with Prince Deerrunner cut the session short. Moonbear spoke. "Deerrunner wishes to talk with you before our departure."

Hurriedly, Taziar slid his sword into its sheath. Uncertain whether to bow or kneel, he stood still and met Deerrunner's stare. The prince's eyes were as sharp and gray as the distant crags.

Deerrunner uttered a few short words, and Moonbear translated. "He welcomes you to his tribe."

"Thank him for me."

Moonbear and Deerrunner exchanged sentences. Moonbear explained. "He asked where you come from and I told him. He wants to know if you served in the baron's army."

Shaken by the direction of Deerrunner's questioning, Taziar replied quickly. "Please. Tell him no."

Again Moonbear passed conversation with Deerrunner in the Northern tongue. He then addressed Taziar. "He wants to know if your gods fought in the wars."

The statement floored Taziar. "My what?"

Moonbear chuckled at his own mistake. "Your *ancestors*. The words mean the same in our language."

Though intrigued by this concept, Taziar found the prince's query more pressing. He considered for some time before attempting a reply. "Moonbear, I can't lie to you. I still feel guilty teaching you 'thief' is an honorable profession." Unnerved by the information he was passing to Moonbear, he fidgeted. "My father led the baron's troops during the barbarian wars. But, by Mardain's mercy, don't tell Deerrunner."

Moonbear accepted the confession with unexpected composure. He conveyed some information to Deerrunner. The Danwaldian's reply was brief. Moonbear switched to the barony's language. "He says your father was a brave warrior."

All color drained from Taziar. His fingers knotted into bloodless fists. Uncertain which shocked him more: Moonbear's direct betrayal of his request or the prince's reply. Taziar stammered. "M-my father killed his people. Why would Deerrunner praise an enemy?"

Moonbear drew breath to reply, but Deerrunner laid a hand on his arm. The old prince spoke in an awkward, broken form of the barony's tongue, yet his voice still commanded respect. "Your father . . . warrior. He chose enemies not. Baron did." He stepped toward Taziar. "Your father warriors slaughtered not women . . . children. Burned not . . . cut apart not our . . . gods."

Moonbear clarified. "He means your father's soldiers never dishonored our dead."

Taziar chewed his lower lip, suspecting Deerrunner understood much more of the language than he could speak.

Moonbear answered Taziar's unspoken question. "Deerrunner knew the answers before he questioned you. He wanted to see if you would reply truthfully."

Taziar recalled how he had identified himself when the barbarians surrounded him in the first clearing. "He recognized me from the moment I entered camp. Why didn't he have me slain?"

Moonbear and Deerrunner stared, apparently finding his query ludicrous. "The day the wars ended, my cousins no longer wished your father any harm. But even had he killed children, like the men of other troops, how could we hold that offense against you? Would your people punish you for another man's crime?"

They might. Taziar hesitated, unable to find the words to explain stereotypes and prejudice. For generations, guards' tales of barbarians' ferocity and cruelties had sparked hatred against the wild men throughout the barony. Enveloped by an emotion he could not name, Taziar felt as if he had always watched life's procession through a reflecting pond. Now, a pebble had fallen into its waters and, after the ripples subsided, the world's image would no longer be the same.

Thinking back, Taziar could not recall his father ever speaking specifically of the barbarians. He limited his tales to descriptions of guard work, soldiers, war and its consequences. But some of the guardsmen spoke freely on the streets and in the taverns. They glorified their own efforts in the battles and referred to the barbarians as animals. Reminded of the mistreatment of a beggar woman in Cullinsberg's streets, Taziar wondered who more aptly deserved the insult. Yet, still fiercely loyal to his own people, Taziar pushed aside his judgment against them. He found himself with nothing to say.

A warrior dressed in bearskin with animal claws braided into his hair rushed to Deerrunner's side. As he spoke, he gesticulated wildly. Drawn from his thoughts, Taziar watched the three barbarians converse. Shortly, Moonbear translated, "The scouts have identified guards from the barony. They're tracking us with hounds. Recently, the horsemen split off from the others and now they are rapidly closing the distance between us."

Taziar cursed. Aware Deerrunner knew his language, he suppressed the urge to chastise Moonbear for wasted time.

With a conspiratorial smile, Deerrunner addressed Moonbear in the Northern tongue. In response, Moonbear's face darkened. His reply seemed uncharacteristically angry. The Swede caught Taziar's sleeve and jerked him toward the woods.

Taziar hastened after Moonbear, pausing only long enough to toss one sentence over his shoulder. "You're good people."

Taziar caught up with Moonbear a few paces

into the brush. Before he could ask, the barbarian explained his odd behavior. "Deerrunner suggested his warriors fend off the guard patrol while we escape."

Taziar wrestled with branches, wondering why Deerrunner's kind offer enraged his companion. "What did you say?"

"I forbade it." Moonbear paused to keep from moving too far ahead of Taziar. "You saw nearly all that remains of Deerrunner's great tribe. They lost many brave men and women to the war. The forest shows their children no mercy." Moonbear hunched through a dense overgrowth. "If my time to die has come, I accept it. I will not have even one innocent life lost for me."

The tangle of untraveled brush closed in on Taziar, his efforts to break through it drenching him with sweat. Though he knew Moonbear was right, he felt less certain of his own ability to evade hounds and horses. It came to him suddenly that Moonbear could escape far more quickly without him. *Surely the political aspects of a prince's ransom outweigh the consequences of my theft. If we separated, the soldiers would probably track Moonbear. He might be able to elude them alone.*

Even as the option presented itself to Taziar's mind, it raised another issue. Moonbear's presence and Mordath's jadestone in his pocket had become his last links with a familiar civilization. Without a guide or a hunter's knowledge, Taziar might perish in the forest long before he came upon a town. Plagued by these thoughts, Taziar worked his way through the brush as quickly as possible. When he again caught up with Moonbear, he phrased his confusion as a question. "Moonbear, how do you make a difficult decision?"

Moonbear replied without hesitation. "I ask the advice of my father."

Taziar shied from a bramble patch. "Mmm, not much help here. Besides, my father is dead."

"Mine, too."

Taziar and Moonbear swam through a final growth of briars to emerge into a less clustered area of forest. "What? Could you repeat that?"

Moonbear paused, staring at the peaks which obscured the northern horizon. "We will need to veer east to find a crossing through the Kolding Hills. And I said my father is also dead."

Intrigued by the paradox, Taziar questioned further. "If he died, how can you speak with him?"

Moonbear continued toward the crags. "I simply think what I want to say. It is quite easy."

Taziar scrambled after his companion. "I suppose so. But surely you don't think he answers you."

"Always."

"Forgive my ignorance, but how does a dead man talk?"

"It's hard to explain. Try it. Ask your father a question."

"Fine." Feeling foolish, Taziar concentrated on his dilemma. *Should I remain with Moonbear or would we both be safer apart?* The redirection of his thoughts raised a flurry of emotion. He had grown to like the barbarian and his people. He felt a loyalty to his huge companion which transcended common sense. *I've promised to bring him home safely. I owe him my life. Yet, my slowness may cost his.*

Moonbear interrupted Taziar's train of thought. "Did you ask him?"

Taziar ducked beneath a fallen tree. "Yes."

"And he answered?"

Taziar broke into a trot. The forest was thinning, and the ground becoming more rocky as they approached the Kolding Hills. Now he could discern distant rolling rises carpeted with greenery. The crag he'd mistaken for mountains was the bare granite of a single vertical fault. "Of course not. He's dead."

Moonbear quickened his pace. "He answered. You do not know how to listen. Right after you stated your problem, did you find an answer which came straight from your heart? The option which required no thought?"

"Yes. But that came from me."

Moonbear snorted. "You do not know how to listen."

As Taziar and Moonbear approached the granite cliff, they headed eastward. Taziar considered his next argument, recalling how his father used to chastise him for responding without thought. *The best verbal offense consists of deep reflection and careful wording. Nothing unnerves an opponent more than a long drawn pause.* Even as Captain Taziar's suggestion emerged in his memory, the Shadow Climber realized Moonbear was right. More than once in the past, Taziar had turned to memories of his dead father for solace and direction. "Perhaps you have a point. Is that why your language uses 'god,' 'dead,' and 'ancestor' interchangeably?"

Now Moonbear hesitated. "We believe our ancestors have a great influence over us and the world. We learn from them."

Taziar smiled. *Finally, a religion which makes sense to me. Each man has his own personal god to watch over him. There's no organization or rules, no temple, and no greedy priests to wring money from his followers.* His thoughts took a different turn. "If your father died, doesn't that make you king?"

"Prince," Moonbear corrected. "My father is king. When I am killed, I shall take his place. I hope I can do as well as he . . ." He broke off suddenly, listening.

Taziar noted Moonbear's distraction. "What do you hear?"

Moonbear replied softly, but his single word carried the force of a whipcrack. "Hounds."

Anxiety ground through Taziar. Within seconds, he too could hear the dogs yapping with murderous eagerness. Though distant, the sound carried the deadly promise of a bowmen's volley. Every tendon in his neck pulled taut. "Come on." He ran, straight for the vertical rock formation. He had no other destination. The hounds had found their fresh scent, and there was no time to seek a pass.

After a few steps, Taziar felt the familiar, wild rush of euphoria. His race to the cliff face brought memories of adventurous thefts and impossible escapes. Always before he'd found a way out, whether through a tight hole, a crack, or a door. But, as he drew near the fault, he could tell that in places it stood sheerer than any wall he had ever scaled. He paused at the base, aware he'd left Moonbear behind in his haste.

The baying of the hounds grew louder. Taziar waited only until Moonbear drew to his side. "Up. There's no other way to go." He started climbing the white-gray rubble.

Moonbear hesitated, apparently as unfamiliar

with ascending granite as Taziar was with forests. Picking his route carefully, he followed.

Taziar knew frustration. He took the first few ledges at a run. At the level of the treetops, Taziar saw the lead dog broach the forest. *Aga'arin's blood.* Goaded to reckless speed, Taziar forced his concentration on each handhold. The climbing grew more difficult. Pits and crags became more sparse the higher he went. In his haste, he seized a loose stone for support. It wrenched free, tumbling down the cliff face. Taziar fell. His throat pinched closed, strangling his cry. He scrabbled for a hold. His fingernails shattered. Pain jarred through his hands. From habit, the callused edges of his fingers caught faults in the granite.

Pressed to the stone, Taziar felt his heart pound a rapid cadence. He heard a horse's whinny and a man's shout, but he dared not take the time to look. He continued his climb, each new hold a full, deliberate movement. He pulled himself up to a rock-strewn shelf. He could hear Moonbear a short distance below him on the cliffs. A straight stretch of stone rose above Taziar, smooth as the polished jadestone in his pocket.

Discouragement assailed Taziar. Cornered against unscalable stone, he was reminded of his imprisonment in the baron's dungeon without hope of escape. But Taziar would not accept despair. He examined the slick granite with the intensity of a hunting hawk. As Moonbear pulled up beside Taziar, the thief's search was rewarded by the discovery of a miniscule fissure which ran the remaining length of the cliff face, scarcely large enough to admit Taziar's fingers.

A late summer wind blustered around Taziar,

snapping the hem of his cloak. Desperation drove him to remember the youthful boasts of his gang brothers. *Taziar Medakan could climb an icicle.* Burdened with the obligation of two lives, Taziar swore to achieve the impossible. Wedging his fingers into the cleft, he hugged the granite wall. The jagged sides of the crack scraped skin from his digits. Using the sides of his feet for what little traction they could offer, he inched his way up the cliff side.

Effort fired elation through Taziar. Blood trickled along his hands, but he felt no pain. Grim concentration narrowed his world to the surface of stone. Each new handgrasp was a triumph. Forty feet of granite cliff seemed to span miles. Still, Taziar edged upward.

Dried grasses tickled through Taziar's hair. Clinging to what little surface the crevice allowed, he groped with one hand. His fingers crested the rise. With a grunt of realization, he hurled his body over the top. He lay in a thin layer of brush, staring at a gray-streaked, early evening sky and a nearby line of pine and birch. Dirt clotted his eyelashes. Pain descended like a wasp swarm. Limbs aching, he pushed to his feet and gazed into the valley.

At least twenty mounted soldiers spread across the flatlands. Hounds jabbered at the base of the cliff; some had clambered to the lower ledges. Trapped on the shelf below Taziar, Moonbear fingered a gathered pile of rocks, a defense against men or dogs who dared the climb.

Taziar hollered to Moonbear. "Stay there. I'll find a better route." Sparked with urgency, he ran along the hilltop. His flight nearly carried him into a man, a sudden sidestep was all that saved them both from collision. Surprised to find another person so far from civilization, Taziar studied the stranger. He was tall and thick. Lines of hardship creased his features. His closely-cropped, dark hair sported a tinge of red. Dried sweat and plant sap darkened his buckskins. He carried a leather bow case and a full quiver. A sword graced his hip. Taziar read relief and interest in the man's demeanor.

The hunter spoke first. "Ho, child. What's your hurry?"

The howls of the hounds cut Taziar like knives. It was not in his nature to trust a stranger, but dire necessity usurped caution. If the bowman carried something as simple as a rope, Moonbear's life and freedom might be spared. "My friend is trapped on a ledge."

The stranger seemed remarkably calm. "Show me."

Hurriedly, Taziar led his new acquaintance to Moonbear. In the valley below, several of the cavalrymen had drawn bows, but none dared to fire. Taziar watched as the man in buckskin judged the distance to Moonbear. Then, with enviable composure, he traced the distance to the timber line. He singled out a tall yellow pine, freed his sword and brandished it like an axe.

Taziar's breath caught in his throat. His voice emerged as a hoarse croak. "What are you doing?"

The sword bit twice into the tree trunk. With a groan, the pine leaned toward the cliff face. Suddenly, the stranger's plan seemed morbidly clear to Taziar. Careful to stay clear of the falling timber, Taziar raced to the crest. "Moonbear!" he shouted. The blade thunked against wood. Moonbear looked up. He dove aside. The treetop crashed to the ledge. Its upper branches pummeled him to the shelf.

Taziar shouted. "Karana's hell! You crazed maniac. You could have killed him." He watched Moonbear stagger to his feet. The remaining woodgrain held the pine in place while Moonbear climbed its jutting branches as easily as a ladder. At the base of the cliff, the guardsmen scrambled to the lower ledges in pursuit.

The stranger muttered. "Idiots." He waited until Moonbear gained the crest then splintered the last few strands of wood from the stump. The tree clattered down the cliff face, smashing hounds like toys. The guardsmen sprang aside. Their zebra steeds scattered across the valley.

Taziar drew a ragged breath. For now, they were safe. The baron's men would need to regroup and find a passage through the crags. Likely, they would wait for their infantry, gaining Taziar and Moonbear more time. Recognizing the nearness of their escape, Taziar resolved not to underestimate the army's power again.

Moonbear's voice broke through Taziar's troubled maze of thought. "Shadow!" He made a broad sweep of his arm, beckoning Taziar toward the timber line.

Taziar approached Moonbear and his new companion. Recalling the barbarian's disdain of appreciative gestures for actions he considered simple courtesy, Taziar drew the burden of graciousness upon himself. He met the stranger's eyes; they were the soft brown of a deer's. "I'm sorry I yelled at you. Thanks for saving Moonbear." Not wishing to explain his alias, Taziar introduced himself with the same name Moonbear had used. "They call me Shadow."

The stranger spoke with the blunt abrasiveness of one unused to company. "Aird Moor. Why are you running from Cullinsberg's army?"

Taziar ignored the question, trying to decoy Aird Moor with one of his own. "You from Cullinsberg?"

"Once," Aird Moor confessed. "Years ago, I served in their army. That was back when the commanders did more than babysit."

Taziar seized the opportunity to steer the conversation completely away from himself. "What are you doing out here alone?" He asked more to ascertain that Aird Moor had no companions than from real curiosity.

Aird Moor thumbed his bow case. "I'm a hunter and woodsman. I live 'out here alone.' Right now, I'm also a traveler headed for Norway. My sister's getting married."

Before Taziar could think to stop him, Moonbear spoke. "We're headed in the same direction. Want to join us?"

Taziar stifled a gasp, wishing his companion was less trusting. "Moon," he said slowly, as if chastising a child. "We're not looking for company."

"Neither am I." Aird Moor snorted. "The last thing I need is a troop of half-trained soldiers trailing me and a pair of fugitives." He pointed upward. "And I'm not happy about him either."

Taziar peered into the sky. A hawk circled the clouds, eagerly revealing their position. "What's it doing?"

"Telling the world where to find you." Aird

Moor followed the bird with his gaze. "It's a karahawk. Years ago, men taught its forebears to hunt both game and renegade slaves. Even after their handlers released them, the hawks continued to pass the old signals to their fledglings."

Taziar frowned. "So, you knew we were here."

Aird Moor met Taziar's stare. "Of course. The hawk told me." He pointed upward. "And I was curious what sort of man could climb a straight cliff face. I guess even an old soldier hasn't seen everything."

Pleased with Aird Moor's backhanded compliment, Taziar relented. The woodsman's confidence and no-nonsense attention to detail reminded Taziar of his father. *Perhaps we do have need of a quick thinker who is also observant and knows the woods. He did save Moonbear's life and slow the patrol. And we seem to share a common dislike for Cullinsberg's soldiers.* "You're welcome to join us, Aird Moor. If we come with you, at least your trip won't be boring. The guards want us dead. Does the reason really matter?"

Aird Moor looked over the crags and studied the carnage below with a strange smile. "I hadn't planned on company, but camp for three is no more difficult than for one. And there's more people to share the work. I doubt those soldiers will prove much trouble. Come on. I'll show you a short route to Port Calrmar." He strode eastward.

Thinking he had gained a valuable ally, Taziar followed.

CHAPTER 9

The Days of Glory

"Not once or twice in our rough island story
The path of duty was the way to glory."
—*Alfred, Lord Tennyson,*
Ode on the Death of the Duke of Wellington

A vague familiarity had plagued Ilyrian nearly
from the time Mordath joined Salik's patrol. It
seemed as if he had met the Dragonmage some-
time in the past. The thought was surely madness.
A short distance from the sleeping soldiers, Ilyrian
watched Mordath slouch over a rectangle traced
in the dirt at the edge of the Danwald Wilderness.
Surely I would recall an encounter with a legend; his
arrogance alone is memorable. Yet the memory remained elusive. Ilyrian could only assume he was
mistaken.

Night cloaked Mordath in shadow, broken by a
line of moonlight which glittered through his
golden hair. His eyes flicked closed in concentration. Hunched and intent, he wore an expression
of vulnerability which reawakened Ilyrian's feelings of twice meeting. Before him, the shape in

the dust glimmered. Harsh white light shot through the matrix, then muted to a wavering pattern of gray and black.

Ilyrian stared, blank with shock. Mordath leaned closer until his face nearly touched his sorceries. "North and east," the Dragonrank informed his companion. The pattern on the ground winked. As if emerging from a dark tunnel to regained sight, Ilyrian watched images take shape in the dirt. A flickering fire lit a camp in a stand of scrub pine. He easily identified the men stretched or curled on the ground. Aird Moor lay with an arm curled around his bow. Moonbear slept in a crouched position which looked uncomfortable. The borders of Mordath's spell neatly decapitated Taziar.

Mordath explained. "I focused on the Swede. We saw the others because they happen to be nearby." He dispelled his magics with a wave. "They've hardly moved from the cliff."

Ilyrian frowned, recalling how he, Salik, and Mordath had arrived with the infantry to find most of the hounds dead and two of the cavalrymen injured. "They didn't need to go far after they finished playing with Salik's second in command and his men." The possibility of manipulating Mordath to help gain control of the army convinced Ilyrian to sow the first seeds of dissent. "Cullinsberg's soldiers are fierce and noble fighters. They would fare far better with capable leadership." He regarded Mordath's face for any hint that his treasonous utterance had overstepped boundaries.

But Mordath's feline eyes had gone dull. His proud head sagged. Initially, Ilyrian assumed the long, hard journey had tired the Dragonrank mage. But the change seemed too sudden and too soon after the location spell to be coincidence. Ilyrian realized the use of sorceries taxed Mordath's physical endurance. And the wizard's humble pose suddenly sparked a memory.

Ilyrian recalled a day, years ago, when a young Norseman entered Vesberg near Ilyrian's father's estate. Disheveled and dirty, he had not been welcomed by the populace. But his mission piqued Ilyrian's curiosity. The Norseman sought to slay Aird Moor, a pursuit which fell within Ilyrian's own designs. The shy, eager Norseman of his memory bore little resemblance to the haughty sorcerer now before him. Yet Ilyrian realized they were one and the same. He also dredged reason from recollection: a sister's thwarted marriage and a newborn child.

Seeking to sunder any residual loyalties between Aird Moor and Mordath, Ilyrian took advantage of his newly recovered information and the sorcerer's current weakness. "Unpredictable bastard," he muttered. Having gained Mordath's attention, he continued with more volume. "Have you noticed Aird Moor already plots against us? He's so damned vengeful, he dropped a tree on our cavalry because he dislikes a single soldier. Surely he could have ingratiated himself with the fugitives without taking our men's lives."

Mordath nodded without replying. His features appeared drawn.

Ilyrian drove home his point. "One of the cavalrymen heard Aird Moor shout something about killing an old lover who'd ruined his child. Can you imagine any sane man holding a grudge like that?"

Mordath jerked to attention. His fatigue seemed to disappear, but the hand which gripped his dragonstaff trembled slightly. "Which man told you this?"

Ilyrian tossed his head and named the soldier he knew could be most easily bribed. "Herwig. But he may have misunderstood with the hounds barking and the distance." He adopted an expression of innocence, secretly thrilled by Mordath's obvious discomfort.

"Perhaps," Mordath said, but his tone precluded the possibility. "For now, we sleep. But my patience has worn thin. I won't tolerate incompetence. If Aird Moor has not led the gem-stealing insect and his friend within our grasp by this time tomorrow, we'll find them. They'll be dead and the jadestone returned to my possession, if I have to lead these men myself."

Ilyrian's lips turned upward in a thin smile.

Morning dawned over the Kolding Hills, its glory dampened by a veil of clouds. Completely disoriented, Taziar awoke to the smell of cooking meat. For an instant, he thought he lay on a pallet in Shylar's whorehouse. But the floor carried an aroma of moist earth, and the acrid reek of the campfire roused him more fully. He opened his eyes. Aird Moor and Moonbear conversed over the flames, speaking too softly for Taziar to understand. His neck ached; he had slept with his head propped against a log. Every leaf and twig seemed to have left a permanent impression on his back.

Taziar rose and raked knotted, black hair from his eyes. "Good morning." He joined his companions at the fire. Aird Moor roasted strips of rabbit over a green twig.

Moonbear waved in greeting. Aird Moor merely grunted. He picked meat from his stick with his fingers and passed a few strands to Taziar.

"Thank you." Taziar accepted the food gratefully, now glad to have a hunter among the party. He ate in silence while Aird Moor packed up his bow and prepared for departure.

They traveled east; the sun glared in their eyes despite the scattered trunks. Yet, after days spent in dense forest and brush, Taziar welcomed its blinding intensity. At least he no longer had any difficulty keeping up with his forest-seasoned companions. He remained pensively silent while Moonbear and Aird Moor argued directions. Aird Moor insisted he lived in the area and therefore knew the best way to Calrmar Port. Moonbear's rejoinder that he had traversed the route just prior to his troubles in Cullinsberg was not as convincing. Therefore, the morning was passed following Aird Moor's shortcut with no heed given to the barbarian's suggestion to veer northward.

Life in the woodlands gave Aird Moor and Moonbear many interests in common. By midday, Taziar had found no opportunity to speak. Jealousy twinged through him at the fast friendship which had developed between his companions. At a lull in their talk, before they could once again begin to dispute the route, Taziar addressed Aird Moor. "Your idea to rescue Moonbear with a tree was quick thinking."

Aird Moor shrugged off the compliment. "I've done it before, boy. War makes men resourceful."

Excited at the possibility of finding another man who might have served with his father, Taziar did not take the time to phrase his query appropriately. "What was it like, the war, I mean? Did you enjoy it?"

Aird Moor stopped dead. "Enjoy?" He repeated the word, louder. "Enjoy." Suddenly his control burst. His calm and cautious exterior crumbled, admitting a raging beast with little resemblance to the stranger Taziar had met on the cliff. "Would you enjoy stewing in summer sweat, two days shy of food, waiting for a silent enemy to come and kill you? Would you enjoy having friends bleed to death in your arms? Could you find enjoyment in taking the lives of fathers and sons in the cause of advancing the baron's lands a few fingersbreadth farther into the forest?"

Wrenched by the verbal onslaught, Taziar cringed away. "Hey, I'm sorry. I really didn't mean . . ."

But the gates of Aird Moor's conscience had opened wide and could not be easily shut again. However, his tone did become less accusatory and more regretful. "We killed them; they killed us. We fought for small gains in territory. They sought to save the only home they had. Their copper swords and spears were no match for steel. But it was their forest and they knew it. With predatory patience, they would fade beyond sight in the woodlands, then pepper us with arrows or slay us in our sleep."

Aird Moor continued eastward. Surprised by the ferocity and bitterness of his words, Taziar followed in silence.

"Our men were of two types: those who served the baron and those who served his money. Our survivors also embodied two kinds of soldiers: men who learned from the forests and cowards." Aird Moor's mouth formed a quiet smile. "When the baron finally realized he'd lost the majority of his true warriors to death and many more to desertion, he called us in, no richer for land or gold."

Horror etched Taziar's features. None of his father's descriptions had prepared him for Aird Moor's revelations.

Aird Moor spoke more softly, as if to himself. "Despite our failure, the populace greeted us as heroes. Heroes." He bit back a sarcastic laugh and his voice again gained volume. "As if ripping men's guts with the point of a sword makes you special. But heroes they called us, and the consequences of our mass murder they called glory." He addressed Taziar directly, no longer angry. "Boy, glory is a farce, an abstraction. It has no meaning. It exists only to allow weak men and statesmen to justify immorality. The cowards returned home to bask in the peasants' awe. But survival and the forest had become my life."

As the sun descended behind Taziar and his companions, clouds coiled like wraiths about the Kolding Hills. Disdain deepened the pitch of Aird Moor's story. "Enjoy, indeed. Listening to the biased stories of those soldiers who survived and also chose to return to Cullinsberg, a child might come to believe such a thing. The baron's current army contains a few good patriots who believe in his causes. In the name of the most holy, I would never find fault with a man who fights for what he believes. But most of his men live off the so-called glory of the previous generation. They wear their free uniforms like medals of courage. They hold themselves above their families and display their competence against the helpless: prisoners, beggars, and street orphans."

Aird Moor fell silent. Taziar gnawed his lower lip, unable to find the right thing to say in the wake of Aird Moor's revelations. He recalled the many times Cullinsberg's young guardsmen treated his gang brothers with unnecessary cruelty and the abuse of the beggar woman in an alley near the alehouse. At least for the moment, Taziar felt safer keeping his father's identity hidden. In the wash of emotion which Aird Moor's tale inspired, many of the elder Medakan's parables of war and duty took on a new meaning.

Moonbear, too, seemed impressed with Aird Moor's display. He ceased insisting they turn north and allowed Aird Moor to steer eastward until they chose to make camp that night. Over a dinner of quail and roots the conversation returned to more benign matters. But memories of Aird Moor's descriptions haunted Taziar well after his companions succumbed to sleep.

Around a parallel campsite at the base of the cliffs, Ilyrian and Mordath stared into a crude rectangle of sorcery. Ilyrian studied the slumbering forms of Moonbear and Aird Moor. His mouth curled into a bitter smile. "This will be simple."

"No." Mordath's tapering fingernails bit the flesh of Ilyrian's forearm like a claw. "Never undervalue Aird Moor. The snap of a twig could send him skittering into the forest like a deer. Without constant use of my location spell, a service I haven't enough power to provide, we would never find them again."

Ilyrian licked lips dry with anticipation. "Do you have a spell which could silence the army?"

Mordath glared. "Do you have a sword form which could kill fifty men? If you wish miracles, enlist a god. The best I can do is mute the sound of half a dozen men and their horses." He focused his gaze on Moonbear. "I want capable soldiers with me. You, perhaps?"

Ilyrian blanched. "I'm along for statecraft and strategy. I can fight," he added carefully, "but Salik could serve your purposes better. He is their commander."

"Salik then." Mordath screwed up his eyes and advanced nearer to his magics. "I can't be certain which of my spells will become necessary in the coming battle, nor how much of my life energy they might drain. We mustn't lose. If the thief reaches the Kattegat ferry, my promotion to garnet level of mastery and our chance at wealth may fail."

Ilyrian's sandy hair bracketed his sharp features. "Why is that?"

Mordath shook his head and refused to answer.

Curious, but not wishing to antagonize the sorcerer, Ilyrian changed the subject. "Where's Taziar?"

Mordath paused a moment, his eyes distracted as if he collected his thoughts. "He's not within the radius of the spell."

"Can't you channel your energy in on him?"

Mordath dismissed the image. "Not as long as he carries the jadestone. If he's tossed it, I can find him. The only way to know for certain is to try. But my life aura is spent whether or not the spell meets with success. I can't waste it."

Ilyrian climbed to his feet. "Come now. Let's prepare Salik and his men for battle." With the captain away, Ilyrian realized command of the remaining forces might fall to himself. The thought left a pleasant taste in his mouth.

Taziar Medakan wandered without a conscious goal; Aird Moor's descriptions had cut deeply into his soul. For the first time, he understood the cynicism which had hovered like a cloud about his father, a level of mental isolation which Taziar could never bridge. It had lent the captain an aura of mystery. But now, Taziar thought he could finally understand the torment which had consumed his father's mind, even while in the safe confines of his own home. Each year, eager youths joined under his command. Despite his best attempts at weapons training, every battle claimed more lives. The guilt must have seemed unbearable. Mothers' sons came to him, shiny new swords scratched from sparring and training. And he returned them in caskets or not at all.

Taziar's walk took him to the bare face of granite. The pale circle of moonlight revealed a pass through the crags. He crouched in the darkness, uneasy with his own thoughts. Wind whipped strands of hair into his eyes. Even as he brushed it away and wistfully remembered his last visit to Cullinsberg's barber, the muffled clink of metal startled him.

Taziar went utterly still. Tension chased his skin into gooseflesh. He strained every sense, but heard only the steady hum of cicada and the distant whoo of an owl. The foreign sound did not recur. Yet Taziar remained silent several minutes longer.

Finally, attributing the noise to imagination, he shook a cramp from his leg. As he moved, seven zebra steeds with riders emerged from the crossing.

Taziar froze. Near enough to recognize Captain Salik Kanathul as well as the Dragonrank mage he had robbed in Wyneth's tavern, Taziar hoped darkness and inactivity would hide him from their sight. The scene seemed strangely unreal. But the early stirrings of excitement convinced him the guardsmen were no dream.

One of the steeds snorted. The sound emerged no louder than a whisper. The phenomenon was not lost on Taziar. *Seven enemies on horseback moving with no more sound than a fox. How?* No answers came. But Taziar knew it had something to do with the blond wizard who, even mounted, held his staff aloft with blithe confidence.

The guardsmen dismounted. The red-trimmed uniforms which had filled Taziar with excitement as a child now seemed a mockery of glory and justice. Apparently oblivious to Taziar's presence, the soldiers hobbled their horses. Mordath's gaze swept the crags unhurriedly. Taziar held his breath as the emerald stare played over him. But the sorcerer made no sign he had seen Taziar. Instead, he followed the guardsmen into the scrub pines toward the dense copse of trees which hid Moonbear's and Aird Moor's camp.

Concern struck like madness. Taziar fingered his sword hilt, aware he could not hope to battle a sorcerer with capabilities beyond his understanding and six warriors as well. The moment he revealed himself by sound or gesture, he would die. He knew he could serve his companions better alive and unnoticed by Mordath, but he did not

want the sorcerer and his followers to catch Aird
Moor and Moonbear sleeping. Burdened with un-
satisfying options, Taziar trailed Mordath with the
stealth he had gained from his last few days in the
woods.

Taziar stopped at the border of the camp.
Mordath halted no more than ten steps away. The
soldiers continued forward, slow and silent in the
gloom. Taziar shivered. He clung to a tree trunk;
bark gouged his chest. He waited, hoping the soldiers would make some noise to betray them and
awaken Moonbear. But the men moved, ominous
as shadows in the unnatural quiet of Mordath's
spell.

Still Taziar waited, aware that the guards' necessity to capture Moonbear alive would buy him
some time. He watched as the soldiers split into
unequal groups. Salik led three to the far side of
Moonbear, and the remaining two poised over
Aird Moor. Irony penetrated the urgency which
goaded Taziar to action. *They, too, recall the battle in
Wyneth. They won't underestimate Moonbear again.* With
this realization, Taziar stared in dreamlike detach-
ment as Salik approached Moonbear, the haft of
his sword raised for a stunning blow. Another
Cullinsbergen positioned himself over Aird Moor.

Now devoid of choices, Taziar cried out a warning. Suddenly, Aird Moor moved. The bow in his
fist swung in a wild arc. It crashed against the legs
of a guardsman, staggering him. The maneuver
gained Aird Moor enough space to stand. Hurling
the bow at his other assailant, he drew his sword
to do battle. The last dying coals of the campfire
lit the steel red as blood.

Moonbear awoke no less swiftly. His huge hand

locked on Salik's ankle and jerked inward. Off
balance, the captain's blow fell short. With his free
hand, Moonbear drew his sword. Its blade skimmed
across Salik's abdomen. The captain screamed, a
sickening, strangled sound thanks to Mordath's
magic. Moonbear changed the direction of his
strike. He buried his sword in Salik's ribs as the
other three guardsmen closed in on him.

The sight of Salik's violent death made Taziar's
stomach twitch. A hard glimmer of blue-white light
drew his eye. The sky went suddenly dark as storm.
Thunder boomed. The gem in Mordath's staff
blazed green fire. Lightning flared across the heavens. It shot downward in a bolt of incandescence
which bounced from the gemstone and shot straight
for Taziar.

Taziar dove aside. He struck the ground hard,
rolled to his feet, and dodged behind a tree. Behind him, the backlash of Mordath's spell streaked
ruddy sparks across the forest floor. The odor of
ozone seemed suffocating. A sinuous twist of steam
rose into the treetops.

Mordath screamed a coarse blasphemy. Taziar
cringed behind bark as the sorcerer's ruthless gaze
sought him in the brush. Driven backward, the
two guards battling Aird Moor came dangerously
close to Mordath. Self-defense forced the sorcerer's attention to them. In the brief reprieve, Taziar
freed his sword and raced down on Mordath's
unshielded back.

A rush of panic turned Taziar's limbs weak as
rags. Memories of his mother's slaying came unbidden. His skin wept clammy sweat. His hands
felt wet with the recollection of blood he could
never wash away. He fumbled the sword in his

grip. *Karana's damned, not now!* But morality burned
his conscience like hellfire. He could not raise his
hand to kill again.

Mordath backstepped; exhaustion robbed him
of his usual arrogant grace. The distant crash of
steel revealed that the sorcerer's sound-muting spell
covered only the guardsmen. And, by the sound,
Moonbear at least was still up and fighting. Again,
Taziar tried to turn his sword on Mordath. His
pulse pounded in his ears. Dizziness swam through
his head.

Fatigue tempered Mordath's movements. He
made a muffled noise of concession. Lightning
cracked open the heavens. It struck the green
depths of Mordath's stone and shattered in twain.
Its energies raged forward with a human scream.
Half plowed into Aird Moor, dropping him to the
ground. The remainder shot for Moonbear. The
bolt struck, scattering starred points of light. The
barbarian plummeted, and Mordath, too, fell to
the ground in a silent faint.

For several seconds, no one moved. The guardsmen
stood like crafted statues. Taziar slunk into the
trees, heavy with guilt and anguish. The storm
clouds dispersed as rapidly as a lifted veil, making
the moon seem unusually brilliant. Taziar waited
in restless horror for some sign of life in his friends.
Similarly concerned, the guardsmen ran to their
captain. But even from the farther side of the
camp, Taziar could see that Salik lay in an unnatural position. Blood stained the leaves around him
like wine.

Taziar felt bitterly cold. A breeze wove through
the brush, lamenting the senseless loss of lives in
the clearing. Sprawled around Moonbear's prone

form, two other guardsmen lay dead. The three survivors checked bodies in grim silence. One glanced up from Moonbear. Apparently, Mordath's spell had faded, for his words wafted softly to Taziar's ears. "This one's alive." The man with Aird Moor raised his head. "This one, too."

Relief flooded through Taziar, but the third man's reply sent a shiver through them. "Kill them then. Let's be done with this." His sword rasped from its sheath.

Another guard seized his eager companion's wrist. "Wald! Are you possessed! The baron commanded us to bring the barbarian back alive. And Salik insisted we leave Aird Moor unharmed as well." He unclipped a length of heavy rope from his belt. "Bind them. Guard your back and your tongue. The thief's out there somewhere."

Grudgingly, Wald knotted the line around Moonbear and Aird Moor. The third Cullinsbergen approached Mordath and pressed his fingers to the sorcerer's throat. "Aga'arin's gold! Strangest thing. There's not a mark on him. His heart's going, but slowly, like he's asleep or something."

The guard who had rescued Moonbear from his companion's angry thrust made a religious gesture. "Leave him there. Didn't you see what he did? He commands a god's powers. Who can guess what may come of even a touch?"

The soldier shrank away from Mordath. His red cuffs flicked back to reveal crisscrossing scars of battle. He returned to his companions and addressed the man who appeared to have taken command. "What now, Derich? Back to the horses?"

"No." Derich examined Moonbear's bonds with satisfaction. "We're all tired. Ilyrian knows where we are. We can't risk moving the captives in the dark."

Ilyrian's name charged hatred through Taziar. *So, the traitor joined the hunt. As if he hasn't done me enough damage.* Prickling with impatience, he waited while the guards settled for the night at the farther edge of camp. Derich and his unnamed companion sprawled near their captives. Wald remained awake and watchful, guarding the perimeter with a darting gaze. Already, Taziar could see Aird Moor stirring within his bonds. Nor far from his own position, Mordath lay in supernatural sleep, his life aura nearly emptied on a desperate spell.

Night intensified, cloaking the camp in gray-black mist. Taziar could no longer discern more than silhouettes at the opposite side of the clearing. A brief conversation revealed that both of his companions were now conscious. Moonbear's crisp singsong rose in question. "Where is Shadow?"

Wald replied with unconcealed hatred. "He's dead, you repulsive animal. Just like my captain."

Taziar winced, aware Moonbear could not know the guardman's statement was a bald-faced lie. He felt the deep pain which must have twisted through the naive and kindhearted barbarian. Taziar read no intention in the ensuing silence, but he knew he would need to act quickly. Daylight would bring the army and destroy any chance of rescue. Wald's alert presence by the prisoners made any attempt to free Moonbear and Aird Moor impossible. Somehow, Taziar would need to lure the guardsman from his post.

Again, Taziar studied the comatose sorcerer. Sleep softened Mordath's chiseled features, lending him an air of childlike innocence. *Surely he carries some object which could be used to distract a soldier.* Dropping to his belly, Taziar slithered toward the Dragonrank mage. Even in slumber, Mordath's bearing and the carven staff at his side seemed intimidating.

Taziar hesitated, affected by Derich's warning to his companion. Until his encounter with Mordath in Wyneth, Taziar would have dismissed the idea of magic, mortal or god-sanctioned. *Handling Mordath or his possessions might well prove dangerous.* Immediately, Taziar found the flaw in his own logic. *I robbed him with impunity in Wyneth's tavern. He would never have noticed the jade was missing without its revealing flash.* He caught the hem of Mordath's robes. With the quick, capable hands of a professional, he emptied the sorcerer's pockets.

Taziar found Mordath's effects disappointingly normal. His search revealed only a handkerchief; a pouch of coins; a gaudy, silver ring; and a small knife with an ivory hilt studded with tiny emeralds. The haft was worn smooth from use, the blade clean and well-tended. *At least now I have something less bulky than a sword to cut bindings.* Uncertain whether he would find any use for the other objects, he transferred them to his own pocket.

Wald shifted position with a loud rustle. Taziar paused, not daring movement. There followed the scratch of a twig against grit as the guardsman drew bored circles in the dust. Mordath stirred slightly, then again went still.

Only a fool could surrender an opportunity to slay an opponent this strong. But Taziar recognized his conscience as a witness more dreadful than any man. *I couldn't even take Mordath's life to save my friends. I certainly can't do it now.* Cursing his weakness, Taziar prepared to leave. His gaze fell on the dragonstaff. Its jadestone still shimmered, like the few persistent rays which follow the sunset. *I can't kill him. But perhaps I can cripple his power.* Filled with new purpose, Taziar crawled to the dragonstaff.

Four black-nailed toes gripped the jadestone like a vise. Grasping the dagger, Taziar steadied his trembling hands. He set the sharpened edge against the darkly-stained surface of one claw. With quiet, deliberate strokes, he sawed through the wood. Chips flaked into his palm. After several cuts, one toenail snapped free. The knife blade scratched across the surface of the jadestone.

Light streamed from the injured gem like blood. Mordath cried out from his trance. Instinct flattened Taziar to the leaf-strewn ground. To his relief, the gem's beam faded to darkness. Mordath groaned, rolled, and dropped back into sleep.

Wald leaped to his feet. His sandy hair seemed beaded with moonlight, framing his shadowed face. He peered through the darkness, studying the sorcerer. Then, he looked back at his sleeping companions. With a shrug of feigned disinterest, he returned to his idle dust pictures.

Afraid to risk waking the sorcerer, Taziar gave up his attack on the staff. Carefully, he crawled to the perimeter. Hoping the insect chorus would mask the sounds of his passage, he worked his way slowly around the clearing. He kept his attention fixed alternately on his route and Wald. The sentry occasionally turned his eyes to Mordath. Apparently curiosity warred with his natural mistrust of the supernatural.

Wald stood upright. He threw a brief glance around the clearing. Satisfied nothing had changed, he headed toward Mordath.

Taziar quickened his pace, hoping Mordath and his flawed staff would hold Wald's attention long enough for him to take action. Ahead, Moonbear's tremendous bulk appeared reassuringly familiar. Taziar covered the remaining distance in a bound. He set the knife to Moonbear's bonds.

The barbarian went taut, resisting. Taziar put his mouth to his companion's ear and whispered, "It's Shadow. Be still until I free Aird Moor."

The razor edge of Mordath's dagger sliced through the ropes. Having cut Moonbear loose, Taziar started on Aird Moor. A glance in Wald's direction revealed the sentry returning at a trot. Taziar chopped faster. The strands broke with a hiss of parting hemp. Moonbear and Aird Moor struggled to their feet.

Wald shouted. His companions responded sluggishly. Swords whipped free, silvered by moonlight.

Taziar ran toward the cliff. "This way." Realizing a sprint into the woods seemed a more sensible move, he added, "Trust me."

Aird Moor followed on Taziar's heels. But Moonbear remained behind long enough to reclaim his and Aird Moor's swords. Taziar slowed. Aird Moor caught his arm. "Moonbear'll catch up with us. No need for another battle."

Steel chimed a grim suffix to Aird Moor's words. Concerned for Moonbear, Taziar turned. Reflected moonbeams highlighted the barbarian moving toward them rapidly. Behind, the shadowy figures of the three guardsmen gave chase.

The forest opened out suddenly. Taziar wound

through the scrub pine into the open ground before the cliff face. A horse's snort echoed eerily
along the crags. Striped necks lifted, arched tautly.
"Mount up quickly." Taziar brandished Mordath's
dagger, carefully slashing the steeds' hobbles.

Aird Moor sprang to a mount's back. Taziar
climbed to the withers of a muscular mare and
clutched the reins of the gelding he'd chosen for
Moonbear in a fist gone slick with sweat. The
barbarian ran to him and stopped before the striped
animal. Distress wrinkled the skin around his eyes.
"Not again?"

Too stressed to see the humor in the situation,
Taziar patted the gelding's flank. "Get on and
hold tight. We must ride east along the cliffs. Only
a madman would gallop at night through forest."
He held the horse until Moonbear settled into his
seat, then kicked his own steed into a canter.

CHAPTER 10

Another Betrayal

"It is more ignominious to mistrust our friends than to be deceived by them."
—*Francois, Duc de La Rouchefoucauld,*
Sentences and Moral Maxims

Ilyrian awakened to the early, pink stirrings of dawn. The authority which fell to him in Salik's absence thrilled through him like a fine wine, but he knew from his own war experience it would take more than political power to gain the soldiers' unquestioning obedience. Lacking Salik's popularity or Captain Taziar's confident authority, Ilyrian realized he would lead these men by superstitious fear or not at all. But first, he needed to appraise his opposition. Salik's second in command, Barret, was a foot soldier who held his rank only because the baron had kept the remainder of his officers home to guard the city. The young commander might well prove ineffectual and easily dominated. Ilyrian felt compelled to test Barret's limits.

Ilyrian jabbed the nearest guardsman with his toes. "You, there. Start the fire."

The soldier startled awake. He fixed sharp, dark eyes on Ilyrian. "Start your own fire. I'm not your errand boy."

Ilyrian pretended to be infuriated by the man's insolence. He leaped to his feet. "You ignorant, dirt-eating peasant! Who do you think you're talking to?

Ilyrian's shout roused the camp. From behind him, a bass voice rang with challenge. "Stop it, Ilyrian. The men are my charge until Salik's return."

Ilyrian whirled to face Barret. He sat, enmeshed in a dirty, woolen blanket. Brown hair hugged his head in tight curls. A beard encased his jutting chin like foam. Carefully Ilyrian channeled his anger against the second in command. "Witless fool. I'm the ranking officer."

"Ranking political officer," Barret corrected. "I'm the ranking military officer. You hold an advisory position. For now, I lead the soldiers, and I can use or discard your designs as I see fit."

Ilyrian feigned raw fury, seeking to undermine Barret's command. "You power-grabbing worm! Would you see more of our soldiers injured? Wasn't that fiasco at the cliff face enough for you? Political or military, I have far more war experience than you."

Barret freed his broad-boned frame from his covers. His face went wooden with offense. "Enough of this cat fight! We can settle our differences in solitude. Let the men have what little sleep remains to them." He snatched up his blanket and withdrew a short distance from the campsite.

Ilyrian stalked after him. He waited only until Barret settled into position on the ground. "Adviser only? Fah! I was a part of this army while you still suckled your mother's breast."

Barret hesitated, apparently previously unaware of Ilyrian's revelation. His demeanor went deadly calm. "You've overstepped your bounds. One more outburst, Ilyrian, and I'll consider this mutiny." His fingers clamped about his sword hilt. "It's within my rights to slay you for treason."

Bitter irony checked Ilyrian's game. His expression went bland in recognition of temporary defeat. Silently, he cursed Barret's strength, knowing he would need to dispose of both commanders before he could gain control of Salik's patrol. "Forgive me, Barret. I've spent too long in court and grown accustomed to the servants there obeying my every whim." He sat beside the second in command and forced a tremor into his voice. "Salik's long absence has my nerves wound in coils. I'm sorry."

Barret accepted Ilyrian's apology with an unconvinced grunt. He wrapped himself in his blanket again in an obvious attempt to recapture sleep.

Ilyrian remained awake, calculating, attentive to the distant, whispered conjectures of the guardsmen. As the sun's edge gained the eastern horizon, their conversations died to snores. Beside Ilyrian, Barret's chest rose and fell in the heavy pattern of slumber.

A sudden pulse of light blinded Ilyrian. Surprise wrenched him backward. Barret jarred awake. Before them, Mordath stood, his dark robes torn and dirty. One nail of his staff was neatly snapped off at its base.

"Mordath!" Ilyrian pressed toward the sorcerer, eager for news. "What happened?"

Bitter scorn colored Mordath's reply. "I nearly killed myself covering your guards' incompetence. The fugitives are gone, mounted now. Hel's icy citadel will dance with flame before we ride them down again."

Barret ignored Mordath's blatant insult. His harried question revealed his own concerns. "Our men?"

Mordath turned indifferent eyes on Barret. "The three survivors await our arrival at the camp."

Barret's sinews went taut. He clambered to his feet. "Salik?" he asked tentatively.

Mordath made no attempt to soften the news. "The barbarian cut him down with a single stroke."

Ilyrian went tense with excitement. Barret's face crumpled to a mask of regret. "Aga'arin," the commander whispered.

Mordath spoke through morning glare. "Swiftly now. Rouse the men. The ferry sails in five days, and we must make haste to Calrmar Port."

"No!" Grief wrenched the authority from Barret's command. "Salik's last order was to break the hunt and return to Cullinsberg in the event of his death."

A hiss of anger escaped Ilyrian's lips. "We must chase the barbarian until captured, by the baron's direct order. Now who suggests treason?"

Barret's rebuke rattled with warning. "I answer directly to Salik. His command has passed to me, and I will not go against his final order."

Fury jangled against Ilyrian's control. He hesitated, barely restraining his hatred.

In the ensuing stillness of Ilyrian's struggle,

Mordath spoke with haughty assurance. "Let them leave. They're dung beetles in a contest between lions. We're better off free of them."

Barret wisely held his tongue and headed toward camp to organize his men. Ilyrian pulled Mordath aside. Charged with purpose, he addressed the sorcerer with impudent harshness. "Has a single failure addled you? Your casual indifference will lose us an army."

"No great loss." Mordath shrugged. "So far, Cullinsberg's soldiers have served no other purpose than to get in my way."

Ilyrian's tone went deceptively soft. "Not so. The sword strokes which took the lives of three soldiers would otherwise have been aimed at you. At worst, the effort it would take Moonbear and Aird Moor to hew through nearly fifty soldiers would buy time for your magics. At best, given the proper circumstances, you will discover the guardsmen are more than capable fighters."

Apparently, Mordath's rash dismissal was the product of emotion, for his intentions were easily swayed. "Fine. But how do you propose we convince Barret? He seems determined."

Ilyrian's lips wreathed into a grin of cold purpose. Grimly, he plotted, thoughts clustered like a cancer within him. "With your help. I've no knowledge of sorceries. What abilities do you have at your disposal?"

Mordath frowned disapprovingly. "I have a vast repertoire. But I expend the least energy controlling weather: snow, wind gusts, parching heat."

Ilyrian licked his lips, his thoughts hungry for power. "Storms?"

"Storms," Mordath confirmed.

Ideas jostled through Ilyrian's mind, forming to a clear path of resolution. His expression was as cold as an arctic wind.

The sun crept into view, a full golden eye which illuminated the blue arch of the morning sky. Cullinsberg's soldiers scurried to prepare for departure. Bits clacked against horses' teeth. Men strapped rolled blankets to their backs. Perched on a large stone, Commander Barret sharpened his sword blade. The whetstone slashed across the steel edge with a snakelike hiss. In the center of camp, the cook for the day stirred a huge kettle of breakfast soup with a wooden ladle.

Leaving Mordath hidden in the brush, Ilyrian walked to the cooking fire. Bold certainty characterized his movements, but it was a feigned confidence. Beneath his calm exterior, the nobleman felt twitchy as a rat. He knew only a drastic action would gain the soldier's interest.

With a quick motion, Ilyrian seized the spoon from the cook's hand, bashed it against the kettle with repetitive, ringing strokes, and tossed it. The ladle flew in a wide arc, splattering soup across the nearest guardsmen. It struck the ground and rolled; its surface coated with forest silt.

Suddenly, Ilyrian held every man's attention. The cook stood astounded, his mouth opening and closing in silent outrage. Ilyrian shouted over the angry protests of the soup-splashed guardsmen. "Friends and warriors, I've a message from our lord, Baron Dietrich of Cullinsberg."

A murmur of grudging acceptance passed through the gathering. Barret pocketed his whetstone, and his eyes followed the nobleman with dark mistrust.

Ilyrian continued. "As you know, the baron rules by the divine right of our gods: Aga'arin who supplies our gold and silver, Mardain who controls our births with the sun or moon and places a star for the soul of every brave man or woman who dies; and the host of lesser divinities who sanction his rule. Long live our baron!"

From habit, the men repeated the platitude. "Long live our baron." They fidgeted, impatient with affairs of state.

Ilyrian focused his attention on Barret. "As you also know, Baron Dietrich sent us after a barbarian and a thief with explicit orders to bring them home at any cost. Our brave captain, Salik, led us toward that goal. But those of you who noticed a new star in the heavens realize he lost his life to the baron's cause." Head bowed, Ilyrian worked sadness into his voice. "May Mardain hold his soul as sacred."

Horror etched many of the guardsmen's faces. Conversations broke out through the ranks. But Ilyrian had gained their full attention, and an exuberant wave of the nobleman's hand silenced their talk.

Ilyrian's exposition gained a fevered determination. "My friends, despite my deep and heartfelt grief, it has become my duty to inform you of a great wrong. Were he alive, Salik would still lead you to fulfill his promises to the baron. But circumstance has left a coward in his place, a man who would abandon Salik's trust and convince you to return to Cullinsberg empty-handed."

Barret sprang from his rock, sword clenched in fists white with anger. "You calculating bastard! I warned you."

Ilyrian's voice rang over Barret's threats. "Warriors, *your leader proposes treason!*"

Barret advanced. His curled, brown hair clung damply to his temples. His sword was poised for a strike. "Enough, Ilyrian. It is you who proposes treason. If I bring the baron nothing else, I'll hand him your lying head."

Ilyrian backstepped, suddenly afraid. His prepared speech nearly caught on his dry tongue. "If you oppose me, you also stand against the gods who sanction me and this quest!"

The sky went ominously dark. Wisps of gray fog obscured the newly risen sun. The soldiers waited, uncertain, as Barret lunged forward. Ilyrian retreated with a growled threat. From habit, his hand dropped to the hilt of his own weapon.

Thunder ground through Ilyrian's ears, covering Barret's furious expletive. The clouds split open. A jagged bar of lightning lanced for Barret like a striking snake. It crashed against his raised sword. Energy pulsed through the commander, hurling him limp to the ground.

Nothing in Mordath's description had prepared Ilyrian for the grandeur of the sorcerer's attack. The force of the backlash toppled the nobleman. The odor of burnt flesh pinched his nostrils, and pinpoints of light slashed his face. Shock emptied his memory of the next step in his own plan.

The guardsmen gawked in blank surprise. Blood-colored sparks cast an eerie red glow on their pale faces. Ilyrian knew these men had never before witnessed even the simplest of Mordath's magics. To them, the furious assault from the heavens could only be attributed to an angry god. Ilyrian used the few extra seconds his foreknowledge gained him to crawl to Barret's side. He placed his fingers on the guardsman's neck.

A pulse throbbed against Ilyrian's touch. Unobtrusively, he caught the cartilage of the commander's throat between his thumb and first finger. A quick, subtle twist crushed Barret's windpipe. The large man was racked by death throes, then went ominously still. Consumed by poisonous triumph, Ilyrian rose, his face twisted with false sorrow. "He's dead," he informed the horror-stricken guardsmen.

The sky remained shadowed and expectant. Spurred by the glory of murder and control, Ilyrian gathered his scattered wits. "Mardain has spoken in the baron's name. He has slain the traitor and passed his command to me. Any man who would oppose my authority, speak now and face Mardain's wrath."

The clouds bunched tighter. The men watched in silence, throttled by a hush of superstitious belief. To Ilyrian's relief, no man stepped forward. Mordath had expressly stated he would not repeat the grand performance and risk his life energy again. Suddenly, Ilyrian realized that the three survivors at the fugitives' camp were aware of Mordath's abilities and could not be allowed to rejoin the troop. Their speculations would surely reveal the deception.

Ilyrian continued, his voice resonant in the awed stillness. "The plan has changed. The barbarian slaughtered our captain. The gods will it that he pay with his life. Kill him on sight. Any who stand in our way must be slain as well."

Bored by the seemingly endless chase and desperate for war and a chance at heroism, the soldiers rallied about Ilyrian, mad for revenge.

The ride to Calrmar Port seemed unbearably long to Taziar. Once through the passes of the Kolding Hills, his companions' bickering about direction drove him to take the lead of the party. Shunning the forests, he chose hard-packed roadways, following street signs and, when available, strangers' advice.

Taziar's course displeased Moonbear and Aird Moor. The open terrain made them as skittish as caged foxes. From the time Moonbear dismissed Aird Moor's shortcut, the woodsman went sullen. He spoke stiltedly of hunts, battles, and woodlands with Moonbear. He rarely addressed Taziar; when he did, it was usually with an undertone of hostility and always as "boy" or "child." But when they stopped and wandered into the forest to make camp each night, Aird Moor supplied freshly-killed meat to add to the fare of roots and berries. Taziar found the woodsman's presence too valuable to make any strenuous objections.

Each evening, Taziar faithfully practiced sword forms while his companions prepared supper and tended the horses. Without an instructor, he never quite knew whether he had performed the maneuvers correctly. His only feedback came on the second night of their journey. Aird Moor glanced up from a mouthful of raspberries. "Shadow," he said. "You know just enough swordplay to endanger yourself." The following night, Taziar trained deeper in the woods, out of sight of his critical companion.

Despite its practical dangers, Taziar's strategy of

using traveled pathways paid off. This six-day trek to Port Calrmar through forest was condensed to a three-day ride with no sight or sound of the baron's army. At midday, still a half-day's walk from the town proper, the horse and cart traffic to the port city thickened. Huge, tarp-covered wagons jounced along the roadways, filled with goods bound for the Northlands. The three dusty travelers and their odd-looking steeds drew more than their share of stares from the merchants they passed.

Moonbear seemed unusually cheerful. "With this many merchants headed for Calrmar, the summer ferry has not cast off yet. Now, let us dispose of these beasts we are riding. My legs are aching."

Taziar laughed, by now familiar with Moonbear's attempts to rid them of the horses. But this time, he found a twisted logic in the suggestion. "You do have a point. Some of these merchants may have come from the direction of Cullinsberg. No need to draw more attention to ourselves with these glaringly ugly steeds." He dismounted and led his horse into the forest. His companions followed. Leaving the animals to graze on foliage, they continued on to the city on foot.

Some distance further, the forest dwindled and disappeared, replaced by square-cut fields of wheat and beans punctuated by clusters of blueberry bushes. Birds swarmed over the low, twisted shrubs, their beaks and talons smeared purple from the feast. Between the neat gardens sat hovels of wood, stone, and mud. As Tazier and his companions drew closer, the cottages became more densely packed, and the crops changed to potatoes, tur-

nips, and beets. Taziar's dreams of beer and a
warm bed inched closer to reality.

The last desperate entreaties of merchants in
the marketplace echoed through the graying streets.
The sound cut through Taziar like a knife, bringing memories of his own stand and its carefully
lettered promise: *I can get anything*. Attuned like a
musician to the seller's boasts, Taziar felt comfortable within the confines of the city.

Aird Moor led Taziar and Moonbear along a
crowded side road. "If recollection serves me,
there's an inn down this way. Interested?"

Taziar replied before Moonbear could open his
mouth. "Nothing," he said with enthusiastic sincerity, "would make me happier."

They continued down the alleyway as the calls
in the market grew distant. Peasants with greasy
hair hovered in the cottage doorways, their homespun hanging in untidy wrinkles. No one seemed
to take notice of Taziar and his companions. Apparently, the populace was quite accustomed to
strangers.

The inn stood alone at the end of the street, its
weathered sign battered and unreadable. Stone
steps led to its lighted interior. The door was
wedged open to admit the last few rays of sunshine before twilight. From a distance, Taziar could
see the bobbing shadows of people, moving inside.
Boisterous voices leaked into the alleyway which
reeked of drink.

But, for all its noise, the inn seemed a welcome
change from days in the brooding forest. Taziar
was the first to climb the stairs and step inside, but
his companions followed swiftly. The thief was
immediately struck by the odor of sweat and salt

air. Smoke rolled from the hearth fire, shrouding the rowdy patrons. Great barrels and kegs lined the opposite wall beneath shelves of bowls, mugs, and glassware. A stained, wooden bar ran from wall to wall. The patrons clustered here, away from the heat of the fire. So, despite the crowd, Taziar wound his way to an empty table.

Spilled beer discolored the tabletop in spidery outlines. The legs of its four chairs had cut long grooves into the floor. Taziar selected a seat with his back to the fire and the winding stairway which led to the inn rooms above. Moonbear sat beside him, but Aird Moor remained standing.

The woodsman said, "Stay here. I'll go to the bar and get us a room. I'll pick up a few beers, too. It'll give us something to sip until the help gets through this crowd to take our dinner order." He paused looking sheepish. His voice acquired an embarrassed tone. "Either of you have any money?"

Recalling the coins he had taken from Mordath, Taziar reached into his pocket. He flicked open the pouch and explored the contents with his fingers. The metal pieces sifted through his hand. He settled on a large, round coin with a central hole. From its size, Taziar guessed it was a copper. He flipped it to the table. "Mordath graciously agreed to pay for tonight's . . ." He broke off as the coin rolled across the tabletop, ruddy yellow in the hearthlight. It was gold.

The coin spun awkwardly on its edge, each pass bringing it closer to the table's edge. Raised in a city where flashing wealth meant losing it to thieves, Taziar instinctively slapped his hand over the gold piece. Quickly, he exchanged it for a smaller coin and slid the latter to Aird Moor. The woodsman wore a surprised look; but, apparently intent on other matters, he said nothing. He trotted through the crowd.

"Penrger," said Moonbear.

The word had no meaning to Taziar. He tore his gaze from a pair of fishermen carrying a companion who was deep in a drunken stupor. "What?"

"The coin you have is a penrger. It is worth about fifty of your ducats."

"How did you know that?"

Moonbear shrugged his meaty shoulders. "It is a Scandinavian coin."

Taziar persisted. "But I didn't think barb . . . your people had a monetary system."

"We do not," Moonbear admitted. "But many of our neighbors in the cities do. We have only few dealings with them. But a man who wintered with my people bought supplies there. He brought coins from your city and exchanged them for Scandinavian ones."

Interest spiraled through Taziar. "You have cities?"

Moonbear laced his fingers on the tabletop, wearing a smirk of wry amusement. "Did you imagine Sweden as one big forest?"

Taziar stared at his toes, his misconception embarrassingly evident. "I . . . didn't think about it. My people tell stories of the wild Northlands across the sea." He flushed. "I suppose you don't really have dragons or sorcerers either."

"It is rumored the Dragonrank School grounds lie in Norway. But I never saw a wizard until Wyneth." Moonbear leaned his chin on his clasped hands.

Taziar smiled, more confident with his decision to remain with Moonbear. Once across the Kattegat, he could remain in a Swedish city, well beyond the baron's influence.

Moonbear added conversationally. "Of course, the language is completely different."

Jolted by the realization he would need to learn a new tongue, Taziar discovered self-doubt. Before he could reply, a seaman bellowed for a barmaid to fill his tankard. His heavy dialect distorted his words. Taziar paid more heed to the bawdy conversations around them. The patrons spoke in a slurred, simplified version of the barony's tongue, liberally colored with foreign syllables and inflections.

Aird Moor returned, balancing three foam-capped mugs. He set them on the table, casually selected two, and slid them to his companions. He sat across from Taziar. "Sorry I took so long. I checked the room. It'll be cramped sleeping tonight." He addressed Taziar directly. "Want your change, boy?"

"You keep it." Taziar wrapped his fingers around the mug, eager for the taste of beer. "And it can't be any worse than sleeping on sticks and dried leaves." He raised the drink to his lips and quaffed hungrily. Immediately, a bitter taste coated his tongue, gagging him. His face pinched in revulsion. His voice went thin and strained. "Gods! This is the sourest beer I've ever had."

Aird Moor met Taziar's pronouncement with a scornful chuckle. "Can't handle a man's drink?" He downed half his mug with a single gulp.

Aird Moor's mocking challenge infuriated Taziar. It reminded him of a day eight years ago in

Cullinsberg's alleyway. Then, giddy with stolen wine, Taziar had amused his gang brothers with an awkward fall to the cobbled street which scraped a gash in his arm. Berin had hoisted his drunken companion to his feet, jeering. "Ya daisy! Ya hold liquor like a girl." Waren laughed. "Mouse'd drink him under the table." Humiliated, Taziar had practiced bingeing until he handled his beer more easily than any of his fellows except Blade. Now, goaded by Aird Moor's gibes and his own insecurity, Taziar downed the acrid beer. He wiped his mouth on his sleeve and struggled to restrain a grimace. "I'll buy the next round," he said, forgetting in his anger, that he had purchased the last.

"I'll get it," said Aird Moor, accepting the gold coin Taziar pressed into his hand. He tossed down the remainder of his drink and headed back to the bar.

Taziar watched Moonbear sip his drink more slowly. Aird Moor's absence allowed Taziar to regain control of his temper. He confided in Moonbear. "Somehow, that man always makes me feel incompetent. He's treated me like a blundering child since we met him. The more I try to prove myself, the clumsier I seem."

Moonbear finished his drink, nodding sagely. "Why do you care what he thinks?"

Taziar tapped his fingers with puzzlement. "I have no idea. I think he reminds me too much of my father."

Both men fell silent as Aird Moor arrived with the beer. The woodsman divided the drinks. "Barmaid ought to be along pretty soon to take an order."

"No hurry." Taziar's eyes stung from the smoke.

With time, the hearth fire appeared to be becoming brighter. "We have our drinks." He felt an odd complacency.

The beer in the mugs dwindled slowly. Moonbear sipped his drink in silence, but he seemed to have lost his aura of wild discomfort. A swirl of smoke unfocused Taziar's vision. The milling crowd blurred to outlines, and he watched the other patrons with disinterested eyes. Nausea overtook him halfway through his second beer. "I don't think I'm hungry." The words emerged slurred.

A hand brushed Taziar's shoulder. "Are you well?" Sickness rocked Taziar's gut, preventing an answer. He rose. Vertigo dropped him to his knees. The shock of the fall drove purpose through him. His mind responded sluggishly. Gripping the edge of the table, he struggled to his feet.

Taziar forced words between lips which felt numb. "The beer!" With heroic determination, he dove for Aird Moor's mug. His hand struck the tankard, and momentum swept it from the table. Beer sprayed across Aird Moor and the floor. The mug hit the ground with a ring of sound.

"Too much to drink." The apology sounded in Taziar's ears as if from a great distance. He toppled from the table and crashed to the floor. Darkness enfolded his consciousness, cold and silent as death.

Aird Moor marched through the dimly lit streets of Calrmar Port, hoping to find a merchant before they all closed down for the night. Moonbear and Taziar lay bound in the inn room, victims of carefully measured doses of poppy extract. It seemed simple now. Aird Moor knew the silver in his pocket would buy a decent wagon and horse team. If he followed the roadways south, he would eventually reach Cullinsberg where he could turn his charges over directly to the baron.

I can avoid dealing with Salik's band of children. Aird Moor's thoughts went bitter as he recalled the soldiers' attack on their camp. *If they'd allowed me to lead Moonbear and Shadow to Hawk Rock, like I'd planned, things would never have gone this far. At least they had the sense to bind me, too, and divert suspicion.*

A curtain of clouds swept in from the south, claiming the light of moon and stars. Aird Moor cursed. The early darkness would make it even harder to find a merchant in the streets. Resigned to purchasing his horse cart from a farmer, Aird Moor reversed his direction and sidled into an alley. *The man'll probably ask some exorbitant sum for a rattletrap wagon and a doddering fossil of a horse.*

Deeper in the alleyway, a flash of green light drew Aird Moor's attention. Rain trickled from the heavens, further irritating him. Through the haze, his eyes traced the outline of a man clutching a staff, his blond cascade of hair visible even through the storm. "Mordath? Well, I'm glad you're here. I can get your gem."

Mordath replied with a disdainful laugh. "So can I. But I'll have your life first." He made a bold gesture. The rain gusted into opaque sheets. Lightning flared, splitting the sky like hellfire, then sped toward Aird Moor.

"No!" cried Aird Moor in outraged disbelief. He grasped his sword hilt and charged Mordath. A discarded rag wrapped about his ankles, sprawling him. The lightning crashed to the ground before him with a roar of sound. White hot sparks stung his face. Static crackled, raising every hair on his body. He struggled to his feet, struck blind by light. "Mordath! Stop, you idiot! We can talk."

Mordath's curse bounced from the wall stones. Grimly aware he could not battle the Dragonrank's magics alone, Aird Moor whirled and ran. Booted footfalls pursued him. Sightless, he careened down the roadway. He groped the air before him, trying to map the streets in his memory.

Gradually, Aird Moor's vision returned. His running steps grew more confident. Wind rattled against the ancient windows in the few shops rich enough to have glass panes. Thunder shook the cobbled streets. Aird Moor plunged into an alleyway. The looming bulk of the inn appeared before him. By the nearness of his tread, Mordath had already narrowed the gap between them.

Aird Moor sped toward the inn. To his relief, the door still stood open. He sprinted up the stone porch steps and plowed through the milling crowd, arms bent protectively before his face. His elbow drove into a fisherman's chest. The man staggered and clawed, bringing several others crashing down in a wheel of flailing limbs. Aird Moor dodged aside. A hand seized his shirt and a coarse blasphemy hissed into his ear. He twisted, still running. The fringe of his buckskins gave. Momentum carried him forward awkwardly. He jostled an arm. Wine splattered in a sticky stream down Aird Moor's forearm. The glass shattered on the floor, and a heavy foot smashed it to powder.

Aird Moor gained the stairway, unable to sound out Mordath in the screamed cacophony beneath him. He took the stairs two at a time, fumbling in his pocket as he ran. His fingers muddled through silver to the key. Freeing it, he hurtled down the corridor and stopped, before his room. Behind him, he heard the slam of feet on the stairway. He dared not look back. Jamming the key into the lock, he twisted. The panel yielded. Aird Moor blustered within and slammed the door on his heels.

Breath rasped through Aird Moor's lungs. He took in the room at a glance. Moonbear and Taziar lay trussed on the floor, their eyes open and interested. The Shadow Climber had already managed to work his bonds partially free.

Anger tore through Aird Moor at the thought of sacrificing his bounty, but he needed Moonbear's aid to fend off the sorcerer. Aware his companions could not know who'd drugged them, he covered the length of the chamber in three running steps. Something jarred the door. Aird Moor drew his hunting knife and slit the ropes which held Moonbear.

A more benign lightning from the storm flared across the scratched, purple glass of the window. Light oozed like water beneath the doorjamb. Suddenly, the panel sagged on its hinges, and Mordath's black-robed form filled the archway. Aird Moor thrust a sword hilt into Moonbear's hand and drew his own weapon as the sorcerer advanced.

Aird Moor lunged. Inches from Mordath's gut, the sword crashed against an invisible barrier, jolting the woodsman to the elbow. He finished the form from habit. He cut upward. Again his blade impacted something unseen. *What in Karana's hell? How can we hope to win this battle without knowledge of Mordath's powers?* To Aird Moor's left, Moonbear's strokes met the same resistance.

Repeatedly, the swordsmen's blades jangled against the solid form of Mordath's sorcery, seeking a flaw in the bunched magics. Yet, despite his success, Mordath maintained a stance devoid of triumph. His face massed in harried creases of concentration. He made no attempt to strike through his own spell nor to dodge Aird Moor's enraged but ineffectual sword blows.

After a time, Aird Moor backstepped, sword poised. Moonbear imitated his companion's retreat. Uncertain whether Mordath could hear through his barrier, Aird Moor shouted in impotent rage. "You're safe now, wizard! But the moment you drop your guard, I'll kill you."

A movement behind Mordath caught Aird Moor's eye. A small figure flitted across the landing. *Shadow!* Realizing the thief had escaped through the windows, Aird Moor tried to draw Mordath's attention with another futile cut against the invisible shield.

Suddenly, Mordath recoiled. His head twisted toward Taziar. Aird Moor sprang. This time, his lunge met no resistance. The stone in the sorcerer's staff winked, scattering green highlights through the corridor. Mordath disappeared. Aird Moor's sword sliced the air where he had stood.

"Hey!" Taziar cringed away from Aird Moor's frenzied onslaught. "I'm a friend."

Aird Moor swore for a full minute.

When he finished, Taziar caught his forearm reassuringly. "At least he's gone for now. Thanks for freeing us."

Aird Moor grumbled. "Sure." He realized, with some satisfaction, that Taziar believed Mordath had poisoned the drinks. Seeking to reinforce the misconception, Aird Moor continued. "And thanks to you. Your quick action saved me from taking much of the beer, too."

A grin split Taziar's face, and he seemed pleased by the praise. But just as suddenly, his smile wilted. "Friends," said the Shadow Climber, surveying the wreckage from the landing. "I don't think we're welcome in this inn any longer."

CHAPTER 11

Dragonrank Magic

"The anchor heaves, the ship swings free,
The sails swell full. To sea, to sea."
— *Thomas Lovell Beddoes,*
"Sailor's Song," st. 2

The lateen-rigged ship, *Amara* rolled at her mooring, lifted by the gentle swells of the Kattegat Strait. Taziar crouched beneath a tent pitched on her deck, attentive to his sleeping companions. The aftereffects of the poppy extract left him feeling queasy, and the constant motion of the ship intensified his discomfort.

Too alert to sleep, Taziar slipped from the tent. The night sky hovered, dark as pitch, broken only by the pinpoint lights of stars. Strung on pegs, unlit lanterns banged against the bulwark. Taziar wandered to the taffrail and looked out over the black waves which lapped the hull. Awed by the unbridled power of the sea, he contemplated the events which had brought them to *Amara*. Turned away by the innkeeper in Calrmar, Taziar, Aird Moor, and Moonbear sought quarters elsewhere.

The double-rigged lateen ferryboat seemed the ideal place. An encampment on its deck assured them that the ship would not sail without them. And surely the baron's guards would never think to search *Amara* two days before her casting off.

Taziar balanced a foot on the gunwale, recalling his dealings with the sunburned captain. The crude lodgings had cost him a penrger, five times the price of crossing for Taziar and his friends. But money meant little to the city bred thief, especially when it was gained by robbery. And a closer peek at the contents of Mordath's purse revealed nine more penrger, several smaller Scandinavian gold pieces, and scores of tiny silver and copper ducats.

The strangeness of Taziar's surroundings incited his curiosity. The captain's firm insistence that Taziar and his companions remain on the upper deck and out of the way of the crew served only to further pique Taziar's interest. Turning, he skirted the shadowed bulk of the dinghy lashed to the bow and trotted aft.

The mainmast jutted skyward, the black cross-hatching of its riggings blurred by night. Spurred by a childish urge, Taziar caught hold of the wood. It was an easy climb to the boom. He continued up the mast with a constant, rapid rhythm. He ducked beneath the shroud lines and shinnied upward until the creak of the yard warned him he had nearly reached the masthead.

A cold Northern breeze, wet with sea air, wound through the lines. Chilled despite the late summer season, Taziar glanced downward. His position allowed a wide view of the deck. The two sailors who would serve as night crew during the voyage lounged on the quarterdeck. The wind fanned

smoke from an oil lamp before them, splotching
the deck with shadows. Their voices wafted clearly
to Taziar, but their accents so badly mangled the
hybrid language, he could not understand their
conversation. Amidships, a canvas sheet covered
the sand pit where the crew fixed their meals,
protecting the firewood and provisions from rain.
Beyond it, the yawning mouth of the hatchway led
into the darkness below the deck.

Bored with his bird's eye view of the lateen,
Taziar scurried down the mast. Shying into the
shadows beyond the sailor's light, he crept to the
hatchway. A sudden swell jolted Taziar forward,
nearly hurling him into the opening. Legs widely
braced, he waited until *Amara* settled back into her
anchorage, then ran down the companion ladder
into the hold.

The dim outline of baled cargo filled most of
the lower deck. Taziar stood still while his eyes
adjusted to the gloom, listening to the harried
scramble of rats' claws between crates. The glow
from the lantern and stray beams of moonlight
brightened the hold enough to reveal the bulk-
heads of the fore and aft cabins. From an earlier
conversation, Taziar knew the captain occupied
the compartment in the stern. He stepped around
the bilge hatch and wandered forward.

Everything below deck seemed as ordinary as
above, and Taziar felt foolish over defying the
captain's orders to stay above deck. But the captain's gritty warning was merely the latest of many
challenges Taziar could not ignore.

Two mahogany doors broke the solid line of the
forward bulkhead. Silently, Taziar walked to the
leftmost door. He seized the handle and pulled. It

resisted. Pale light from within outlined the keyhole, but Taziar heard no noise to indicate a human presence. Intrigued by a locked door aboard
Amara, he rummaged through his pocket for
Mordath's knife.

The ivory hilt felt smooth against Taziar's callused
palm. He knelt before the key slit, instantly realizing the blade would never fit. Returning the dagger to his pocket, he considered. Never in the
course of his thefts had he been stymied by a
simple lock. But always before he had carried the
proper tools for such a job. Thwarted, but not
defeated, Taziar turned his attention to the other
door.

This one opened easily to his touch. The panel
swung inward to reveal a compartment lined with
chests. Folded canvas occupied the center of the
room, smelling of mildew. An open locker held
coiled lines. *Sailors' personals*, Taziar guessed. He
was turning to leave when a glint of silver from
the locker caught his eye. Two large sewing needles nestled among the ropes. *Perfect*. Taziar pocketed one, abandoned the room, and closed the
door behind him.

Back in the central confines of the hold, Taziar
poised before the locked door. Anticipation chased
sleep from his thoughts. He brandished the needle, suddenly uncertain. *Obviously* Amara's *captain keeps something here he wants unseen. I'm risking
my life involving myself in things which are none of my
affair*. Yet, like the lions which guarded Aga'arin's
temple and the challenge of robbing Mordath in
the tavern in Wyneth, Taziar found himself unable to resist the allure of the forbidden. Grimly,
quietly, he set to work.

The needle fit into the keyhole sideways. Taziar's sensitive fingers felt the metal slide across the workings. He redirected its tip, easing it into the appropriate groove of the lock. Satisfied with its positioning, he pinned it in place with his thumb and turned the end in his other hand a full circle. The maneuver was soundless. Taziar flipped the latch. It creaked. The panel held.

Taziar ducked behind a crate, heart pounding. After several seconds, when no one responded to the noise, he approached the door again. He repeated his attempt with the needle. This time, the door moved freely. Taziar stared into a cabin dimly lit by an oil lamp which swung from a gimbal ring overhead. A wooden chair stood flush with the left front corner. A water-filled basin on its seat flashed the reflected light of the lantern. A straw-covered berth lined the opposite side of the room.

When Taziar's eyes had adjusted to the sudden presence of light, he realized he, too, was being studied. A woman occupied the berth, her legs a pale shadow in the gloom. Her flaxen hair hung functionally short. Her mocking, blue gaze traced Taziar's figure in the doorway, but her expression seemed friendly. She spoke in a low voice, her accent an enchanting singsong. "Are you clumsy or just slow? How long does it take you to open a lock?"

Taziar gawked, instantly recognizing her as the woman who had twice appeared in his dreams. Aware he could no longer run, he stepped into the room. He responded in the same half serious manner, but shock drained his words of confidence. "It . . . takes longer when you don't have a key." He displayed the sewing needle.

The woman blinked in surprise. Closer, Taziar found features with a simple beauty. Golden ringlets framed an oval visage with high, dimpled cheeks. A flannel nightshirt covered her thin frame. Her eyes darted, alert with mischief, and Taziar suspected they missed little.

"You're no sailor." She rose from the berth. Casually, she stretched, arching her back into a delicate curve.

Taziar watched with interest. The woman moved with an acrobat's grace. At least for the moment, she seemed unlikely to reveal his presence to the captain. "And you're no willing passenger. Why does the captain keep you locked in your cabin?"

"I'm expensive cargo." She leaned toward Taziar, examining him in the spinning light. "My name's Astryd. Thanks for rescuing me." Abruptly, she dodged past him and ran for the door.

Caught off guard, Taziar scrambled after her. He dove for Astryd's retreating form. He crashed into her legs, sprawling her to the deck. She twisted. Her feet pounded Taziar's chest. Her fingernails slashed his face. Swearing silently, Taziar seized her arm, spun her, and hoisted her to her feet. He dragged her, struggling, back into the room.

Carefully, Taziar closed the door. "You stupid wench! I'm in enough trouble sneaking about the ship. Risking myself is one matter. But I won't gamble my friends' lives by allowing a stranger to escape." Taziar knew the search which might follow Astryd's disappearance would delay the voyage long enough for Cullinsberg's guardsmen to reach Calrmar Port. And, if *Amara*'s captain discovered that Taziar had released her, the consequences to him and his companions might prove a heavy toll.

The deck lurched. Instinctively, Taziar clutched Astryd tighter. She grasped the berth, and they both managed to remain upright. Taziar felt the woman trembling beneath his grip. Abruptly, he realized she was shorter and slighter than himself. He pushed her to the straw. "Now why did you do that? I don't think much of the captain holding a woman against her will. I'll help you if I can, but not if you're going to endanger me and my companions every time I turn my back." He glared, but sympathy robbed his gesture of purpose. "My friends call me Shadow."

Astryd scowled and pulled away. "So what do people who don't care much for you call you?"

Despite Astryd's sullen rage, her closeness filled Taziar with desire. He had known her only a few short moments, but, for some reason he could not explain, he wanted her to like him. Her resemblance to the woman of his vision seemed eerily unnatural. "I really don't know. I try not to get near enough for them to call me anything."

Astryd met the joke with rancorous silence.

Taziar shifted awkwardly. "Listen, Astryd. My friends and I leave the ship in Sweden. I promise, I'll free you by then, if not sooner. I just can't take the risk until we're out of Calrmar Port."

To Taziar's relief, Astryd turned back to face him. A smile made her features shine. She clasped his hands. In the slash of lantern light, Taziar noticed that a scar puckered the soft, white skin of her knuckles in the unmistakable pattern of a claw. To Taziar's surprise, his mood became protectively angry. "Did someone hurt you?"

"Hurt me? Only you. Why?" Her gaze followed Taziar's stare. She laughed. "That's the dragon mark."

"The what?" Taziar went defensive. The blemish looked like a two-dimensional version of the tip of Mordath's staff.

"Whenever a person destined to become Dragonrank reaches late childhood or adolescence, the symbol appears." Her fingers dragged across Taziar's knee seductively. She continued, apparently misinterpreting his concern. "It doesn't hurt, really. It only means I have the power to learn magic."

Taziar felt betrayed. "You're a witch."

"Sorceress," Astryd corrected. "And you're a burglar! *You* broke into *my* room. I don't hold that against *you*."

Astryd's words forced Taziar to realize he was judging her by his experiences with Mordath. "I'm sorry," he said sincerely. He recalled Mordath's disappearance in the inn. "But if you have magical powers, how can the captain keep you confined?"

"I merely said I was Dragonrank. I don't have any spells, at least not now. My powers have been stolen from me."

"How?" asked Taziar, truly interested.

Astryd sighed. Her face went soft with sorrow. "It's a long story, and you'd best leave before the sailors come to check on me."

With strange regret, Taziar headed for the door. His fingers enwrapped the latch.

"Shadow?" Astryd's voice sounded sweet and musical. "You will come back?"

"I promise." He exited, pausing just long enough to snap the lock closed with his sewing needle.

The trip back to the tent on the upper deck proceeded in a wheel of unfamiliar emotion. Taziar wanted to see Astryd again. Of that, he felt certain. But his reasons seemed less clear. Idly, he wondered if she had thrown some sort of spell over him. He discarded the thought almost instantly. *If so, she would have been stupid to reveal herself as a sorceress, and she surely could have gotten me to release her.*

Taziar mounted the companionway to the upper deck, still deep in contemplation. He supposed it was Astryd's demeanor which attracted him so strongly: her daring attempt at escape, the quick, bold agility which characterized her movements, the impish glimmer in her eyes which told him she could understand his own ongoing quests to master the impossible. He found her size an additional positive feature. Her dream appearances in his mind only made him certain that Astryd was born to be his, although he suspected that his long journey with only male companionship contributed somewhat to her desirability.

Taziar paused at the tent opening and watched one of the sailors head toward the hatchway, his lantern dispersing the darkness in a broad circle. Astryd's timing had saved Taziar from explaining his presence in the hold. He watched the light funnel through the companionway, then turned and silently entered the tent. Moonbear sprawled beneath the canvas, his breathing deep and even. Beside him, Aird Moor's blanket lay, spread neatly across the deck. The woodsman was gone.

Air caught in Taziar's throat. Sudden sweat spangled his forehead. He knelt beside Moonbear. The barbarian opened one eye, grunted a greeting, and turned to his other side.

"Where's Aird Moor?" Taziar whispered.

Moonbear kept his back to Taziar. "He went on shore. He said he was looking for someone."

Rage tore through Taziar. *Aird Moor should never have left Moonbear alone. Together, we can stand against the guards or Mordath. Separated, Mordath could take any of us with a single spell.*

Astryd forgotten for the moment, Taziar flopped to Aird Moor's bedding. Gradually, his anger faded, and he dropped into a wary sleep.

Taziar awakened in the false prolongation of night supplied by the tent. He was alone. Voices wafted along the deck. The captain's rasping accent was unmistakable. "Water's stayed unusual calm. The Kattegat's a monster most times. Most cap'ns won't chance her. That's why my few trips a year's so profitable." Taziar heard the man spit. "Me and them crazy Viking pirates up your way's the only ones what'll brave her. No offense, of course."

Amusement colored Moonbear's reply. "None taken."

Taziar yawned, pressed wrinkles from his clothing, and trotted out to the deck. The sun hung well above the horizon, blazing like torchlight. Smoke trickled from the sand pit amidships. Even from a distance, Taziar could see half a dozen figures before the cooking pit. The smell of salt and fish twined over the deck, reminding Taziar he had not eaten the previous evening.

Taziar quickened his pace. Nearer, he recognized the crew, most of whom had spent the night in Calrmar's inn. The captain sat on one side with Moonbear, apparently pleased with his new audience.

"Course," *Amara*'s captain continued, "I spends half the year ice-locked in the harbor . . ." He broke off as Taziar approached. "Well, here's your li'l friend. Slep the good dawn away. Mornin', Shadow. Hungry?"

Nodding, Taziar sat, cross-legged, beside Moon-bear. The captain rose, went to the cooking pot, and ladled chowder into a wooden bowl. Taziar seized the time his short absence allowed. "Has Aird Moor returned?"

"No." Moonbear watched the captain stride to the rhythm of the swells.

Amara's captain passed the steaming bowl and a short wooden spoon to Taziar. "Ever eaten cod chowder?"

"Never," Taziar admitted. He shoveled some into his mouth. It tasted unfamiliar but pleasant. "It's good," Taziar said around the mouthful.

The captain beamed.

Wishing to capitalize on the seaman's mood, Taziar phrased his query delicately. "Last night in the tavern, I heard one of your crewmen mumble something about a woman aboard. Now, I don't believe in those mothers' stories, but I thought you seamen felt the presence of a woman on a ship is bad luck."

The captain's expression went icy. The crow's feet around his eyes deepened. His gaze played over his crew. "Which man spoke?"

Not wishing to implicate any man with his lie, Taziar continued. "Please, Captain. If I had known my babbling might make trouble for the sailor, I'd have said nothing. The blame is all mine. I've developed a bad habit of listening to private conversations."

The captain seemed to accept the explanation easily. "Aegir's accursed storms, least I knows to curb my tongue with you aboard. We've a missy in the hold. I's paid well to ship her and weller to keep her presence secret. She's a Norse 'un, headed away far north to Mjalmar to become a king's bride."

So Astryd's getting married. Disappointment sifted through Taziar's thoughts.

The captain went on with his disclosure, apparently glad to pass the information. "Small thing, pretty in her own ways, but not the sort men'd kill for."

Well aware of Astryd's attractions, Taziar pressed further. "Why do you keep her in the hold?"

The captain turned his attention to his chowder, as if bored by the subject of conversation. "Strange thing. Keeps tellin' my men we's made a mistake. But I's paid to take her to Mjalmar, and that's where she goes. Can't fathom why a missy'd fight against becomin' a queen."

Neither can I. Taziar pondered the thought, knowing precisely where to find the answer to such a question. *Next time I visit Astryd, there will be explanations.* But before Taziar could push the matter further, one of the sailors approached his captain.

The crewman spoke in a rapid patter of pidgin Scandinavian intermingled with punctuated bursts of the barony's tongue and an unrecognizable language which matched his coarse accent. His swarthy features and the coiled black hair which covered his skin marked him as a foreigner. His tone was conversational, but the word "Cullinsberg" sifted clearly from his broken speech. Taziar turned to Moonbear, hoping the barbarian would know enough of both languages for clarification.

Moonbear did not disappoint Taziar. "He told the captain an armed patrol camped last night a half day's walk outside of Calrmar." He paused, listening, then continued. "They wear red and black uniforms. Calrmar's constabulary rode out to meet them, but they have not returned yet."

Taziar drew a ragged breath. Impatiently, he waited until the sailor finished reporting to the captain and returned to his fellows. Pushed to quick action, Taziar did not trouble to hide his motives. "Captain, can we sail today?"

Amara's captain studied Taziar from beneath beetled brows. "Are you mad, son? The sails are furled. There's merchants still headin' in. An early cast off would cost me gold."

"Gold?" Concerned for his friends' lives, Taziar was annoyed by the captain's obsession with money. He jabbed his fingers into his pocket and jerked free Mordath's purse without bothering to secure the string. The pouch flopped open in his hand, spilling its contents. Gold, silver, and copper fell like glimmering rain. A spray of coins scattered across the deck. Some rebounded from the hatch coaming and the cooking pit. They settled on *Amara*'s rolling deck.

In the shocked silence which followed, Taziar's voice emerged unusually loud. "Will that cover your losses?"

Amara's captain treated Taziar to an intensely unpleasant scrutiny. His gaze snapped to the coins which littered the otherwise spotless deck. Abruptly, he bellowed at the crew. "Unfurl the sails. Fetch your companions from the tavern. We weighs anchor today."

Without question, the sailors rushed to obey.

The captain rounded on Taziar. "Clean the mess. And don't dare tells me or the crew why's you're bein' chased by soldiers. If I'm goin' to harbor fugitives, it'll be from ignorance." He turned on his heel and tromped down the quarterdeck.

Aird Moor returned on the dinghy which brought *Amara*'s remaining crew, his buckskins slashed and stained. His hands looked sore with abrasions, his features drawn. Accepting a steadying hand from a sailor, he staggered to the deck and offered Taziar no explanations.

Taziar waited until the sailor's footsteps faded, then confronted his companion. "Where in Karana's hottest hell did you run off to in the middle of the night?"

"Leave me alone, boy." Aird Moor brushed past Taziar, headed for the tent.

Taziar caught the woodsman's arm, his fury from the previous night blazing anew. "You left Moonbear alone and asleep. I need a better reason than that."

Aird Moor stared at the small fist which gripped his sleeve. His face went red with rising anger. "Take your hand off me, child, before I remove it at the wrist." He whipped his sword from his sheath.

Behind them, wind rattled through the riggings. The sailors' voices sounded distant. Taziar recalled how, eight years ago, Blade had resented Taziar's presence in the street gang until the tiny thief physically challenged the muscled ruffian. The fight had never happened; Blade's newly gained respect made the two fast friends. Now, aware a display of raw courage would impress Aird Moor more than words, Taziar rebelled against the aloofness which tainted all of the woodsman's dealings with him. He freed his own weapon, aware he could never hope to win such a battle. "I'm twenty-one. Aga'arin's blood, quit calling me child!"

Aird Moor gave him a look vicious with scorn. "You know I could kill you with a stroke."

Taziar flinched, but he met the threat with brazen honesty. "I've endangered my life for worse causes than Moonbear's safety. If you would really rather slay me than explain your whereabouts, I can accept that." He crouched, hoping he had not misjudged the woodsman.

Aird Moor's sword went lax in his grip. Rage fled from his features, leaving him looking old beyond his years. "Shadow, I underestimated you. You've got a lot of fire for a Cullinsbergen of your generation. Come along, and I'll tell you what I've been doing." He replaced his sword. "I assume Moonbear's in the tent." Without waiting for a reply, he strode forward.

Taziar followed cautiously, his sinews still taut from anticipated combat. It had been a long time since anyone had praised his courage, and the words took on a special meaning when spoken by a man of Aird Moor's war experience. He wondered who or what had left the woodsman in such a disheveled state and infuriated him enough to draw steel against a companion.

Aird Moor and Taziar entered the tent where Moonbear waited, shielded from the clatter of the sailors checking lines and planking. The woodsman hurled his tattered frame down on his sleeping blanket. "I went out looking for information about Mordath and his powers." His voice gained volume, and Taziar recognized the same ravenous anger which had driven Aird Moor to pull a sword up on deck.

"I slogged through every scummy, disgusting, backwater dive in Calrmar. I tracked down each piece of human ratdung I thought might give me answers. I fought with foul, shit-stinking bandits and assassins so repulsive I washed my knuckles after every punch." He ran a dirty hand over his abraded fingers. "The only thing more rampant than filth was ignorance. I didn't learn a damned thing." He added as a growled afterthought. "Accursed thieves."

Taziar cringed, feeling slightly insulted. "You risked your life to get information about Mordath?"

Wearily, Aird Moor stretched out on the blanket. "He's coming back for us. We can't fight him effectively until we know what he can do."

"Agreed," chimed in Taziar. "But there are better ways than battling street people and announcing our presence all over Calrmar. Get some rest. Tonight I'll take you to someone who may have answers. And we won't even have to leave the ship."

Despite fatigue, Aird Moor seemed interested. "There's someone on board who . . ."

Taziar silenced him with a wave. "Hush. It's a secret. Now close your eyes."

Aird Moor's lids drooped shut. Within moments, he dropped into deep slumber.

Taziar and Moonbear headed to the deck. A second tent lay pitched beside their own, housing for the night crew. The remainder of the eight sailors scurried purposefully about *Amara*, completing the last few tasks which would allow the ship to cast off a day earlier than planned. Taziar could see the aft sail already flying from the mizzenmast.

Wide-legged in the bow, *Amara*'s captain shouted. "Weigh anchor!" The clank of chain reverberated through Taziar's ears as the anchor rose from the ocean. "Hoist the main!" Two of the men hauled on the halyards. The yard rattled up the mast unfurling the triangle of sail. The sailors looped the lines about their belaying pins and prepared to meet the captain's next command. "Shorten sails." The canvas drew taut, and *Amara* skated from her anchorage on a starboard tack.

Aware he would spend much of the night awake with Astryd, Taziar tried to sleep through the afternoon and evening. But anticipation of seeing the sorceress and the novelty of sea travel denied him rest. At length, wearying of watching Aird Moor dream, he joined Moonbear in the bow. Soon, the pitch and roll of *Amara*'s deck became familiar. Taziar stared at the white-capped swells which curled from the hull, his thoughts strangely full of Astryd.

Dinner passed in light conversation. The haggard faces of *Amara*'s captain and her crew revealed an effort which belied the smooth tacks and turns. As the sky darkened, Taziar practiced sword forms amidships while the sailors prepared *Amara* for the night. The anchor sank to the sea bed. The sails again hugged the boom, and all but the two night crew crawled into their tents to sleep.

Taziar waited only until the men settled in before he led his companions down the hatchway into the hold. The cargo still occupied most of the area, now canvas-covered and strapped in place. Moonlight pinned luminous eyes until a rat scrambled out of sight beneath the tarp. Swiftly and silently, Taziar crept to the locked door of the fore cabin. He snapped the mechanism open with his sewing needle and waited for his companions to catch up.

When Aird Moor and Moonbear came up beside him, Taziar turned the latch and pushed the door. The panel swung inward soundlessly. Before Taziar could step within, Astryd hurled herself into his arms with a whispered greeting. "Shadow! Thor's justice, you did return."

Taziar returned the embrace, feeling suddenly warm and excited. Reluctantly, he pulled free, ushered his friends into the room, and latched the door behind them. "Astryd, this is Moonbear and Aird Moor." He indicated each in turn, then addressed the woodsman. "Astryd is Dragonrank."

"Is she now?" Aird Moor looked deeply thoughtful. He crossed the room, removed the pan of washing water from the chair, and sat. "Would you be willing to answer some questions?"

"Certainly," Astryd replied. She, Taziar, and Moonbear took seats on the berth. Astryd caught Taziar's hand and squeezed encouragingly.

Suffocated with desire, Taziar felt awkward as a child. He scarcely heard Aird Moor's question. "What precisely is Dragonrank?"

"It's a method of magic which draws upon the caster's life energy. Any person with the ability to call chaos and channel it for more than minor sorcery eventually becomes naturally marked with the dragon symbol." Astryd held out her right hand to display the claw-shaped scar. "Once it appears, the person can join the Dragonrank School, if he hasn't already killed himself experimenting." She laughed. The sound held a sweetness which made Taziar giddy.

"Killed himself?" Aird Moor leaned forward.

Astryd continued, her face shadow-streaked by the uneven swing of the lantern. "As I said, directing chaos costs life energy. The amount any spell drains depends upon the strength of the caster, the amount of power he's already spent, and how well he's practiced the chosen spell in the past. It's an inexact art. If the sorcerer taps his life energy too far, he dies."

Aird Moor wore a look of bemused puzzlement.

Astryd clarified. "Think of a sword spar. You don't know how much any particular strike will tax you before you make it. But well-rehearsed maneuvers fatigue you far less than wild slashes."

Aird Moor nodded his understanding. Taziar flushed, reminded of his own exhausting practices.

Astryd went on. "The Dragonrank School teaches us to expand our consciousness and endurance, gives us a place to try out sorceries, and supplies the basic information from which to attempt specific spells. Gaining strength consists of refining power so the same spell takes less energy. The transport which taps a quarter of my aura might take only one sixteenth or less for a diamond-rank master."

Taziar freed his damp hand from Astryd's grip and slid his arm behind her.

Aird Moor pressed further. "What's the significance of rank?"

Astryd smiled with girlish allure, obviously aware

of Taziar's unsubtle maneuver. "It's a symbol, arbitrarily represented by progressively more valuable gems. We gain ranks by mastering certain skills. A promotion usually requires several years during which we must spend eleven months of every year on the school grounds. Otherwise, we sacrifice any chance for advancement." Her voice acquired a pained tone. "If I'm not released soon, my chance to regain my powers and continue my training will be forever lost."

Taziar winced, aware her final pronouncement was directed at him.

Aird Moor returned the conversation to its original tack. "What's your rank?"

"Jade."

Taziar was startled. *The same as Mordath.* "Would a sorcerer know his classmates?"

Astryd turned her face to Taziar. The lamplight carved dimples in her fair features, and he felt embarrassed by a rush of adolescent desire. "Not necessarily at early levels. We have a number of glassranks. But magic is a cruel and demanding mistress. We lose many lives to attempts at spells beyond the caster's strength. Others die of more natural causes such as illness or warfare. Remember, too, practice refines skills. Those who daily drain themselves to exhaustion become the most powerful, but the art is inexact. The slightest miscalculation may result in death." She paused, as if attempting to recall the original question. "The answer is yes. As a jaderank, I know all six of my classmates."

"Mordath?" said Aird Moor.

Astryd glanced up as if slapped. Her voice went icy. "I know him."

Aird Moor grinned, displaying stained teeth. "What can he do?"

Astryd scooted back against Taziar's arm. "Anything, like all trained Dragonranks. It's possible for any of us to attempt spells which no one else has ever chronicled. But the cost in power would be unknown, too great for anyone short of ruby-rank to try." Her gaze flitted, from Moonbear's unrevealing visage back to Aird Moor. "He can do nearly anything. But he's most likely to use spells he's practiced. It eventually becomes necessary for every Dragonrank to strictly limit his repertoire to make the spells he knows more powerful and less costly. In other words, if a sorcerer concentrated on a single spell, he could learn to cast it with hardly any expenditure of energy, and as often as he needed it. Additionally, the same way some men have a natural leaning toward swords or bows or polearms, Dragonranks often have tendencies toward certain types of spells. Magics of a specific bent might be more easily learned, thereby costing less life energy. The strongest Dragonranks are usually ones with such a bias who concentrate on their natural strengths."

"Mordath?" prompted Aird Moor.

Astryd patted back strands of yellow hair. "Weather spells mostly. It gives him a nice balance of attack, defense, and general purpose. Of course, he knows the basic fillers: transport, weapon shields, and the like. Anything more you wish to know?"

"That'll do." Aird Moor grunted thoughtfully. He rose to leave.

Wishing for more time with Astryd, Taziar pushed further. "What's your specialty?"

Astryd shifted her weight against Taziar's shoulder. "Summonings," she murmured. "It's a hall-mark bias. The Dragonrank took its name from the ability to call forth dragons. They're not exactly normal fauna."

Taziar pulled Astryd closer, too awash with desire to concern himself with her revelation. Still, needing more answers, he questioned further. "But if Dragonrank magic is based on life energy, and you're alive, how come you've lost your powers?"

"Because I'm an idiot." Astryd leaped to her feet and paced angrily. "I was practicing a spell which concentrated all my ability into my rankstone. It probably sounds stupid to you, but the spell has its purposes. It keeps the caster untraceable. A Dragonrank's worst enemy is a rival Dragonrank. This spell protects me from discovery and a myriad of attacks which affect only another caster." She stopped abruptly and faced Taziar. "Unfortunately, it also gave Mordath a chance to steal my rankstone and all my power. Without spells, I'm helpless against him. To keep me from tracking him with the help of another Dragonrank, he booked my passage aboard *Amara*, ensuring I would be trapped until after our vacation time ended. I'd return too late for promotion."

Taziar shook the sliding comma of hair from his eye, confused. "Why would Mordath do that?"

Astryd resumed pacing. "Because only one Dragonrank can rise to garnet each year." Her strides grew shorter and stiff with agitation. "It's our only competitive rank and the reason Dragonranks below garnet are forbidden by law to slay one another. But Mordath knew the master would choose me over him."

Aird Moor mumbled something uninterpretable.

"What's that?" Taziar encouraged the woodsman.

"Nothing," said Aird Moor, too quickly.

Astryd reclaimed her seat, and her eyes pinned Aird Moor. A jarring silence followed.

Aird Moor sprang to his feet. "I said I meant nothing. And I think I have the information I came for. Thank you, Astryd." He walked to the door and opened it. Darkness crushed in, held at bay in the archway by lamplight.

Moonbear also stood. "We will meet you at the tent," he told Taziar. The two men departed, closing the door behind them.

Taziar studied Astryd's slim figure in the glow from the lantern. Her movement had raised sweat, and the flannel of her nightshirt clung, revealing soft curves. Embarrassed to be caught staring, he spoke. "If you're looking for Mordath, stay with us. He's chased us all the way from Wyneth."

Without replying, Astryd wrapped her arms about Taziar. Breath caught in his throat. Warmth suffused him. She pulled his face to hers and kissed him with a fierce tenderness which shocked him. His fingers looped around her, and he grasped the fabric of her nightshirt. Passion goaded him onward. But the same heavy-handed morality which would not allow him to kill held him back. "Astryd. I promised to free you. Nothing you do or don't do is going to make me break my vow. You don't have to pretend you like me."

"Pretend?" Astryd breathed a long sigh of admission. "All right. I confess. I was going to seduce you, then break free when I thought I had a chance."

Taziar dropped his arms and turned away, suddenly shamed and disinterested.

Astryd continued quickly. "But I couldn't do that to you, Shadow. There's not a man on Midgard vile enough to deserve such deceit. Besides, this may sound like another one of my lies, but . . ." She fidgeted. "I really think I love you already."

Taziar whirled back to Astryd, angered by her game. "Just how stupid do you think I am?"

Astryd looked stricken. "I can't blame you for distrusting me. I'm pulled to you. It's almost like . . . well, like Dragonrank magic. We belong together; I'm certain of it. I only hope my desperation hasn't driven you away completely."

Trusting his intuition, Taziar studied Astryd's face in the pale light of the lantern. The sincerity and concern in her features could not be feigned. "I . . . believe you Astryd. Someone or something wants us together. I don't know how, and I don't know why. But I do know I've no wish to fight it." He caught her by the shoulders and drew her closer. Burying his face in her hair, he thrilled to the warm press of her breasts against him.

They talked deep into the night, revealing secrets with an honest innocence Taziar had never before shared with another person. They chuckled over the difficulties of short people in a world of seeming giants. And, in the end, they made love with a greedy passion Taziar had never experienced with Shylar's girls. Then Taziar returned to his companions only minutes before the night sailor left to check on Astryd.

CHAPTER 12

The Dragon's Wrath

"Come not between the dragon and his wrath."
                    —William Shakespeare,
                    Othello

Taziar awakened in the late morning to the slap of shroud lines and the tent-muffled conversations of the sailors. Alone, he lay in lazy contentment, contemplating his evening with Astryd. Her lovemaking made every past partner seem stale and boring. His instant attraction to her appeared understandable; Astryd was a beautiful woman. But the sorceress' desire for a puny thief and their mutual physical and mental commitment seemed too sudden and complete. Since first seeing the flash of Mordath's jadestone in Wyneth' tavern, Taziar had come to believe in magic. He hoped whatever force had brought them together would remain long enough to allow him to win Astryd's affection in his own way.

Taziar rolled to his side. Absently, he kneaded the jadestone through the fabric of his pocket. Visions of Astryd filled his mind, stronger than in the past. He watched in calm fascination until the images faded. His thoughts turned to the future. Moonbear had informed him that the barbarians' territory lay only a half day's journey from *Amara*'s port. *Surely the Cullinsberg patrol will return home now. They wouldn't dare battle a prince in his own kingdom.*

Taziar rose and dressed, ideas swirling through his mind. He realized, with some satisfaction, that their arrival in Sweden would not end his obligations nor his restlessness. He would need to help Astryd regain her powers from Mordath and he'd have to confront Ilyrian to learn the truth about his father's execution. The new direction Taziar's thoughts had taken filled him with the kind of excitement he felt whenever he agreed to perform a challenging theft. Sparked with purpose, he emerged from the tent to the sallow spread of sunlight.

Sailors trotted the length of *Amara*'s deck, speaking the mangled language Taziar had long ago learned to ignore. He passed them with a gestured greeting and headed aft. Once past the hold and the cooking box, he paused on the quarterdeck, away from the lines and belaying pins. Careful to leave a lane for the sailors, he began a sword practice with newly found exuberance.

Charged with cheerful vigor, he launched into a complicated series of sword forms. The cuts, sweeps, and strikes felt smooth, if slightly awkward. He held the final position, considering what criticisms his father would have made if he were still alive.

"You're dropping your right shoulder." The

words were Captain Taziar Medakan's, but the tone was distinctly different.

Taziar froze, shocked. Slowly, he turned his head, recalling Moonbear's accusation that he did not know how to listen and concerned he might have imagined the voice.

Aird Moor sat amidships, his legs dangling over the coaming into the hatchway. "I said you're dropping your shoulder."

Taziar sheathed his sword, surprised. It was the first time Aird Moor had shown an interest in his practice. "That's exactly what my father would have said."

"You should have listened to him. It sounds as if he knew what he was doing."

Taziar laughed. "I would hope he did. He was Cullinsberg's guard captain for fifteen and a half years."

Aird Moor's features crushed together in puzzlement. "Shadow, what's your real name?"

Taziar wandered amidships and knelt beside Aird Moor. "Taziar," he said. "Taziar Medakan, same as my father."

"Captain Taz was your father?" Aird Moor seemed incredulous. He studied Taziar in the morning sunlight.

"Yes."

"He told me about his son. He said his child was small. But you're scarcely big enough to be a girl."

"Thanks, Aird Moor. I guess I deserved that after asking if you enjoyed the war." Though insulted, Taziar seized the opportunity to uncover more information about the captain's death. "You knew my father?"

"Knew him well. I served under him ten years."

Sudden excitement swept Taziar. He pressed. "What happened to him? How was he killed?"

"He died on the gallows."

Taziar scowled, annoyed with the answer. "Don't you think I know that? The statesman called him a traitor and a coward. I know my father was neither of those things."

"So do I," Aird Moor agreed.

"He was betrayed."

"I know."

"By whom?"

Aird Moor sighed loudly, shaking his head. "Taz, your father was killed by his own morality. He was too honest and kindhearted, always ready to give some deceitful bastard another chance. He would do anything to keep his men alive, yet his ungodly courage made his own life worthless to him. The soldiers loved him. But they were too stupid to understand why. Otherwise, a slick-tongued worm named Ilyrian would never have been able to contrive the charges against him."

Rage boiled through Taziar. "Ilyrian." *I knew it all along. Why am I so surprised?*

"Your father told me he confronted Ilyrian about peddling drugs to the troops, and thereby destroying their ability to fight," Aird Moor said. "Treachery and character assassination, those are Ilyrian's weapons. He could never have faced Taz in fair combat."

"Ilyrian," Taziar repeated. His anger funneled unexpectedly against the man before him. He sprang to his feet. "You knew Ilyrian slandered my father, your captain! And you let him have my father executed. You allowed the town to crush my family, kill my mother, and force me out to live on the streets?"

Aird Moor threw up his hands in disgust. "Believe me, I tried to help. I cornered Ilyrian on the road to the baron's castle and battered the bastard until he confessed to everything. I would have killed him, too, but I needed him at the trial to prove your father's innocence." Aird Moor's hands balled into fists. "Ilyrian had me locked in the dungeons until after the execution. By then, it was too late. I found your mother dead . . . by her own hand, I think . . ."

Taziar winced.

". . . And you had disappeared. The other soldiers wouldn't let me near Ilyrian again. I had no reason to remain in Cullinsberg."

Taziar paced, his earlier contentment swept aside by anguish. "Well, now you'll have another chance. Ilyrian has joined the patrol chasing us."

Aird Moor swore. "That explains a number of things." His gaze followed Taziar's path. "But Ilyrian is no longer my problem. When you were a child, I willingly took that burden upon myself. But Taz Medakan was your father. His vengeance has become yours to fulfill."

"Ilyrian," said Taziar. He felt nauseated. "I'll kill him." Even as he spoke, an image of his mother filled his mind. He recalled the blood, warm and slick on his fingers and the hollow glare of recrimination in the corpse's eyes. Taziar went still. "I won't kill him. I won't kill anyone. I can't . . ."

Aird Moor's voice gained all the savage force Taziar's had lost. "Of all the worthless stupidity! You have none of your father's size or strength, yet you inherited the very things which killed him:

his insane sense of morality and his damnable courage. You can't kill Ilyrian, or you don't want to? Sometimes you have to do things, whether you want to or not, even if you know it will tear your heart apart. There are some things which have to be done."

Taziar turned away, unable to face Aird Moor and his accusations. "I knew you couldn't understand. Death doesn't bother you."

"The first time I killed a man, I vomited until my guts felt on fire. I had nightmares for weeks." Aird Moor caught Taziar's shoulder, his grip painfully firm. "Anyone who can kill without caring doesn't deserve to live. He's contemptible garbage. He's crazy. No sane person could kill another and not feel something evil. I still have dreams which make me wake in a cold sweat. But nothing can give life back to the first man I killed."

Taziar said nothing.

Aird Moor continued. "Nobody wants to kill. You kill because you must. Sometimes you have to make a decision. Some things are important enough to kill for: ideals, family, friends. Taz Medakan is dead. But he's still more important than that slime, Ilyrian. Yesterday, you were willing to die for Moonbear, and you told me you've only known each other a few weeks. Your father should seem as important to you as Moonbear. And if you're willing to spend your own life, why not someone else's?"

Taziar tried to explain an emotion he scarcely understood himself. "Killing is wrong . . ."

Aird Moor interrupted. Impatience colored his words. "I can talk all afternoon, and it won't mean anything. But with all the violence surrounding you now, I guarantee there will come a time when you will need to kill. Either way, a life is lost: yours or your opponent's. The choice is yours to make. If you would rather die than kill, that's your decision. But remember, there's more than your own survival at stake. If you go down, there's a greater chance Moonbear will also. And no one will have slain Ilyrian. Once you die, you leave no one to avenge your father."

Taziar continued, aware his argument had become futile, yet still morally bound. "I can't kill. Not even Ilyrian."

"Fine." Aird Moor released Taziar. "Let Ilyrian kill you, too. Teach him Medakans *are* cowards. Someday, he'll deceive someone who will kill him. Until then, all the men and women he destroys and all the orphans he creates will have been harmed because you made the decision you would rather die than stand and fight." Without another word, he rose and marched toward the bow.

No answering defense came to Taziar's mind. He remained still, staring at his interwoven fingers. Despite Aird Moor's reassurances and the simple wisdom of his points, Taziar knew his conscience would never allow him to kill another human being. He stood and shuffled to the railing. The sea lay calm as glass beneath him. Wisps of cloud appeared and curled around the sun. Off to starboard, the sky went suddenly dark.

The captain shouted. From nowhere, wind gusted, streaming through the riggings. The sails jibed then crashed back to port tack. *Amara* lurched. Taziar slammed into the rail, the breath driven from him. Pain ground though him. His fingers tightened about the railings. *This is no normal storm!*

"Aegir's mercy!" An abrupt battering of rain nearly drowned the captain's commands. *Amara* was tossed to her side. Water sloshed across the deck. Taziar tumbled amidships. His shoulder smacked against the mast. A sailor's garbled words went past him unheard. Then a gruff voice screamed in his own language. "Cut the line!"

Gusts slapped the hull, rolling the ship violently. One arm wrapped around the mizzenmast, Taziar pulled Mordath's dagger and slashed the halyard. The rope parted, spilling wind, and *Amara* inched windward. The sea anchor rattled from the bow. The sailors scurried about the deck, brought to life by this unnatural, murderous storm. Two fought the bucking tiller in the stern. Taziar saw water fountain over the coaming and into the hold. *Astryd!* Realization slapped him with the force of the gale. There was a sickening splinter of wood.

Taziar clawed his way to the hatchway. Shifting his weight with the ceaseless floundering of the deck, he scrambled halfway down the companionway. Suddenly, bile green light split the darkness. A figure appeared on the bow, blurred by distance. Mordath's familiar voice thundered across the deck. "Captain, the gale is mine. Surrender the fugitives."

Tazier ducked beneath the deck level. The captain's reply drifted to him, much softer and filled with hesitant uncertainty. "Begone, demon. Me cargo and passengers aren't for bargain."

Mordath's words went haughty with annoyance. "Then I'll smash your ship to timber: cargo, passengers, and crew. Three lives or all, captain. The choice is yours."

Taziar's heart slammed against his ribs. Aird Moor's challenge rang clear. "I'll kill you, traitor." A sudden gust whipped the bow. *Amara* reared. Wild footfalls shook the deck.

"Stop!" cried Moonbear. "I will not have innocent lives lost for me. I surrender."

Taziar awaited Aird Moor's inevitable searing rebuttal, but the woodsman said nothing. Concerned, Taziar strained his ears for some evidence Aird Moor still lived.

Mordath's tone rose in triumph. "Chain them and place them aboard the dinghy. I want the thief, damn it! I need him most of all."

Stung to action, Taziar ran down the ladder. He knew he would also give himself up. There were too many lives at stake. But first, he needed to fulfill his promise to Astryd. He sprinted through the hold, jammed open the locked door, and caught the Norsewoman in his arms. She felt warm against him. He embraced her with a selfish violence, aware he might soon lose his life.

The ship heeled to starboard. Shouts wafted from above deck. Taziar spoke, his voice thick with grief. "Astryd, I love you. I promised I would free you before the ship reached the Northlands. This is my last chance." Purpose drove through him before she could reply. He seized her hand and hauled her to the companion ladder. "Mordath may claim my life, but he'll have nothing more. I'll deny him anything I can. Good-bye, Astryd. Good luck." Taziar kissed her quickly, then scurried up the companionway.

As Taziar emerged from the hatchway, he heard a cry of recognition. Spurred by a single obsession, he sprinted to the rail. Behind him, he heard yells and muffled footsteps. The captain shouted. "Hol' your gale! My men's too busy fightin' *Amara* to ketch your thief."

The lateen went suddenly still. Taziar grabbed the rail for support; his other hand fumbled in his pocket for Mordath's possessions. He seized the handkerchief and the ring and tossed them as far out to sea as he could. The cloth fluttered, gently as a feather. The ring struck the water with an impotent splash. Taziar heard the sailors closing in on him. Furiously, he dug through his pocket. He wrapped his fingers about the stolen jadestone and cocked his arm to throw.

"Wait!" Astryd's voice surprised Taziar. He had not expected her to follow him above deck. She caught his wrist and pried the faceted gemstone from his fingers.

Before Taziar could turn and question Astryd's odd behavior, a wave of arms buffeted him to the deck. Pain lanced through his chest. He lay still, allowing the sailors to pin him down and bind him. The ropes bit into his wrists and ankles. He felt himself hoisted into the air. Taziar searched frantically for Astryd, but the sorceress was nowhere he could see. *God's mercy. At least let her escape safely.*

Caught in the unyielding grip of two sailors, Taziar stared into the blue-gray expanse of sky. Under Mordath's control, the winds had dwindled. The sails hung limp from the yards. While the men carried him forward, Taziar quietly, calmly explored the bonds on his wrists and ankles with as much finger motion as the ropes allowed. The knots were the work of experts accustomed to securing lines. Taziar loosed a sigh of grim resignation. *But the fight's not over yet.*

The captain averted his eyes when Taziar reached the bow. Feeling obligated because of the captain's initial staunch defense, Taziar addressed him soothingly. "It's all right, captain. It makes no sense for you to lose your life and your ship for us. We never meant to cause you any trouble."

But Taziar's words seemed only to distress the captain further. His voice cracked, and he gestured feebly toward the taffrail. "Puts 'im with the others."

Closer to the rail, Taziar could see the dinghy resting in the water beside the ship. Mordath sat within it. Moonbear and Aird Moor lay, gagged, on its bottom, their hands and feet bound together behind them. The sight of his two strong companions as helpless captives of the Dragonrank sorcerer sickened Taziar. He offered no resistance as the sailors lowered him to the dinghy by the rope which connected his wrists to his ankles, though the maneuver strained every muscle in his body and pain seared through him like fire.

The dinghy rocked sharply as Taziar settled to the deck with his companions. His discomfort settled to a dull ache. The sailors cast off. At Mordath's command, the winds strengthened, driving the dinghy leeward without the necessity for sail or oars. Scarcely beyond earshot of *Amara*, Mordath seized the ropes which held Taziar and hoisted the thief to his knees.

Taziar shifted awkwardly for balance, his face at Mordath's knees and his friends flat on the floorboards behind him. He focused his gaze on Mordath, but his fingers picked diligently at the ropes. Vowing to stall for the time he needed to free himself, he addressed the sorcerer. "What do you want from us?"

Mordath's brows puckered to a scowl. "My gem, Taziar. The rankstone. Where is it?"

"Gem?" Taziar twisted his face in a look of exaggerated puzzlement. A picture of the diamond-cut jadestone filled his mind, an exact duplicate of the gem in Mordath's staff. *Rankstone.* Realization jarred him to silent self-loathing. *The jade I carried as carelessly as a toy is Astryd's rankstone. So that was the attraction. If only I hadn't blinded myself to everything but her beauty, I could have restored her magic before it was too late. Karana's damned! I hope the sailors haven't hurt her.* Taziar's finger snagged a loop in the knot. He feigned ignorance. "What gem is that?"

Mordath's hungry patience snapped. "You thieving little bastard! You know which gem. The jadestone you stole from me. Where is it?"

Tazier fought the ropes, swaying with the toss of the boat to disguise his movements. "I believe I last saw it in Wyneth." He pretended to consider. "Is that right?"

Quick as a cat, Mordath seized Taziar's cloak at the throat. His angry, green eyes seemed to lay Taziar open. "You still had it on the ship just before I boarded. My spell couldn't track you there." He pulled suddenly. Cloth tore, Taziar staggered on his knees.

Sudden anger swept through Taziar. The sea breeze chilled him. Mordath swore violently. He drew a knife and began slicing the pockets and hems of Taziar's cloak and tunic in a frenzied rage. The search uncovered nothing but the sword which the sailors had not bothered to take from him in their haste. Mordath stood, brandishing the blade. "Odin damn you to coldest Hel! Where are you hiding the jadestone? Tell me, or I'll slit you stem to stern!"

Still kneeling on the deck, Taziar replied boldly. "Then I hope your magics allow you to talk with dead people."

Mordath reacted with thoughtless fury. He backhanded Taziar's face with the sword hilt. Steel jarred against Taziar's head. His thoughts exploded into hot sparks. Consciousness swam. He loosed a whimper of distress, his struggle to free himself from his bonds forgotten in his anguish.

"The jade!" screamed Mordath.

Taziar shook his head dizzily, unable to speak. *I won't betray Astryd. I hope that jade restores her powers.* By now *Amara* had dwindled to a shadow on the horizon. From the corner of his eye, Taziar caught sight of another sailing ship moving north. *The guards,* he guessed. Apparently, Mordath's storm had been carefully localized to damage only *Amara*.

Mordath raised his hand for another strike. Taziar flinched. The wooden seat gouged into his back. Suddenly, Mordath's features twisted into a glare of arrogant calculation. He let the sword drop to the deck. "I haven't gone fishing for a while. I think I might try some trolling ... with Moonbear. Probably the first time anyone ever used 220 weight of bait to catch a worm."

Mordath pushed past Taziar toward the bow. Taziar scowled. "Don't bluff me, wizard. I know the baron wants Moonbear alive." Taziar twisted his head to watch Mordath, once again working at the knots which imprisoned him.

Mordath uncoiled a line in the bow and fastened one end to Moonbear's bonds. "On the contrary. *Captain* Ilyrian has given me direct orders to kill both the Swede and Aird Moor."

Captain Ilyrian? The title seemed a cruel parody. The very thought drove Taziar to fight his bonds even harder. The knot loosened but still would not give.

Clutching the free end of the line, Mordath again stepped around Taziar. His intentions became frighteningly clear. Once in the water, Moonbear would be dragged behind the dinghy. Facedown and tightly tied, he would drown. "No!" Taziar flung himself at the sorcerer. His side struck Mordath, staggering him. The Dragonrank mage scrabbled for balance. The boat rolled sideways. Mordath cursed, regained his equilibrium, and skittered to the bow beyond Taziar's reach.

Taziar howled in frustration. While Mordath secured the line to the stern cleat, Taziar twisted his wrist. The rope burned painfully across flesh. His hand came free, throbbing as the circulation returned.

Abruptly, green light pulsed across the dinghy. The boat rocked dangerously. Mordath whirled. His fiercely hunched posture betrayed surprise. Taziar turned his head to follow the sorcerer's gaze. Astryd stood between Taziar and Moonbear, her golden hair stained an oily black from the combined effects of her transport magics and Mordath's storm. For several seconds, the Dragonrank mages stood like carved statues at opposite ends of a courtyard. Taziar worked his other hand free of the ropes. Still bound at the ankles, he dove for Mordath.

Mordath hissed. He raised his hand and a star of light knifed through the air like a sword. Taziar recoiled. Astryd spoke a single word. Sparks arched protectively before Taziar. Mordath's magics struck Astryd's, and both spells exploded in a blinding pinwheel of color. Again, Taziar lunged at Mordath. Yet as he moved, thick, emerald smoke enwrapped Mordath, and the sorcerer was gone.

Astryd's urgency usurped Taziar's frustration. "Untie them quickly. Mordath's weakening. But he still has control of the winds."

Taziar rushed to obey. He seized his sword. Even as he slashed Moonbear's bonds with its tip, wind shrieked down upon them. A swell of water crashed against the tiny hull. The boat rolled violently to one side. Tossed like flotsam, Taziar swung wildly for Aird Moor's bonds. Momentarily, he met resistance. Blood splashed the gunwale. A wave knocked Taziar overboard. The dinghy lurched like a dying animal, then the sea pounded her to wreckage.

Battered by storm-churned waters, Taziar fought to swim. "Astryd!" he screamed. "Moonbear!" His cries were lost beneath the rain which pounded down relentlessly. A swirl of gale-lashed current dragged him under. The ropes still tangled about his ankles hampered his movements. He gathered his remaining strength and surged to the surface. His face broke water. He found himself staring at a triangular, black head as large as his own torso.

Horror tore through Taziar. *What in Karana's hell!* Before he could swim away, another swell toppled him. This time, he emerged near the snake-like body of the creature he had seen. He was shocked to recognize Astryd astride the creature's thorny back, her head low. Magics shaped in strands between her fingertips. Behind her sat Aird Moor, nursing a gash across his right wrist. Moonbear reached down for Taziar.

Astryd's summonings! Mardain's mercy, it's a dragon. Taziar caught Moonbear's sinewy wrist and allowed the barbarian to hoist him atop the creature's tremendous bulk. The brown-swirled scales seemed as slick as wet tile. Taziar could feel the powerful muscles contracting beneath him. Icy gusts stabbed through his soaked and tattered clothing. He clung, shivering.

Suddenly, Astryd shouted. Light snapped from her fingers and sheeted in a small plane between the dragon and the distant ship. Her magics faded quickly. Around the dragon, the winds stopped as if choked. But the rain still splattered from the threatening, pitch-colored skies, and merciless gusts whipped the sea outside the sphere of Astryd's protection to foam.

Without a word, Moonbear plucked his cloak from over his tunic and breeks, and laid the sodden linen across Taziar's shoulders. Grateful for the cloak's minimal warmth, Taziar drew it closely about him. "Thank you," he murmured. He knew his gratitude meant nothing to Moonbear, but he felt more comfortable voicing it. Able to think more clearly now that the immediate danger was past, Taziar felt as if he were caught in some hero's tale. Despite the rattle of the dragon's tremendous scales and the billowing motion which was transporting them faster than any ship, Taziar's mind scarcely allowed him to believe in the beast's existence.

Taziar turned his attention to Astryd. Her frame

remained as taut as wire. Her hands shook. Her lips were pinched to white lines. It was obvious her battle continued. Mordath's storm battered against her shield, and her sorceries were all that stood between her companions and death. Unable to assist her, Taziar felt as helpless as a newborn baby.

Gradually, the sky dulled to orange. Astryd fell to the beast's neck, exhausted. And the sea dragon swam silently toward the distant shore.

CHAPTER 13

The Price of War

"To weep is to make less the depth of grief."
—*William Shakespeare*
King Henry the Sixth, Part III

Early in the afternoon, Astryd's sea dragon glided to the Swedish shore. Beyond the flat beach where it landed, a forest of spruce and pine swayed in the late summer winds. Shivering, Taziar Medakan slid to the ground. Aird Moor followed. Blood seeped through the bandage on his wrist, speckling the cloth with scarlet, but the woodsman made no mention of Taziar's desperate slash which had opened the wound and saved his life.

Feeling responsible for Aird Moor's suffering, Taziar avoided the woodsman's gaze. He watched in silence as Moonbear clambered down over the dragon's dripping, black scales and lowered Astryd to the sand. The dragon disappeared into the sea, and beyond it, Taziar saw a square-rigged sailboat running, wind astern, for shore. *Cullinsberg's guards are still chasing us.* Though worried by Ilyrian's persistence, Taziar's first concern was Astryd. She

lay as still as death, though she breathed deeply
and evenly. Taziar knelt beside the sorceress, called
her name, and prodded her arm forcefully.

Astryd opened eyes glazed as if with fever. She
made a feeble gesture, and her voice emerged in a
thin whine. "I'll be all right." Her lids drifted
closed.

Distressed by Astryd's helplessness, Taziar caught
her hand.

Aird Moor stepped between Taziar and Astryd.
"She just needs rest. You heard what she said
about Dragonrank magic costing life energy." He
seized Astryd by the armpits, hoisted her to her
feet, and tossed her to his shoulder. "There's nothing more Mordath can do to hurt her. Her battle
is over and won, but ours has just begun."

Grimly, Taziar nodded. Cullinsberg's patrol
seemed a distant threat. For now, he was more
worried about his relationship with Astryd. *I no
longer hold the jadestone which drew me to her, yet I still
care deeply. When she recovers from the spells which
sapped her strength, will she remember or care about
the affection we shared?* Taziar watched Aird Moor
carry Astryd toward the woods, stung with jealousy and self-doubt. *Astryd needs me, and I'm too
small to protect her.* Ire rose against the woodsman
who transported the sorceress' frail form with natural ease. But Taziar quelled his rising resentment. *It's not Aird Moor's fault I'm slight. Astryd and I
are fortunate to have strong companions.* The rational-
ization did little to dispel Taziar's feelings of inadequacy. Quietly, he followed Moonbear and Aird
Moor to the tree line.

Moonbear questioned Aird Moor's statement.

"Do you think the guards will continue following us now? So close to my village?"

Aird Moor slipped between two pines. Needled branches muffled his reply. "I'm certain. I saw their sailboat heading for shore; it's probably mooring now. Mordath said Ilyrian has taken charge. That worm can only be after three things: money, power, or vengeance. Somehow, he's decided killing you will bring one or all of those. And he's willing to waste every life but his own to get it."

Taziar trailed his companions like a shadow. Aird Moor's revelations raised memories of brave promises made in Shylar's whorehouse, vows to discover his father's slayer. But the knowledge of Ilyrian's guilt did nothing to ease his restlessness. *I need Ilyrian's confession and some evidence of remorse. I can't fight an army. But at least I've no need to return to Cullinsberg to confront Ilyrian.*

Moonbear led the journey through the forest. The sky was as still and calm as glass, with no evidence remaining of Mordath's storm. A northern breeze wound between the trees, rattling the needles in a soft chorus. Taziar felt numb with cold. Astryd's weight burdened Aird Moor enough to slow the woodsman to Taziar's pace. In the interest of speed, no one made much effort at silence.

A short distance deeper into the forest, Moonbear brought his companions to the bank of a narrow river. "Follow the water. It's the easiest route to my village."

Aird Moor waved him on. "Quickly then."

The three men jogged along the riverside. Taziar winced each time Aird Moor's motion bounced Astryd on his shoulders. But soon the burble of water and the constant movement became familiar. Their path continued inland. The river formed a deep gorge. Its sides cut sharply upward to granite cliffs which became steeper as they traveled farther north.

Idly, Taziar studied the sheer sides of the gorge, instinctively assessing it to see how stable it was. *I could climb it. It would prove difficult. I doubt too many other people could do it.* Staring at the forested top, Taziar felt vulnerable. *One man with a bow and good aim could take my life, and I'd never see him coming.* Discomforted by his thoughts, Taziar quickened his pace.

Gradually, the cliffs diminished, melting into the landscape. The river meandered through a vast plain of conifers. The afternoon sun flashed rays clear as diamonds from the surface of the stream. Astryd's eyes were open now, and she spared Taziar an occasional crooked smile which soothed his doubts.

Suddenly, Aird Moor froze as a man appeared directly ahead of them. He stood as tall as Moonbear and was nearly as heavy. Brown bearskin covered his burly frame. His hair hung in a tangle of gold. Jabbering in an excited singsong, he ran for Moonbear.

Taziar scrambled from the barbarian's path, then watched with interest as the huge men embraced. The stranger clapped Moonbear's face between hands as large as a lion's paws. Abruptly, he turned and trotted off into the forest.

Moonbear explained. "He is a scout from my tribe. We are not far from the village. He will run ahead to let them know we are coming."

Taziar smiled, remembering his earlier encounter with the Danwald barbarians. Yet, his joy was tempered by the knowledge that their enemies were close behind, trained soldiers with steel swords who would probably outnumber Moonbear's tribe. From his father's descriptions, Taziar recalled the barbarians' greatest handicap was their lack of modern weaponry. *I'm the only one with a proper sword. Even Moonbear and Aird Moor lost their blades to the sailors aboard* Amara. Taziar's realization goaded him to question his friend. "Moonbear, why didn't you warn your scout about the patrol?"

Moonbear's shoulders rose and fell with a maddeningly simple composure. "We will tell them, soon enough, when we arrive. Meantime, let them have a few moments of happiness at discovering their captured prince returned intact."

Though not wholly comprehending Moonbear's reasoning, Taziar assumed the barbarian understood his own people. The thief did not press further. He trailed his companions as they moved from the river and wrestled their way through the densely-packed pines.

Later that afternoon, Taziar, Moonbear, Aird Moor and Astryd came upon a manmade clearing. A moss-chinked log longhouse rose in the center. At the periphery, half a dozen huts surrounded the central stucture. A few fur-clad, blond men and women, all tanned and robust, descended upon them. Shouts of welcome drew several more from the longhouse.

The barbarians caught Moonbear and his companions in vigorous hugs, not discriminating in the least between the strangers and their long absent prince. Taziar felt suffocated by the warm embraces. Lost beneath the barbarians' greetings,

he was forced to ignore the spatial taboos of his
city breeding. The instincts of a thief rose, unbidden, and Taziar realized with wry amusement that
he could rob any or all of the barbarians without
the slightest effort. *But I'd have no reason to do it.
Like Moonbear said, if I needed something he had, he
would give it to me.*

Put at ease by his thoughts, Taziar began to pay
more attention to events around him. The barbarians had relieved Aird Moor of his burden by
taking Astryd to their longhouse. The woodsman
conversed with the wild Swedes in their odd language. As Taziar threaded toward Astryd, he vowed
to learn the northern tongue fluently before leaving Moonbear's people.

Astryd sat with her back propped against the
longhouse, her face unusually pale. Taziar crouched
beside her, his side touching her lightly. When she
made no objection, he looped his arm through
hers and waited for the chaos around them to sort
itself. From his position, he estimated the number
of barbarians at sixty, including a dozen children
and half again as many elders.

One of the young barbarian men made an an-
nouncement. A great cheer rose from the crowd.
Then Moonbear spoke, and the tone of his followers shifted from excitement to sober intensity. Most
rushed into the longhouse. A few sprinted for the
cottages at the outskirts of the clearing. Moonbear
trotted toward one of the huts. Aird Moor approached Taziar and Astryd. "Moonbear's people
wanted to celebrate his return, but he warned
them about the guardsmen. They've gone to gather
weapons. We'll meet to plan our strategy in that
hut." He pointed after Moonbear's retreating fig-

ure. "If you've any of your father's common sense, we could use you."

Taziar flushed, aware he knew too little of battle to be much help. He rose and aided Astryd to stand on her still shaky legs. "Here." Taziar unhooked his sword belt. "You or Moonbear could make better use of this than me."

Aird Moor swept a hand through his curled locks. "On the contrary. You need it more than either of us." He did not trouble himself to explain further but moved to Astryd's other side. "Come on."

Astryd waved Aird Moor away.

With a shrug, Aird Moor started toward the cabin. Taziar refastened his weapon and followed. Astryd leaned heavily against him, but she had at least regained enough strength to walk. Despite the urgency of impending war and the knowledge that he would soon have to fight, Taziar felt reassured by Astryd's closeness.

When Taziar entered the cabin, he found Moonbear seated on the floor with three other barbarians, two males and one female. Aird Moor sat cross-legged beside Moonbear. Taziar took a place with his back to the door and Astryd sank to the floor beside him. Aird Moor used the language of Cullinsberg so Taziar could understand what was being said. "How many fighting men do you have?"

"Fighting men." Moonbear considered. "Eighteen."

Aird Moor winced. "A standard Cullinsberg phalanx has about fifty. A massed frontal defense will get us all killed."

Taziar's mind raced, disgusted by the huge waste of life which was about to occur because of one man's greed. He thought about their journey from the beach to the barbarian village. "Moonbear, where would a sailboat dock after crossing the Kattegat?"

Moonbear shrugged. "Anywhere on the southern shore. Probably the port at Sverigehavn. It is the safest landing."

Aird Moor took over the questioning. "How would an army get from the port to here?"

Moonbear scratched his head. "The same way we came would be best. Along the river. It is not the shortest path, but it is certainly the easiest."

Aird Moor spoke softly, as if to himself. "And since they'd have to track us, that's undoubtedly the route they'll take." He turned to face the barbarian prince. "We'll need scouts."

"They are out all the time."

Taziar could hear the barbarians outside organizing with awesome speed. It seemed strange to imagine these friendly people gathered in a cause of war. But that these barbarians had great strength and were skilled in combat he already knew from seeing Moonbear in action.

Suddenly, a young woman burst into the meeting. She addressed Moonbear from behind Taziar and Astryd, her words unintelligible to Taziar. She appeared disheveled and breathless, but her voice was calm. Astryd whispered a translation. "She's discovered thirty or forty uniformed soldiers headed for the river. 'Foreigners,' she called them. She found another twelve who remained behind. From her description, I think Mordath's at the camp. Now she's giving the locations. Hel's coldest citadel, Shadow. What have you and your friends done?"

Taziar ignored the barbarians' exchange and turned his attention to Astryd. "Do you remember when I broke into your room, and you called me a burglar?"

Astryd nodded.

"I'm afraid I really am. One of my thefts and the aspirations of a power-crazed, vengeful child of minor nobility are responsible for this. I'm sorry I involved you."

Astryd snorted weakly. "Nonsense. If not for you and the jade you . . . um, acquired . . . from Mordath, I'd be a king's slave or, at best, a wanderer lost in northern Scandinavia. If I ever returned to the Dragonrank School, it would be too late to continue my training. I wouldn't get through the gates."

The scout exited the tent, followed by the other three barbarians. Aird Moor and Moonbear rose. The woodsman asked, "Moonbear, I thought you just told your captain to gather thirty warriors?"

Moonbear nodded assent.

Aird Moor threw up his hands in exasperation. "You told me you had only eighteen fighting men."

"We do. Also we have twenty-three women. We do not have a large tribe. We all learn to fight, if we must. Our women know weapons as well as our men." Smiling, Moonbear nodded through the open door at the female who had sat in on the strategy meeting. "Some better."

"Great." Aird Moor seemed surprised but pleased by the information. He caught Moonbear's arm before the prince could leave the room. "One thing more. You can't lead the ambush."

Taziar held his breath, appalled by Aird Moor's bold undermining of Moonbear's command.

But Moonbear maintained his gentle dignity. "Why not?"

"Mordath." Aird Moor interrupted his explanation to address Taziar. "Moonbear plans to arm his people with bows and spears and place them on the cliffs over the river gorge. The Cullinsbergens won't stand a chance."

Taziar recalled the sheer, granite sides and realized the barbarians probably would not lose a single warrior. He nodded his understanding.

"But," continued Aird Moor, "Mordath can magically locate people he knows: people like me, you, Moonbear, and Astryd. If he discovers us, the ambush will be ruined."

Astryd stood. "Don't worry about Mordath. He drained his life energy even more than I did. He won't have the strength to cast spells."

"And he, too, is getting stronger with time." Aird Moor turned his gaze on Astryd. "Can you tell me for certain he's too weak to cast? Can you guarantee he won't regain his power before we spring our trap?"

"Of course not. I can only guess," said Astryd. "But I'm reasonably certain . . ."

Aird Moor interrupted with jarring force. "Certain enough to risk thirty lives?"

Astryd lowered her head. Taziar curled a comforting arm across her back.

Aird Moor turned back to Moonbear. "There are two places we cannot let Mordath find: the current location of your warriors and this village. And there's only one way I know to render Mordath's spell useless. *We* need to find *him* first."

Taziar winced, alarmingly aware of what Aird

Moor's plan meant. "The four of us are going to challenge a dozen soldiers at their camp?"

Moonbear allowed the door to swing shut. "I could bring some of my warriors."

"No." Aird Moor said quickly and with more force than necessary. "We need your warriors for the ambush and to guard your children and elders if the fighting fails." He considered. "Besides, your warriors may misunderstand my methods. Ilyrian and Mordath want us. I'll not risk your people's lives unnecessarily." He glanced down. "Astryd, is the person carrying the jadestone still undetectable to Mordath?"

Astryd stood gracelessly. "This was a property of my spell, not the gem. The moment I reclaimed my powers, Mordath could once again locate me."

"Then you'll have to come along." Aird Moor headed for the door.

The suggestion charged Taziar with concern. He leaped to his feet. "Enough, Aird Moor! She's too weak to go traipsing through the forest."

Aird Moor's voice went gritty with annoyance. "Then Moonbear can carry her. She can't stay in the village. And she's safer with us than alone in the woods. Come on. We're wasting time." He pushed through the doorway into the clearing. Moonbear followed.

Alone with Astryd, Taziar paced. He had no choice but to accept Aird Moor's plans. The woodsman knew much more about combat, and his explanations seemed logical. But the promise of war weighed heavily upon Taziar despite his natural thrill for action. Pinned beneath the loathsome burden of his mother's death, he studied Astryd in the gloom of the cabin. *I can fight for her. I could*

*die for her if necessary. But even for Astryd's survival, I
don't know if I could take another life.*

Struggling against his own conscience, Taziar
tightened every muscle until his arms ached with
effort. Unless he could overcome his own com-
punctions, he knew he would be slain in the coming battle. He turned to memories of his father
for direction: *To become a warrior, a man must kill
himself inside. Once he has reached this realization, he
fears nothing. No one can do him harm.* But, for once,
the elder Medakan's words failed to comfort. Even
the anticipation of performing against steep odds
lacked its usual allure; this time, success would
require Taziar to kill.

Astryd spoke softly, apparently misunderstand-
ing Taziar's distress. "Aird Moor's right, of course.
It's unlikely, but if Mordath has regained enough
strength to cast spells, you will need me along."

Lost inside himself, Taziar did not reply. One
by one, he forced his muscles to relax. "Let's go."
He held the door for Astryd, then trailed her into
the early evening haze.

In the clearing, skin-clad barbarians massed in
grim expectation, clutching spears, bows, and clubs.
A few carried swords of copper, bronze, or steel.
Moonbear gave some final instructions to his commander, then accepted a pair of crafted longswords
from a woman nearly as large as itself. In no
formation, the barbarians melted into the forest.

Moonbear stared after his departing warriors,
his face twisted in a grimace of concern. Without
looking toward Aird Moor, he offered him one of
the swords. Taziar watched while Aird Moor examined the length of a crudely made bow. A quiver of turkey feather-fletched arrows balanced

across his back. He took the proffered sword and jammed it, sheathed, through his belt. "Ready?" His gaze flitted from Moonbear to Astryd and settled on Taziar.

Sweat prickled Taziar's skin despite the first stirrings of excitement. "Let's do what we must."

Softly as a deer, Aird Moor slid between the gathered pines. Moonbear glided silently after him. Taziar and Astryd followed with less grace and dignity. The sorceress clutched Taziar's arm with trembling fingers and did not speak, but otherwise she seemed to have physically recovered from her ordeal. As they pressed through stands and clustered copses of evergreen, Taziar monitored her location carefully. The spines of pine and spruce stabbed through the drying remains of his clothing, but anticipation dulled pain beneath a steady wash of adrenaline.

The heavy snows of Scandinavia which limited the coastal woodlands to conifers also kept the lower areas freer of vines and underbrush. A layer of brown needles crunched underfoot with far less noise than the broad oak and hickory leaves on the southern continent. Aird Moor held the lead. At times, he told Moonbear, Taziar, and Astryd to wait while he scouted ahead, then returned to gesture them in a different direction. Often, the woodsman consulted with Moonbear, but he never allowed the barbarian prince to take command of the group. And, in his quietly accepting way, Moonbear never complained nor demanded.

An hour crawled to the next. The sun sank toward the western horizon, forming a tail of colored semicircles. Now more familiar with forests, Taziar reveled in his own developing stealth. He

no longer wasted time dodging deadfalls or wres-
tling vines; he'd learned to judge pathways at a
glance. Though still slower than his more experienced companions, he managed to maintain a rea-
sonable pace. And Aird Moor's frequent stops made
keeping abreast of Moonbear even easier.

A quarter of the way through the third hour,
Aird Moor returned from one of his scouting
jaunts wearing a strange half smile. He grasped
his long bow in his left hand and again scrutinized
it for defects. He looped the string over one end
and allowed it to dangle. "Stay close."

Before Taziar could question him, Aird Moor
pushed through the trees with Moonbear at his
heels. Taziar caught Astryd's wrist and straggled
through the needled branches. They emerged into
a vast clearing hemmed by scrub pine. Ten soldiers lounged around a central fire, wearing the
red and black uniforms of Cullinsberg's guardsmen.
Their shields and weapons lay spread across the
dirt. Smoke curled from the blaze in a weak parody of the gray-tinged sky. At the farther edge of
camp, Mordath sagged, his back propped against
the trunk of a towering spruce. Beside him, Ilyrian
studied his own hands in the evening haze.

Shocked by Aird Moor's direct approach to a
camp full of enemies, Taziar inched into the shadows beyond the brightly-lit circle of the campfire.
For several seconds, nothing happened. Then a
guardsman glanced in their direction. He shouted
an alarm, and the others leaped to attention. Ilyrian
rose, shrieking blasphemies an octave above his
normal voice. "Men, kill them!"

The soldiers scrambled for swords. Red highlights bounced from rising shields, spinning like

wraiths between the trees. As the Cullinsbergen guardsmen closed, Taziar forced Astryd behind him. He reached for his sword hilt.

The sorceress whispered. "Keep your attention on Ilyrian. Mordath and I are both still too weak to cast."

Aird Moor's voice, though deadly calm, boomed over the crash of readying weaponry. "Stop! Stand where you are or Ilyrian dies."

The men hesitated, glancing toward their captain. Ilyrian stood, still and tense, his face locked in an expression of murderous outrage.

Aird Moor addressed Ilyrian directly. "You haven't enough soldiers here to keep me or Moonbear from killing you. Call off your men. Right now."

Ilyrian looked from the massed soldiers to Aird Moor. His glare withered to a frown of discomfort. "Men, stand in formation. Stay alert. Don't trust them."

The soldiers held their positions, their weapons readied.

Mordath yelled suddenly. His tone was harsh, but it lacked his usual resonant authority. "Fools! Slay them all!"

The guardsmen shifted nervously, awaiting their captain's signal.

Aird Moor took a bold step toward the guards. Taziar squeezed Astryd's fingers reassuringly while the woodsman spoke. "I've brought them, Ilyrian. If you can keep them, you can have them. But I want you to know I'm on their side."

The soldiers remained still and anxious. Ilyrian's face framed the same calculating grin he'd worn when he had confessed his betrayal to Taziar in the baron's dungeon. "That wasn't our deal, Aird Moor. You promised to deliver the barbarian and the thief unarmed."

Taziar loosed a startled gasp of realization. *So, Aird Moor, too, would double-cross friends.* Uncertainty sank beneath a wild rush of anger. Memory surfaced with glaring clarity. He recalled Aird Moor's insistence on fetching the drinks in Calrmar Port, mugs of beer which had turned out to be poisoned. Taziar berated his own blindness. *City born, street-raised, enmeshed in the underground, and I'm still too damned gullible.* He edged deeper into the darkness, no longer certain whom to trust.

Aird Moor countered Ilyrian's challenge. "The way things were doesn't matter. What's important is how they stand now. You have a choice, Ilyrian." He dropped his voice to an unsettling growl. "The remainder of your soldiers, the ones you were too much of a coward to lead, are being slaughtered by barbarians in an ambush. The barbarians will finish their play soon and arrive here before nightfall. It won't take long for them to . . . clean up . . . what few of your men might have had sense enough to learn to fight."

Moonbear said nothing, his stance characteristically relaxed. Taziar remained poised and wary, awaiting Aird Moor's next pronouncement. The brooding tension of the guardsmen seemed tangible.

Aird Moor continued. "If you attack us, between Moonbear and myself, we'll kill at least half, if not all of you. The three survivors aren't going to be enough crew to sail your ship. The barbarians will hack down whoever remains. Now, if you want a chance for some of these men, and possibly you, to leave alive, all you must do is fight, Ilyrian.

One man against one man. Fair combat, something you know little about."

Taziar's rage dispersed, leaving him feeling cold and empty. *Of course Aird Moor joined us when his loyalties were with Cullinsberg. Did I expect him to league with criminals? At least he's shown enough common sense to switch his alliance to us. And his brave challenge may save the lives of ten soldiers—Moonbear's, Astryd's, and mine as well.*

Ilyrian's reply went shrill. "I can't fight you. You know you'd kill me. That's the only reason you're willing to resolve this conflict one against one."

Aird Moor fingered his bow. "I'm not expecting you to fight me." He patted his sword, and the guardsmen pressed forward. "I have a decent blade. I wouldn't soil it by splitting your ugly head. If I just wanted you dead, I would have remained in the woods and put an arrow through your chest. But Taziar here . . ." His gaze probed the evening haze. He sidestepped and waved toward the location Taziar had occupied before his careful fade beyond the firelight. "Taziar *Medakan* must avenge a murder you committed."

Horror shattered Taziar's composure. *He wants ME to fight!* He knew raw fear for the first time since childhood. His throat tightened, strangling speech. A wild surge of excitement made him giddy.

Ilyrian's voice came to Taziar as if from a great distance. "What are you talking about?"

"You may as well admit it." Aird Moor's hands balled to fists, but his features remained placid. "We both know you killed Taz's father. Eight years ago, you had your captain executed because you never had the courage to challenge him to fair combat."

Ilyrian went rigid. "Liar!" he screamed.

Casually, Aird Moor strung his bow. "You calling me liar is as ludicrous as me addressing you as woodsman. The men you command now know you're a devious, manipulative worm, or at least the stupidest bastard on the beach for getting thirty or forty of their companions killed. If you walk away from this shore, your own men will probably murder you before you return to Cullinsberg. I know I would were I among them." His eyes goaded each of the guardsmen in turn. "Ilyrian, you've nothing to lose by admitting you contrived the charges against Captain Taziar except you won't die with a lie on your lips." He fingered an arrow fletching.

Ilyrian turned scarlet with rage. "Attack!"

Quick as a cat, Aird Moor nocked the arrow and aimed for Ilyrian. "Freeze!"

The soldiers went still.

Aird Moor finished. "Fine, Ilyrian. Do you think they're faster than an arrow? I'll bet none of them dives in front to catch it for you. Now, call them off."

Ilyrian's head sank in subdued dejection, but Taziar recognized an alertness beneath the nobleman's feigned demeanor. "Men, stand as you were. Fine, hunter. I'll fight the thieving little coward. But I want some assurances. If I win, my men and I can leave undisturbed."

"Agreed," said Aird Moor. Moonbear nodded assent as the woodsman continued. "And if you lose, I want your men to promise to go immediately. The men, Ilyrian, because I don't trust your vows."

At a word from Ilyrian, the soldiers dispersed to the edge of camp. Mordath staggered to his feet, clutching the tree trunk for support. Ilyrian remained, his eyes locked on Taziar. He wore an expression of calm indifference, as if he found the outcome of the conflict a foregone conclusion.

Sweat soaked Taziar's palms. His mouth felt as dry as cotton. "I'm not going to fight," he whispered hoarsely. "I told you, Aird Moor. I *just can't kill.*"

Aird Moor replied, as softly and matter-of-fact as an instructor explaining a difficult sword form. "You've run all your life, son. You've come to a corner. Now, you either fight for your life or lose it. If you refuse to face Ilyrian, you still fight, only with odds of twelve against four. Would you see Moonbear and Astryd dead to avoid doing battle with the worm who killed your father?"

Taziar loosed a strangled cry of frustration. "You bastard! You backed me into that corner."

Aird Moor shrugged. "The method doesn't matter. The conflict is between you and Ilyrian. It always was." He turned away, but not before Taziar recognized concern in the brown depths of his eyes.

Taziar steeled himself. He approached Ilyrian, hiding fear behind an outward calm confidence he had learned from his years in Cullinsberg's street gang. Anticipation blurred the nobleman to dark shapelessness. Ilyrian's sword slid from its sheath, lit red by the sunset. Taziar curled steady fingers about his own hilt.

Ilyrian waited only until Taziar stepped within

sword range. He hissed. "I did kill your father. *It was easy!*"

An anguished gasp escaped Taziar's throat. In the moment of hesitation, Ilyrian lunged. An instinctive sidestep spared Taziar's life, but Ilyrian's blade slashed his left arm. Pain jarred to Taziar's shoulder. Off balance, he raised his sword to block a second blow. Steel hammered on steel. The force sent Taziar lurching backward.

Ilyrian pressed his advantage with a cold enjoyment. Repeatedly, his sword swept for Taziar, only to meet a harried web of defense. Each well-aimed stroke drove Taziar further back. Soon, the nobleman's superior strength wore on Taziar. His arms ached. Blood dripped from his torn arm and rolled down his crossguard. Pine needles pricked through the back of his torn cloak. He realized, with alarm, that he could no longer retreat.

Determination rose within Taziar. Ilyrian's sword crashed against his with jarring force. Taziar riposted. He slashed with fierce desperation. Ilyrian backstepped. Taziar's blade clove air. He followed the strike with wild sweeps for Ilyrian's head. Inexperience made him unpredictable. His strokes were frenzied.

Ilyrian retreated before Taziar, meeting the crazed lunges with defensive flicks of his sword. He bided his time, apparently seeking a pattern to Taziar's rabid assault. Suddenly, he skipped aside. Taziar's blade descended on air, throwing him off balance again. Ilyrian hooked his foot around Taziar's heel. The thief crashed heavily to the ground and rolled. Ilyrian's sword howled next to his ear and swept past. With practiced agility, Taziar regained his feet.

The combatants squared off. Taziar paused, catching his breath. Ilyrian's sneer of triumph emphasized Taziar's weakness. Again, he raised his sword. Ilyrian bore in. He hacked at Taziar's unprotected side. Taziar blocked. Before he could return the stroke, Ilyrian lunged again. Taziar met the sword in midsweep. Abruptly, Ilyrian changed the direction of his attack. Surprised, Taziar sprang aside. Ilyrian's blade opened a ragged hole in Taziar's thigh. Blood spilled forth, but the steady high of exertion precluded pain. Taziar staggered to one knee, overemphasizing the severity of the wound. *Let the bastard think he has me.*

With a howl of wicked victory, Ilyrian hewed for Taziar's head. From the ground, Taziar arched his sword in defense. His blade slammed into Ilyrian's knee and bit through flesh. The nobleman dropped instantly. Taziar yanked his sword free and leaped to his feet. Blood sprayed from the wound. Taziar raised his blade for a killing stroke.

Ilyrian cringed against the dirt. His dark eyes were wide with fear. His face twisted into a pall of panicked accusation.

Wind streamed through the clearing, throwing the fire into a wild dance. Taziar's sword arm shook. Pain descended upon him in a mad rush. Every muscle in his body ached. The steady trickle of blood from his wounds made his stomach lurch. He studied Ilyrian's lined features in the dying sunlight and realized what he'd known all along. *I can't take a man's life, not even one who would kill a friend and live a lie.*

Taziar lowered his sword. "Ilyrian, get up. Get out of here before I change my mind."

Ilyrian struggled to a sitting position, and his lips pressed together in relief and triumph.

"Stay where you are, Ilyrian." Aird Moor's voice echoed through the gathering darkness. He addressed Taziar. "Taz, if you really wish to free him, it's your decision. He's your problem. You have to live with the consequences of your choice. I only ask that you think before you decide."

Ilyrian remained, unmoving. Sweat beaded his upper lip.

Moonbear's voice emerged in a soothing singsong. "Shadow, ask your father."

Taziar locked his eyes on the nobleman. He searched his mind for father's advice which had come to him so easily in the past. But this time, memories of the elder Medakan eluded him. The words which echoed through his head had been spoken by Aird Moor. . . . *all the men and women Ilyrian destroys and all the orphans he creates were harmed because you made the decision you would rather die than stand and fight.*

A scene sprang clear in Taziar's mind, a day in Cullinsberg's dungeon when he stared at a wall splashed with his own blood. Ilyrian's ratlike features hovered over him. His voice had rattled with malicious joy. "Years ago, your father menaced my rise to power. You can see which of us was destroyed by it."

Self-righteous anger goaded Taziar to action. *Better Ilyrian than the innocents who stand in the path of his rise to power.* Taziar reversed his grip and drove the blade through Ilyrian's chest. The steel jarred around the breastbone and glided easily through flesh. Ilyrian flopped to the ground, his expression oddly peaceful.

Torn by grief, Taziar dropped to his knees. Tears burned his eyes like fire. The voices around him muted to distant noise. He hunched, weeping over the pale, still corpse of a man he had hated. But the figure which filled Taziar's mind was a heavily-muscled warrior swinging, lifeless, from the gallows, a man for whom Taziar had never been allowed to cry.

The lapse in Taziar's defenses lasted scant moments. Years among the street-toughened gang of orphans had taught him to hide weakness, and the expression he turned toward Moonbear was placidly composed. He leaped to his feet. His face bunched to a defiant glare which dared friends or guardsmen to acknowledge his tears. But the Cullinsbergens' interest in their captain ended with his death. Instead, they stood in attentive silence, watching a grim trio at the other side of the clearing. Taziar followed the direction of their gazes.

Mordath crouched. His damaged Dragonstaff supported much of his lean, haughty frame, but his feline eyes fixed sharply on Astryd. Beside her, Aird Moor held a relaxed stance. One tip of his bow rested on his foot; his other hand draped casually across his sword hilt. The woodsman's voice sounded eerily unfamiliar through the evening fog. "I thought we had settled our differences and joined in your sister's cause. Why did you betray me?"

As Taziar watched the unfolding drama, Moonbear bound his wound, and then the barbarian placed his arm across Taziar's shoulders. Though he said nothing, his gesture was heavy with meaning: deep, heartfelt, fatherly concern without a hint of condemnation. They both awaited Mordath's reply.

Mordath backstepped. A rock rolled beneath his foot, making him stumble. His face locked in an expression of impassive fearlessness. "Ilyrian told me about your cruel and ignoble past. What my sister needs is an assassin to free her from an overbearing, pirate husband not some old lover who would slay her in vengeance."

The hand on Aird Moor's sword hilt tensed to a bloodless fist. "What your sister needs is a brother who cares more for her happiness than the ludicrous ramblings of a power-mad nobleman who never spoke a true word in his misery-making life. I love Inge. I would do nothing to harm her. And I believe she loves me. But she loves her father and brothers, too, enough so we sacrificed our happiness together for your father's decree. Enough so that I will spare your worthless life because I know your death would break her heart."

"My death?" Mordath laughed with withering disdain. "I've more than enough power to destroy you." He made a gesture so sudden even Moonbear cringed aside.

Astryd spoke softly, yet her tone was as bold as Mordath's motion. "He's lying. His life aura has grown faded and thin as an old cloak. It'll be well past nightfall before he can use something as simple as a transport escape."

Mordath hissed a savage blasphemy.

Aird Moor's tone went crisp. "If that school has done nothing else, it's given you an inflated sense of self-importance. Barring you from completing your education there may prove the best thing for you. This world has much to teach you, at the very least, how to tell real friends from manipulating rats who would use your power and play your ego like a puppet only to cast you aside or kill you." He turned away. "See you in Norway, Mordath. Under friendlier circumstances, I hope."

The sun slipped beneath the western horizon. Night winds whipped down from the north, chilling beneath the tatters of Taziar's cloak. He shivered. The movement jarred his overtaxed muscles, and he realized he would pay for the evening's exertion with days of pain.

Moonbear gripped Taziar's shoulder. "Are you well?"

Taziar considered. The restlessness which had hounded him since his father's death had departed, lifting a burden far heavier than Moonbear's thickly-muscled arm. But Taziar's passion for excitement was not dulled in the least, only less directed. He'd become aware of a whole new world which was opening before him. Scandinavia's stunted forests promised the challenge of exploration; her crowded cities were ripe for the agility and wile of a western-born thief. Taziar ducked beneath Moonbear's arm, then caught the barbarian's enormous hand. "I'm fine," he said softly. "Let's go home."

EPILOGUE

". . . How many things, too, are looked upon as quite impossible until they have been actually effected?"

—*Pliny the Elder*

The longhouse door banged shut a dozen times, admitting broken rays of morning sunshine. In the clearing, barbarians laughed and sang in their gruffer version of the Scandinavian tongue. Taziar sighed, no longer able to sleep. He rolled to his side. Pain pounded and throbbed through every muscle in his body, a constant reminder of the events of the previous night.

Taziar glanced around the building which was crudely-constructed from logs of varied sizes. The barbarians' bedding consisted of fur pieces spread across the floor, now rolled up and tucked away for the day. The only occupants of the longhouse were Aird Moor, Astryd, and himself. Taziar sat up, evoking a chorus of aches. He suppressed a grunt of discomfort.

"Good morning." Aird Moor approached and

crouched at Taziar's bedside. "Moonbear's people are celebrating his return and their victory. Want to join them?"

Taziar winced. "Not just yet." He met his companion's doelike eyes, and his question was deadly direct. "Aird Moor, did you really promise to deliver Moonbear and me to Ilyrian?"

Aird Moor pressed his fingertips to the dirt floor. "Not Ilyrian specifically. I'm a bounty hunter. It's my job. The baron hired me to catch a pair of fugitives. I tried." He smiled. "Luckily, I failed."

Taziar shifted position painfully. "What exactly made you decide to fail?"

Aird Moor considered. "I liked Moonbear almost from the time I met him. He's a capable forester, and his philosophy on war is similar to mine." He settled to one knee. "Discovering you were Taz Medakan's son forced me to think about what I planned to do with you. Taziar, your father would be proud of you."

Taziar lowered his head. Warm satisfaction suffused him, and he could think of no greater compliment.

Aird Moor continued. "But the barbarians themselves inspired my final decision. They have a peace with the forest neither war nor civilization can take from them. *And I suddenly realized I was siding against them to please a baron I no longer served and his troop of half-trained incompetents.*"

Smoke twined into the longhouse, carrying the aroma of fresh meat and roots. The calls of the barbarians in the clearing grew louder. Taziar picked at the bandage on his arm. "What about Mordath? Surely his sister could forgive your slaying him in self-defense. Why did you let him go?"

Aird Moor shrugged. "I'd no reason to kill him. I can't blame him for protecting his sister. Smarter, more socially experienced men than Mordath have fallen prey to Ilyrian's manipulations." Aird Moor rose. "Mordath's selfish, but not evil. His arrogance is mostly an act."

Astryd approached. Her short, blonde hair feathered away from her round face. Sleep had restored beauty to her slight, lithe frame.

Desire rose heavily within Taziar, despite his aches. "Astryd, wouldn't you rather have seen Mordath slain?"

Astryd slid to the fur bedding beside Taziar. "It would be against the rules of Dragonrank for me to raise my hand against him. But our laws say nothing about eliminating an opponent without harming him. In some ways, they encourage it. Plans like Mordath's require creativity, an asset for a Dragonrank mage. His trapping me on a ship was a ploy to allow him to continue his education." She caught Taziar's uninjured arm. "In his position, I might have done the same thing."

Taziar nodded his understanding.

"Shadow?" Astryd seemed uncomfortable. "I have to leave now."

"Leave?" Taziar caught her hand in both of his. "What do you mean? Why now?"

"My month of vacation is over. If I don't go today, I'll lose my chance at garnet rank. Mordath will have won."

Grief dulled Taziar's physical discomfort. "I'll come with you."

Astryd freed her hand and brushed the black

hair from Taziar's eyes. "I have to arrive today, magically. I can only do that alone."

Taziar's mind raced. The thought of losing Astryd tore at his sensibilities. "Give me directions. I'll get there in time."

Tears blurred Astryd's blue eyes. "Only Dragonrank trainees can live on the grounds. We're allowed no visitors, and we may leave the school for just one month every year." She wrapped her arms around Taziar and buried her face in his chest.

Taziar pulled Astryd closer, feeling her tears wash through the thin cloth of his cloak and tunic. *I'd thought to start a new life today, in a strange world with a woman I love.* Anger tore through Taziar. *I can't expect Astryd to give up the Dragonrank and everything she's worked for. I can't force her to surrender a chance at great power any more than she could make me forsake my ardor for adventure.*

Astryd spoke, her words muffled in Taziar's clothing. "I love you, Shadow. I'll find you again next year, if you've not discovered someone better to share your life."

Gently, Taziar pulled Astryd away and met her sorrowful gaze. "I love you, too, Astryd. We'll get together again. I'm certain. Go now. I understand."

Taziar pressed his lips to Astryd's in a long and passionate kiss. Then Astryd spoke a few harsh syllables. Green light flared like an exploding star. Smoke rolled through the confines of the barbarian's longhouse. Then Astryd was gone, and Taziar felt as if she had left him crippled and alone.

"I'm sorry." Aird Moor's voice startled Taziar. He had forgotten the woodsman's presence.

An odd smile dragged across Taziar's harried

features. "Don't feel bad. As soon as I learn the location of the Dragonrank school, we'll be together again. This world hasn't a barrier which could keep me away."

"Are you insane?" Aird Moor stared at Taziar, his expression probing. "A wall twice Moonbear's height surrounds the school. Dragonrank initiates prowl the grounds, eager to practice death spells on any thief stupid enough to break into their confines. Taziar, everyone knows sneaking into that school is impossible."

Taziar smiled, his interest piqued by Aird Moor's words. As it had so many times before, the intimation he would fail became an all-consuming challenge. He recalled the many walls, gates, and holes he had broached, suddenly grateful for the small stature and dexterity which allowed him to consider tasks other men deemed beyond the realm of possibility. "Impossible, you say?" Taziar grinned with eager anticipation. "Thank the gods. I was afraid it would be too easy."

DAW

MORE MAGIC FROM THE MASTERS OF FANTASY

DAW

Savor the magic, the special wonder of the worlds of
Jennifer Roberson

THE NOVELS OF TIGER AND DEL

☐ SWORD-DANCER   (UE2152—$3.50)
Tiger and Del, he a Sword-Dancer of the South, she of the
North, each a master of secret sword-magic. Together, they
would challenge wizards' spells and other deadly perils on a
desert quest to rescue Del's kidnapped brother.

☐ SWORD-SINGER   (UE2295—$3.95)
Outlawed for slaying her own sword master, Del must return to
the Place of Swords to stand in sword-dancer combat and
either clear her name or meet her doom. But behind Tiger and
Del stalks an unseen enemy, intent on stealing the very heart
and soul of their sword-magic!

CHRONICLES OF THE CHEYSULI

This superb fantasy series about a race of warriors gifted with
the ability to assume animal shapes at will presents the Cheysuli,
fated to answer the call of magic in their blood, fulfilling an
ancient prophecy which could spell salvation or ruin.

☐ SHAPECHANGERS: BOOK 1   (UE2140—$2.95)
☐ THE SONG OF HOMANA: BOOK 2   (UE2317—$3.95)
☐ LEGACY OF THE SWORD: BOOK 3   (UE2316—$3.95)
☐ TRACK OF THE WHITE WOLF: BOOK 4 (UE2193—$3.50)
☐ A PRIDE OF PRINCES: BOOK 5   (UE2261—$3.95)

DAW
DAW Presents
Epic Adventures in Magical Realms

MERCEDES LACKEY

THE VALDEMAR TRILOGY

Chosen by one of the mysterious Companions, Talia is awakened to her own unique mental powers and abilities, and becomes one of the Queen's Heralds. But in this realm, beset by dangerous unrest and treachery in high places, it will take all of her special powers, courage and skill to fight enemy armies and the sorcerous doom that is now reaching out to engulf the land.

☐ ARROWS OF THE QUEEN: Book 1   (UE2189—$2.95)
☐ ARROW'S FLIGHT: Book 2   (UE2222—$3.50)
☐ ARROW'S FALL: Book 3   (UE2255—$3.50)

and — coming in July '88 — a new series set in the same world as the Arrows books starts with:

☐ THE OATHBOUND   (UE2285—$3.50)

PETER MORWOOD

THE BOOK OF YEARS

An ambitious lord has meddled with dark forces, and an ancient evil stirs again in the land of Alba. Rescued by an aging wizard Aldric seeks revenge on the sorcerous foe who has slain his clan and stolen his birthright. Betrayed by a treacherous king, can even his powerful friends save him as he faces demons, dragons, and wrathful fiends?

☐ THE HORSE LORD: Book 1   (UE2178—$3.50)
☐ THE DEMON LORD: Book 2   (UE2204—$3.50)
☐ THE DRAGON LORD: Book 3   (UE2252—$3.50)

NEW AMERICAN LIBRARY
P.O. Box 999, Bergenfield, New Jersey 07621

Please send me the DAW BOOKS I have checked above. I am enclosing $_____
(check or money order—no currency or C.O.D.'s). Please include the list price plus $1.00 per order to cover handling costs. Prices and numbers are subject to change without notice.

Name_____

Address_____

City _____ State _____ Zip Code _____
Please allow 4-6 weeks for delivery.

DAW

Attention:

DAW BOOK COLLECTORS

"A Bibliographic Retrospective of DAW Books, 1972-1987" entitled:

FUTURE AND FANTASTIC WORLDS
by Sheldon Jaffery

is now available from Starmont House and certain selected bookshops.

It contains a complete coverage of every DAW Book, its logo and order number, number of pages, cover artist, and date of publication, as well as descriptive material about the book. Also included are three indexes: an Author-Title Index, an Artist-Title Index, and a Title Index.

The book is available by mail from:

STARMONT HOUSE
P.O. Box 851
Mercer Island, WA 98040

and costs $29.95 for the hardcover edition, $19.95 paperbound. DAW Books will not be selling this title directly—please do not order it from us.

This notice is for the benefit of our readers and is not a paid advertisement.

—*D.A.W.*